THE OUTLAW WITH NINE LIVES

Spot Lester was like some kind of hunting cat. He'd strike fast, then steal off into the night. Nobody could capture him, though some were positive they'd killed him. They never had, of course—or else Spot Lester had nine lives.

Durfee and Bunce figured they'd scared him off after he'd tried twice to kill them and failed. "He was pretty near killed, at the wind-up the first time," said Durfee. "It turned his hair white, what he went through. The second time he was caught and beat and slammed into prison. I think he's learned his lesson."

Suddenly Henry St. Clair was laughing. "Oh, you don't know him, you fellows," he said. "You don't know him because you haven't seen him as I have, close up, with his teeth grinding, and Satan in his eyes. He won't forget us, I tell you. All the time that he's been in prison, he's been dreaming about us and how our throats would feel under his thumbs. No, don't make any mistake. He'll be here before long!"

D0733353

Max Brand
AMBUSH AT TORTURE CANYON

PUBLISHED BY POCKET BOOKS NEW YORK

**POCKET BOOKS, a Simon & Schuster division of
GULF & WESTERN CORPORATION
1230 Avenue of the Americas, New York, N.Y. 10020**

Published by arrangement with Dodd, Mead & Company
Library of Congress Catalog Card Number: 78-158344

ISBN: 0-671-41557-3

First Pocket Books printing May, 1973

10   9   8   7   6   5   4

POCKET and colophon are trademarks of Simon & Schuster.

Printed in the U.S.A.

AMBUSH AT TORTURE CANYON

Part One

CHAPTER 1

When Durfee rode up the valley, he found that the country fitted his mind as a glove fits the hand—the sort of glove that he preferred to wear—a little lighter in the leather and more delicate in the make than most of the buckskin gloves that a cowboy will buy.

He liked the look of things, because that look was clean. He saw the gleam of water, here and there; water that looked as though it might be running even in the dry middle of September, after a rainless season. And there were plenty of hills for variety, and yet it was a range that a man could gallop over. Three men, on this sort of a lay, could do the work that sometimes took the riding of ten in worse regions. And then the grass grew thick and short on the ground, the sort of grass that is sweetest on a cow's tooth, that lays the fat round and hard along her backbone, to say nothing of horses. It was a good limestone country, too. He could see the white ribs and elbows of the stone punching through the sides of the hills. And where limestone shows, it will be in the water, and the limestone water makes bone, and bone is the first necessity in the scheme of things, if you want to build a horse.

All that Durfee saw, he liked better and better. He went on for two hours, and did not even curse the flapping of his hat brim up and down before his eyes. For thirty years, more or less, Durfee had cursed a loosely flopping hat brim, but never could persuade himself to wear any other kind.

But on this afternoon he felt such a deep content flowing into him, with the wind and the sunshine and the green flash of the grass, that nothing mattered and nothing could rub his nerves the wrong way.

He could not help smiling, when he saw the cattle gathered under the wide arms of a tree, through which the heat of the midday could never strike. For he knew that restless noontides strip away the poundage of a cow. Peace and plenty make fat steers.

That was why he, perhaps, was so lean. He never had had plenty, and he never had had peace.

Now the valley narrowed a little, and the trees grew thicker. Even a lumberman would have liked the tall, straight look of the pines, and the way they stood together over the ground. Just right for clean, easy lumbering; it made his hands itch for the curved haft of an ax to fit into them!

He saw the house, now, set back among the trees to the right, with the clear green face of a slope running pleasantly down before it toward the creek. It was not too big, but it was big enough. It was not so close to the barns and the corrals that they were under the nose; on the other hand, it was not so far away that work would be made clumsy.

The intelligence that made this valley had brains, in the opinion of Durfee, and so had the men who were working it!

He was not sorry he had made the long ride. He wanted to work for the boss of this layout, even before he laid eyes on the man.

When he rode up and tethered his horse at the long hitching rack that ran before the house, he commented to himself on the good sense of this sort of a front garden. Others might have their silly garden plots, but a hitching rack was far better.

When he knocked on the front door, a Chinese came and opened it, and said that Mr. Bunce would see him; he had only to follow to the library.

That word did not please Durfee. He did not like books, and he had not much use for those who spent hours reading them. But the first glance at the "library" put him at ease. It was just the place to sit on a Sunday, mending bridles and swapping lies. There was a stove in the exact middle, and the fat belly of that stove had a big hollow pipe rail around it, designed by the creator for the heels of cow-punchers to rest against, while they warmed their souls in February weather. There was a big round table covered with newspapers and magazines, and the magazines had a well-worn look.

There was one stain on the fair face of this good weather. That was the little, twisted man who sat crookedly in his chair before a desk in a corner of the room. He looked as though he had just slumped into a freakish posture, the way a chair-weary man will do to stretch himself. But now Durfee saw that it was not a sudden movement, but that the poor fellow was permanently tied in this knot.

Said he: "I'm Silas Durfee. You sent down for me, if you're Thomas Bunce."

"I'm Thomas Bunce," said the little man, craning his head over his shoulder and glowering at the figure in the door.

He added sharply: "Come in here and let me look at you without breaking my neck, will you?"

Most of the brightness departed from the day. Durfee was reasonably sure that he never could work for such a man, no matter in how ideal a place.

However, he walked in slowly, and stood near the desk.

"Sit down," snapped the little man.

He sat down, his hat hanging from one hand.

"Put your hat on the table," said Bunce.

"My hat's resting pretty good the way it is," said Durfee.

Bunce said: "Do as I tell you. You're not nervous, are you?"

"I'm not nervous," said Durfee, speaking more and more slowly. He made no move to obey the order.

"So Latham sent you up to me, did he?" said Bunce.

"It looks that way."

"How old are you? Fifty-one—two?"

"I'm forty-five."

"Five years ago you were."

Durfee said nothing, his eyes grew suddenly obscure, and his mouth hardened.

"You're forty-five, then," said the little man. "I guess a man's as old as he thinks he is, except when it comes to climbing mountains. Any good in mountains, you?"

"Not on foot," said Durfee.

"Suppose you had to be on foot?"

"I don't have to be on foot," said Durfee.

"You might, if you worked for me."

"Then I won't work for you," replied Durfee, in the most polite of tones.

The little man looked at him steadily. His mouth kept twitching to one side. In fact, his whole face was as lopsided as his body. "You live on the back of a horse, eh?" snapped Thomas Bunce.

"I've been on the back of a hoss a few times," said Durfee.

"Why'd Latham send you up here to me?" asked Bunce, in irritation.

"That's what I'm gunna ask him when I get back," replied Durfee.

"You don't like the place, eh? You don't like the looks of the place? Is that it?"

He rattled out the words, snapping his fingers.

"Oh, the place is all right," said Durfee.

"It's me, is it?" said Bunce. "You're one of these lightning calculators, are you? You can add up a man in five minutes, can you? You know all about me already, I suppose. You could teach them in the schools about me, could you?"

"I dunno that I'd apply for that teaching job, either," said Durfee.

He stirred a little in the chair, getting more of his weight on his legs. He was ready to leave.

"Now, you're through, are you? Now you're going to back out, are you?" said Bunce. "I don't know what Latham's thinking about! He's getting old. What did he mean by it? I asked him for—What can you do? Who are you?"

"I'm a man," said Durfee, "by name of Durfee; age, forty-five; condition, single; weight, a hundred and sixty-five; height, five feet ten inches. I can eat three meals a day and sleep ten hours a night, if I get a chance."

"Seven hours for a man, eight hours for a woman, nine hours for a child, and ten hours for a—You were in the Rangers, were you?"

"Yeah. I been there," said Durfee.

"You were with the Texas Rangers, eh?"

"Yeah, I was with them."

"What did you do there?"

"I was sort of roustabout and exercise boy," said Durfee. "I carried water, and cut wood for the cook, and kind of tidied up around. I exercised the hosses, when they was getting fast and sassy, now and then. I was just generally useful all about."

Bunce stared at him with bright, keen eyes.

"Somebody's spoiled you," he said. "Somebody's ruined you. Somebody's told you that you're a wit. A dry wit. A dry wit really means a dried-up brain. You're not funny. I'm asking you questions. I'm offering you a job. Yes, it's a position. I'm talking to you about that. You want to make jokes; you want to be funny. Are you going to talk business, or not?"

"How much business you want to talk," said Durfee.

"I want to talk you, first, and money second."

"Well, go on and talk," said Durfee, with a sigh. "I've rode a long way. I gotta rest before I start back, and I might as well rest my back while I work my jaw. Whacha wanta know?"

CHAPTER 2

"I want to know you. Durfee, can you ride a horse?" said the little man.

"I've been known to. I didn't walk all the way up here," said Durfee.

"I mean, can you ride a pitching bronco?"

"Sometimes I can, and sometimes I can't."

"Did you ever break horses for a living?"

"We've all been young and foolish," said Durfee.

"You did work breaking wild horses?"

"Well, yes."

"How long?"

"Why, off and on about eight years."

"Humph!" said Bunce.

He turned his head and rattled the swift tips of his fingers on the top of the desk.

"Eight years?" he repeated, and cocked his head like a bird, to consider the answer.

Then he said: "You can shoot?"

"Yes."

"Good?"

"I'm fair average."

"How did you stack up in the Rangers?"

"Some were better at one thing; some at another."

"But none of 'em beat you at everything, eh?"

Durfee scowled. "I wouldn't say yes to that, and I wouldn't say no," said he, "unless there was a bet up."

"Rifle and revolver, eh?" said Bunce.

"Yes, I've worn 'em both."

"You're not carrying a weapon now?"

"I wouldn't say that I ain't," said Durfee.

"What sort of a weapon have you? A knife?"

"Yes, a knife, too," said Durfee. "And this."

A long-barreled Colt appeared in his hand.

"Humph!" said Bunce. "Where did you get that?"

"Right from under your eyes, Mr. Bunce."

"Well, well," said Bunce.

The revolver disappeared with a single gesture.

"You're a gunman, are you?" said Bunce. "You're one of these fellows who lives by his gun. Is that it?"

"I didn't say that was it."

"How many men have you killed?"

"None," said Durfee.

"Look here, how long you been in the Rangers?"

"Well, lemme see. Twenty-two years."

"What? Twenty-two years in the Rangers, and never killed a man?"

"No," said Durfee.

"Well, well, well," murmured Bunce. "You rode on active service for twenty-two years, and you had to chase everything from wild Indians to cattle thieves, and yeggs, but you never killed a man?"

"No, I never killed a man," said Durfee.

"Did you ever arrest an armed man, though?"

"Yes."

"How many?"

"Me? Lemme see."

His eyes grew dimmer still. He was looking back down the long years.

"Maybe three-four hundred. I wouldn't trust myself on

remembering. Maybe four hundred, take the average year by year."

"You arrested four hundred men of all kinds?"

"Yes."

"And didn't kill one of them?"

"No."

"Never fired on any of them?"

"I didn't say that."

"Oh, you fired at 'em, and missed the vital spots, eh?"

"I didn't miss the vital spots," said Durfee. "I didn't aim to hit the vital spots, as you call 'em."

Bunce stood up suddenly. He looked smaller when he was on his feet. He hardly came to the head of Durfee, though the latter remained sitting.

"You've arrested four hundred armed men, and you've had gun fights, and you shot for legs and arms. Is that it?"

Durfee held up a thick, brown thumb.

"Take a slug this size," said he, "and slam a man with it from close up, out of a Colt—how's he gonna keep his feet? You tell me that?"

Bunce sat down again, directly facing the stranger.

"I believe you," he said, though his voice cracked and snapped as before. "I believe you, because I know that Latham wouldn't send me a liar, whatever else he sent. That's all I want to talk about you. Now I'll tell you what you're to do."

"Maybe you better talk about wages, first," said the ex-Ranger. "That's an interesting first page to any story that I'm in."

"I'll talk about wages last," answered Bunce. "First, I'll tell you what you're to do. You're to take my nephew in hand. My nephew's name is Henry Vincent. He's been East in school. He's been there mostly for eight years, and he's just come home. You're to take him in hand."

Durfee was silent.

"You're to ride with him, hunt with him, and work the cows with him—you gunman, you, you know one end of a cow from the other?"

"I been told there's a difference," said Durfee.

"What State you born in?"

"Wyoming."

"On the range?"

"Mostly born on the range," said Durfee.

"Lived there?"

"Till I was twenty-three."

"Then you know cows."

"I been introduced to 'em," said Durfee. "But I never had any talent for raisin' the young."

"No?"

"No. Never."

"You'll try your hand with this one, though," said Bunce, irritated again. "And you'll do this for him—you'll see that he never has a quarrel with another man and that he never gets into the saddle on a bucking horse, or a horse that's likely to buck; you'll never let him taste alcohol and never handle a revolver. If you go hunting with him, you'll give him long shots, and few of them, and you'll discourage him in practicing with guns.

"You'll see that he gets to bed early and rises early, too. You'll go fishing with him and riding with him; you'll keep him amused in that way. If you have stories to tell, first and foremost, you'll avoid all tales of bloodshed, and the very mention of the word 'Ranger' is now taboo!"

He struck his bony fist upon the desk.

"You don't need me," said Durfee, shaking his head. "No, all that you need is a broken-down old maid about seventy years old that can still handle a right-smart darning needle and talk the jaw right off its hinges. She'd be better company for the pet boy you're aiming to raise up around here. I wouldn't put my hand to the spoiling of a man, like that."

"You'll do what I tell you to do," said the other. "Don't argue with me. I hate argument. I detest it. I've only started to tell you what your duties are. The most important half has not been mentioned."

"Go right on," said Durfee, "and make it big and hard, will you?"

"You'll find it big and hard enough," said Bunce, with a sneer. "For what you are to do, above all, is to use your eyes and your brains to keep away from my nephew a slender man with a long, dark face, a broken nose and a twisted smile—a man about six feet tall and looking like a bird that's about to drop a field mouse."

The ex-Ranger straightened. "You interest me," said he.

"This fellow, might he have a little crisscross scar over his right eye?"

"Yes. You know him?" asked Bunce hopefully.

"That's Spot Lester, unless I'm dreaming," said Durfee. "Yeah, him and me, we're old friends."

"How? Friends?"

"Yes, friends. We've talked together quite a lot, sometimes a few words, more knife work, and quite a lot of guns."

"Ah-hah!" said Bunce. "You've trailed and fought that man, have you?"

"Yeah. I've done that."

"Well, then," said Bunce, in great excitement, "what I want you to do now is to kill him! That's your job. That's your main task!"

"Thanks very much," said Durfee.

He stood up. I've had a mighty fine little chat with you," said Durfee, "but I gotta be starting back before the day gets much older. I hope you have a lot of fun with Spot Lester. Because there's a lot of fun in him."

"Hold on! You back out?" cried Bunce.

"You bet I back out."

"You mean to say," cried Bunce, "that you're afraid of that man?"

"Yeah, I mean to say it," said Durfee. "I'm scared to death of him. He's licked me good and proper three times, and he's left his marks on me, too. I'm scared of him, and I don't want the job. So long!"

He got almost to the door, and then he was stopped by a voice that called out shrilly: "This job is a hundred dollars a week to you, you fool!"

CHAPTER 3

Said the other: "A hundred dollars a week is fine, fat pay. But I wouldn't be working for myself. I'd be working for the undertaker."

Said Bunce: "Man, you don't realize. If you can kill Spot Lester, you'll get a bonus. You'll get several thousand dollars in spot cash. You understand?"

"I understand," said the ex-Ranger. "But I'm not interested."

He jerked the words out savagely. "I don't want anything more to do with the idea."

He strode through the door.

"A five-thousand bonus," said Bunce.

In the doorway, Durfee turned. His face was working.

"Curse the bonus, and you along with it," said he.

"Ten thousand! Ten thousand dollars in spot cash!" said Bunce, "if you happen to kill him—and a hundred dollars a week, and every possible expense paid, during the time that you work for me!"

Durfee took hold of the edge of the door and braced himself.

"I won't take it!" he muttered.

Bunce began to grin with a sort of fiendish delight.

"You'll take the job, my friend," said he.

"Ten thousand dollars?" said Durfee. His face was puckered with desire and with fear.

"Ten thousand dollars!" said the other.

Durfee loosened his bandanna, though it was already free enough around his throat.

"You get another man," he suggested. "You can get heaps of 'em. You go and get a better than me."

"You ride," chanted Bunce, twisting in his chair, as though he enjoyed the torment of temptation into which he had thrown the other. "You ride, you know the range, you shoot. There's nobody among the Rangers who averages better with rifle and revolver. You said so yourself!"

"I didn't say so," said Durfee.

"On a bet, you'd shoot against any of them! You said that!"

Durfee sat down in a chair, lowering himself wretchedly into it.

"I've gone and let myself in," he muttered. "Look, Bunce. You take ten thousand dollars—and how much land could a man get right around here? What does it cost an acre?"

"Mostly this around here runs to thirty and forty dollars," said Bunce. "But I see what you mean. You've reached the time of life when every man with any sense wants to settle down. You want some land. You want to work your own cows. Am I right?"

Durfee ran his thick fingers through his stiffly curling, iron-gray hair.

"Yeah, I've been dreaming about it, mostly all my life. I've got eight hundred dollars, or something like that, together. That's all. Worked since I was fifteen. Thirty years, and I've got eight hundred dollars. That shows the sort of brains I have."

"You know what I'll do?" said the rancher, "I'll sell you some of my own best land, when this game is finished. And I'll sell it to you for twenty dollars an acre. You can pick up two hundred and fifty acres for five thousand dollars. Land good enough to farm, and to repay careful working. And that'll leave you five thousand to stock up with cows. Yes, and I'll let you pick 'em out of my own herd—the weaker ones at half price. You see what I'll do? I'll pay you ten thousand dollars in cash, but I'll turn that money into twenty thousand dollars in opportunity and land and cattle. Look here, Durfee, you're only forty-five. You've got thirty years ahead of you. Before the end of that time, you may own twenty thousand acres. It can be done. You know the business. You love the range. Men like you can't help succeeding, once you get a start!"

Now, as he poured out this excited stream of words, Durfee twisted and writhed in his chair.

"I tell you what I told you before," said he. "I don't belong in the same room with that fellow, Spot Lester. I'm not on the same street with him. He's faster with his guns, and straighter. He's even faster with his brains, and crookeder. He beats me every way from the start. I wouldn't have a chance against him."

"You'll have a chance," said the rancher, "because you'll have everything that money can do for you to help out. You take the job?"

"Wait a minute," said the other, "how could Lester do any harm if he came close to your nephew? Does he wanta kill the kid?"

"No, he doesn't want to kill him. He wants him to kill himself, and cut his own throat."

"Hold on!" protested Durfee.

"I mean what I say."

"I don't understand what you say, though."

"You don't have to. You take it for granted. I'm right. All

you have to do is to take my word for it—and keep Lester away from the boy!"

"This here boy," said Durfee, scowling to keep a more contemptuous expression of distaste from his lips, "this here kid, that ain't to be allowed to ride no rough horses, nor to bulldog yearlings, likely, nor throw steers, nor handle guns much, nor nothing like that—what kind of a person might he shape up to be?"

"You shake hands on the job and then I'll send for him."

"You send for him first and I'll shake on the job afterward—maybe," said Durfee.

Without a word, the little man at the desk banged on a gong. The slippered feet of the Chinese came at a run.

"Get Henry!" commanded Bunce.

The Chinese disappeared from the doorway.

"How long has this Spot Lester been hanging around?" asked Durfee.

"He hasn't been hanging around, but he will be, within a day or so, before my nephew has been home for a week."

"Humph!" said Durfee. "You want me to work in the dark, do you?"

"That's where you'll have to work," answered Bunce.

"I don't like it," said Durfee.

"You like ten thousand dollars, and this sort of land at twenty dollars an acre. That's what you like!" declared Bunce, with conviction, and Durfee could not reply.

He heard Bunce saying: "This combination is going to work out! I know it is. I feel it in my bones. I'm not a superstitious man, but today I feel lucky. I send for you. I don't like the look of you. And then it turns out that you're an ex-Ranger, and that you're a gun expert, that you've handled badmen all your life almost; and finally you know all about Spot Lester."

"Don't go wrong on that," answered Durfee. "Nobody knows all about Spot Lester. Nobody ever will. A man can't know a cross between a poison snake and a fox!"

"For fifteen years," said the other, "he's committed every crime in the calendar. He's wanted in every state west of the Mississippi, and in most of them east of the same river. He's wanted everywhere, but he's the only man with such a record who hasn't spent the majority of his life in jail."

"He's never had a day in jail, he's never had a conviction," said Durfee. "His record is a lot cleaner than mine."

"They'd hang him for fifty murders," said Bunce.

"Yes, they'd hang him fifty times just to begin with, but they'll never get him in prison."

"Why not?"

"Because he'll die, first."

"How does he work it? Has he so many friends?"

"Nobody knows," answered Durfee. "He may work a lone hand, and he may work with a gang. How are we to tell? Men who work with him are not likely to go about bragging about their friends. And no stool pigeon would have the nerve to squeal on friend Lester, until Lester's dead!"

Here a quick, strong step approached the room, and a youngster of twenty-one or two came in, a big young man with a brown face and with very quiet, large gray eyes.

He was what Durfee called a heavyweight above and a middleweight below. He looked powerful enough to lift a horse and fleet enough to sprint. No athletic coach in the world could have glanced at him without joy. He had the wrist of a fencer and the step of a tennis player, and wrestler's neck and shoulders. And Durfee, who really knew men, filled his eye with this picture.

"I want you to meet my friend, Durfee," said Bunce. "This is my nephew, Henry Vincent."

They shook hands, and Durfee looked up into the eyes and thought that he saw there the answer, the flaw. For there was no gleam in them. They were contented and complacent. They were like the eyes of an ox in the field. The mouth, too, was like the mouth of a child—too full, too regularly and easily curved. The tension of manhood, the strain of effort had never stiffened those lips or made those nostrils flare.

Said Bunce: "I think I'm persuading Durfee to take charge of you, Henry. He's going to show you how to fish and hunt and ride. You want to know the mountains, and he'll show them to you. From the back of a horse, because he has tender feet!"

He laughed a little, and then added abruptly: "That's all!"

Henry Vincent smiled faintly at Durfee and went from the room, and Durfee watched the step, easy, free, perfectly balanced. When the boy was gone, he turned toward Bunce.

"Well?" said the rancher.

"Well," said Durfee slowly, "now that I've seen him, I think that I'd do it for nothing. Not that I'd refuse that ten thousand bucks either!"

He held out his hand and, as the little man grasped it, Durfee said: "But what's wrong with him? He's not like others. What's wrong with him?"

"Nothing's wrong," said Bunce sharply, "and you're to keep anything wrong from happening!"

CHAPTER 4

Despite the assurance of Bunce that there was nothing wrong, a far duller man than Durfee and one with much less experience could have told instantly that something was wrong, and decidedly wrong.

Otherwise, for instance, he, the guard of the young fellow, would surely have been told why the malignancy of Spot Lester should follow young Vincent, and why it was that he wished to harm the boy. Sheer trifling desire to do mischief was not one of the usual features of Lester's work. Cash, or revenge, or some other motive prompted his exploits.

No, Lester had some motive which brought him on the trail of young Henry Vincent, and Durfee did his best to find out what it might be, for he rather naturally thought that, once he mastered the motive for crime, he might be able the better to check the crime itself.

But he could not learn a word from the rancher who was employing him.

His repeated inquiries during the days that followed met with silence, and finally with a blunt command that he was to hold his tongue on the subject.

He tried the other men who were working on the ranch with no better results.

They knew nothing about young Henry Vincent. They simply were told that he was the nephew of their employer. They never had seen him on the ranch before. Neither did they know anything about the father of the boy. Vincent and his ancestors were a blank in their minds.

As for Bunce himself, they knew that he had come into the community fifteen years before, a man in all essentials exactly as he was today, nervous, keen, sharp-tempered, shunning the society of his peers, living alone with his work. He had brought with him a large amount of money and a very thorough knowledge of how cattle should be worked.

Then he had succeeded in picking out an excellent site for his operations, and for fifteen years he had used money, industry, and exceptional intelligence to swell his fortunes. He was the sort of fellow who knew when to hold the crop of baled hay until the middle of winter, when he sold it at a vast profit; he seemed to know when to skip a year of light prices, and unload a double number of beeves when the price climbed up again. And besides a superior intelligence, he seemed to have luck always on his side.

Naturally, he was not a man to be envied, on account of his surpassing physical misfortunes; but somehow his neighbors got into the habit of buying and selling when he led the way.

As for friends, he had none. His manners were harsh, and his soul seemed acrid and sour beneath the exterior. Yet he made, the punchers insisted, an excellent boss. He was always riding out over the range, sitting humped painfully sidewise on his horse, but he used his eyes for his own purposes, not to find fault with the operations of his men.

Sluggards and fools were instantly discharged. But a fellow with normal intelligence and willingness to do his share was not blamed for stampedes or other accidents; his pay was up to the right standard; and there was always an ample staff for the work in hand. Punchers who had labored on worse places—and who among them had not?—declared that this was the sort of paradise for the cowhand.

So when they found that their employer was uncommunicative, they sympathized and shut their mouths and attended to their own concerns. They strongly suggested to Mr. Durfee that it would be better for all concerned if he should imitate their example.

That was all very well for them, but they did not have to keep the figure of Spot Lester in the backs of their minds, and Durfee did. And the thought of the great criminal haunted him continually.

He knew well enough why Lester continued to break the laws and defy them with impunity and much profit. It was because the man combined with a shrewd intellect, a character incapable of remorse, pity, friendship, or affection. He was never rash from overswelling courage. He never rushed into danger for the love of it. Instead, he hunted like a cat, always cautious, bright of eye, suspicious. The waving of a blade of grass could make him pause, but fifty armed guards could not turn him back, eventually, from his purpose.

As secret as a cat's paw, and as dangerous, he glided about his mischief like a shadow. And because scruples never encumbered him, he made swift and successful way always. He had been thwarted, to be sure, but never once had he actually been brought to account.

It was not by cleverness or superior adroitness with weapons that Durfee hoped eventually that he might thwart the prowler; it was simply by luck that he hoped to win out. But he wanted, in the first place, to take every possible measure of prevention. In time of peace he wanted to prepare for war.

What made the thing most trying was that the great criminal gave no sign that he was near. It was true that Bunce gave repeated warning that Spot Lester must now be at hand, watching like a cat before the kill, but there was no token of a prowler.

And day by day, Durfee went on with this ridiculously easy and pleasant work.

He rose when he felt like it and breakfasted on fried trout or similar dainties from the mountain stream. Then he went out to the big corral and sat on the fence, and with a casual glance, picked over the dozen animals which were exclusively reserved for his use and the boy's.

Here Henry Vincent would be found. Apparently he rose at the break of day and, according to the cook, after eating his breakfast he went straight out to the corral and waited there for his companion.

He would not be leaning against the fence, or sitting on a convenient tree stump, but standing erect, easily, never weary or discomposed even though he might have been waiting there, the cook swore, for as much as an hour! And he would greet Durfee with the same half bland and half blank look, and the same meaningless smile.

The cow-punchers made up their minds about him quickly. They said: "The poor kid's a dummy. But that ain't his fault."

Then they forgot about him. Fools are not plagued for their folly in the great West, unless they make themselves obnoxious. And young Henry Vincent never seemed aware of the existence of others more than he was aware of trees and mountains; of himself, as well, he semed to take no thought!

For he cared not what he wore, or what horse he rode, or what rifle was put into his hands. He was willing to walk, or willing to ride. He would climb a mountain as readily as he would stroll over a green meadow. He would hold the horses patiently for hours, while Durfee worked out a trail problem; and he bore messages, chopped wood when a fire was wanted as they camped out; and in all ways he comported himself like a roustabout.

What was in him?

There seemed no ambition, no looking forward from one day to the next, or even from one hour to the next hour.

Once, Durfee asked Bunce how the boy had done in school, and was told curtly that it was none of his blamed business. That was, in fact, the last question that he had cared to ask.

After all, it was the easiest and the pleasantest task that he had ever taken on his hands. He got a hundred dollars a week. And as for Spot Lester, well, when he turned up there would be a chance of earning ten thousand dollars in hard cash, or twice that much in the sort of property which he most wanted in this world.

But for the shadow which Spot Lester cast upon his existence, Durfee would have been happier, now, than he ever had been before.

He wandered over the big range as though he had owned it, with a proprietor's love for his own land. He followed the gay, dancing, chanting little streams over the flat and through the rolling lands, and high up their solemn canyons among the mountains of the back country. He noted all the good pools, some only where fish might be tempted with rod and line, and some deep enough for a swim.

He spotted the worn trails, which were not very numerous, and the inaccessible paths of mountain sheep and goats, and where the deer came down through the woods to find water, or traveled from mountain meadow to a new pasture land. He knew the mountains themselves, the foothills, and the separate groves of trees.

He studied the animals, too, and soon learned the outlines of the separate domains of the three ranges of the grizzly bears who plagued the mountains. He also knew the sign of the buffalo wolves, the big gray, wise-headed rascals who, next to the grizzly itself, are the most cunning of all dwellers in the wilderness. He likewise followed the mountain lions, and whatever he learned, he used to teach to young Henry Vincent at the end of the day.

Then they would sit down with a map of the district which Durfee had sketched out with care. First, they charted in their travels of the day and, next, they talked over whatever had been seen. That is to say, Durfee talked, and the boy listened attentively, gravely, without excitement, but with the childish, meaningless smile on his lips, the smile that never extended to his sober eyes.

For some time Durfee had felt sure he was talking to a blank wall, but after a while he began to get responses. If he asked questions about what he said on other days, he found that everything was remembered, almost word for word!

On that he based his hope, and in the steady progress of his protege in all matters of riding, fishing, and shooting.

CHAPTER 5

Granted a physical machine so magnificent, it would have been strange, indeed, if the boy could not have accomplished almost anything to which he gave his attention; and his attention was always and entirely devoted to what he had placed before him by the forethought of Durfee.

When Durfee told him to get out on the smooth grass of

the meadow near the house and practice fly casting, young Henry Vincent kept it up for three hours, until supper time. And he began again the next morning, though his hand was covered with blisters.

In the art of using an ax, the great thing was to be able to strike the line drawn by the mind's eye, and, to help, Durfee marked a hundred pencil strokes on a log and told the boy to practice on them.

Henry Vincent obeyed immediately. He worked all day at the task and returned to it willingly.

The sign of the animals which appeared on the trail, they studied together. When they got home, Durfee drew the footprints. Vincent then copied them with the easy accuracy of a natural draftsman.

They worked on the birds of the air in the same manner. They drew talons and wings and beak; they examined feathers, and drew them in turn. They looked up the names of flowers, grasses, weeds. They examined the trees. They treated the whole range as a book, to be studied. And presently Durfee found himself making distinct efforts to keep ahead of his pupil, so that every day he would have new lessons to teach him.

He was not exactly a brilliant pupil, but he was steady. He gathered in the words, and he imitated the actions of his instructor. In this way they made famous progress.

The story, as Durfee guessed at it, was that the boy had been kept long and vainly in schools; and, because of his failure, he had been called back to the ranch.

Well, no matter about books. He, Durfee, had no use for them, either. But he would show the punchers on the place what he could do with a "dummy!"

He showed them, too.

Red Al, the foreman, came with them one Sunday and was allowed to fill his eyes with the sight of Henry Vincent riding a mustang uphill and down dale, over slopes that staggered the horse, but never staggered the rider. He saw Henry Vincent sit calmly while the mustang skidded askew to the bottom of a gravel slope. And when Red saw the unchanged, faint smile on the lips of the youngster, he muttered faint oaths which were music to the ear of Durfee.

That was not all.

Later on, Red was permitted also to see the other two screw together the tapering sections of fishing rods, then flick the dry flies over the surface of ragged, white-streaked water, until a little silver streak of dynamite tackled the end of Henry Vincent's line and was duly landed with a touch as delicate as that of a veteran. And he saw the boy clean the fish properly, build the fire, and grill those trout brown, while the coffee was coming to a boil.

On the whole, it was one of the great days in Durfee's life. He said not one word to Red. He let Red do the talking, and what Red had to say was enough!

Thereafter, the punchers took a new attitude toward the boy. They gave him grave advice about his riding. Though they knew that the chief had forbidden the mounting of young Henry on any of the really bad bucking horses, the educated pitchers, they told him how a bad horse is managed; they showed him how to do the thing. They showed him how to master the head of an iron-mouthed brute of a mustang, how to sit for a sunfisher, and how to remain upright when one of the brutes starts to spin in a circle.

They showed him these things, and he watched and listened with the same sober blankness in his eyes.

"He ain't a dummy," said Montana Pete. "He's just an empty bottle that needs filling. We'll fill him, too!"

But to Durfee, rather naturally, all other arts were dependent upon and subordinate to using the rifle and revolver. The revolver was forbidden in the hands of Henry Vincent—because, perhaps, the uncle thought the gun too dangerous for a half-wit to handle? Only the rifle was permitted. Even this was supposed to be used sparingly, according to the first instructions. But Durfee felt that every good teacher must, to a certain degree, arrange the curriculum of the pupil.

So he made the work with the rifle a constant thing every day.

He was a severe, an exact, and a knowing master. His teaching began with the proper cleaning of a gun, and then followed the understanding of every working part. Next he took up range finding, and shooting at every distance from fifty yards to a thousand. For he was not one of those who believe that brilliancy at a target twenty-five yards away, even though the target be a dancing ball on a stream of water, is a real accomplishment. The aim which brings down a running deer a quarter of a mile away—that is what keeps flesh on the ribs of the hunter, even in the leanest season, on the widest desert. He knew how to do those, things, and he proceeded to teach the boy what he could.

After all, he had for a pupil one whose hand never trembled, whose eye was clear as the eye of a hawk. The problems became simply those of shooting at distances, and of striking a moving mark, like a rock thrown into the air, or something foolish, say, like a buzzard, sliding aslant down the viewless path of the wind, somewhat too close to the earth. Even one of these the boy brought to the earth!

And then another and a greater day came for Durfee, when he and his protege were saddled and ready to ride, early one morning, at the very hour when the punchers made ready to take to the range.

A big, long-legged jack rabbit jumped up from the grass and started for the horizon.

"You might try that rabbit, Henry," said Durfee.

And the long Winchester glided swiftly into the hand of the boy.

Red began to laugh; his laughter ended when the first bullet made the jack rabbit dodge, and the second broke its back.

Straightway, Bud McCormick dismounted and paced off the distance.

"Seventy yards!" said he.

"Seventy yards!" muttered a profound chorus.

The punchers were men to whom only certain virtues were of great importance, and only certain accomplishments. If they were presented to a man who was modest and whose tongue was straight, the only diploma he needed was a known ability to ride, to shoot, to catch a fish, and follow a trail.

So they took off their hats, mentally, to the pupil and, above all, they took them off to the teacher.

Perhaps, if Durfee had been entirely perfect, he would have admitted that that was a lucky shot. He would not have winked at the boys when Henry Vincent said: "I don't think that I could do that again—not once in ten."

The punchers took that for modesty; Durfee knew it to

be the truth. But, after all, virtue must have a boundary, and his had been reached. He was not at all prepared for the counterblast that followed this performance.

He was called into the library that same evening, and there he found his employer with a face as white as chalk and even more sour than usual.

Said Bunce: "Red has been telling me a very interesting story about a rabbit on the run, killed with what was practically a snapshot at seventy yards."

"That's what happened," said Durfee. And he grinned. He was sorry for the grin a moment later.

"Never let him have a gun in his hands from now on," said Bunce. "You hear me?"

"Not have a gun?" exclaimed Durfee. "Why, that ain't—" The fist of the little man banged on the desk.

"Don't tell me what it is. It's orders, and that's enough for you!"

Durfee thrust out his jaw.

He had never taken talk like this before. The Rangers were a rough lot, and the rough side of a Ranger officer's tongue could take the hide off a mule at one swipe. But they taught their tongues smoothness, when they dealt with Durfee. Now, however, he held his speech and his breath. He was not thinking of his hundred dollars a week. He was not even thinking of ten thousand dollars and a golden haze for the end of his life. He was thinking, simply, of the boy, and the perfect days they had spent together among the mountains, by the streams, and in the woods.

As the words of the rancher fell like a whip stroke, under the pain of them, Durfee simply winced in silence, for he knew that he loved his pupil. He could not give up this place for the sake of vindicating his proud self-respect.

"All right," he said, "I'll not give him a gun any more. And the range'll lose one of the best natural riflemen that ever looked through sights!"

"A curse on you!" screamed Bunce. "And I suppose that you've let him find that out? Now you've probably spoiled everything. Get out of my sight."

And Durfee left the room, but he did not leave the place. Three times he made up his pack, and three times he undid it again. He sweated. He turned hot and cold. But at last he swallowed his pride and remained.

CHAPTER 6

One thing was very clear after this. It was not Spot Lester, alone, whom Bunce feared. For some reason that Durfee could not fathom, the man feared something in Henry Vincent himself!

Was there some superstition connected with firearms in the Vincent family? Was there some old legend which would explain it all?

The more Durfee pondered, the more convinced he was that if the wits of the boy were not very active, those of his uncle were actively unsound.

And then came the happening which suggested to him that there was more in Henry Vincent than the mere strength of his body and the blankness of his eyes.

For, finally, he saw those eyes lighted. And this was the way of it.

They had gone fishing, and from fishing they had taken their horses along an upper trail, and they had seen a little bank of mountain goats scampering on the rocks above them, gone suddenly mad with terror.

It was a narrow ledge along which the goats fled, and the watchers, looking up, distinctly saw the lithe form of a mountain lion bound after the fugitives, and overtake and strike down one of them.

Durfee unsheathed his rifle, but slayer and slain disappeared among the rocks.

"What brings that blasted murderer on the loose at this time of the day?" said Durfee.

"You told me," said the boy, "that when the female has young, it's apt to hunt even in the broad daylight."

Durfee looked at his pupil. He was continually being surprised in this fashion by his own words coming back to him.

"Well, that's true," said he, at last, "and there may be a litter of cubs at the base of the trail, if we can run it down. We'll take a try, anyway."

So they made the try and climbed a dangerous trail until they came to that upper ledge.

The way was clear enough, for it was dotted with the blood of the goat, which the slayer had dragged or carried down the ledge for a considerable distance, until the mountain gave back in a narrow shoulder, and before them there appeared a heap of great, broken rocks, like the ruins of an immense building. There was a narrow aperture at the base of the heap.

"That may be a cave," said Henry Vincent. "Perhaps they're in there now. Look! There's blood on the rocks just beside the entrance! Will it come out if I throw a rock in?"

"Don't do that!" exclaimed Durfee.

But he was too late, for Vincent had picked up a sizable stone, as he spoke, and flung it underhand through the mouth of the tunnel.

As for Durfee, he had not yet so much as dismounted.

There was a frightful screech in answer, and out into the sunshine flashed the tawny figure of the lioness, straight at the boy.

Durfee's rifle leaped from the bow of his saddle to his shoulder. At the same instant, he made sure that he had only time to make the quickest of snapshots. For, to his horror, he saw that Henry Vincent was not running for his life. Instead, he stood still and straight, and with his hunting knife in his hand.

Durfee's mustang decided to take a hand in the complication, at that moment.

When it saw the mountain lion, it wanted to get away. It wanted to get miles away, moved by a scent which had been a horror in its nostrils from the days of its colthood. Not for nothing were there long, parallel furrows scarred along its hips and quarters!

But the quarters were cramped. There was a precipice behind, and the ledge ran off to the left. So the mustang decided to shed its rider to make the running lighter.

It turned as a cat turns, and bucked at the instant that the rifle came to Durfee's shoulder.

And he left the saddle, and soared high, and smote heavily upon the rocks.

Darkness jumped across his brain, as tropic night at a stride rounds the horizon and lets the stars come through.

Finally, he groped his way back to consciousness and staggered to his feet.

The thought of the danger of the boy was like a hand dragging him back to the light.

And so he saw the little plateau before the entrance to the cave was empty and from within the cave itself came terrible, unearthly howls and growling.

Then the darkness, at a stroke, left his brain. He was himself, though gripped with fear, cold and shaken with it. But the pain that racked his head was nothing, nor the blood that trickled down his face, for those howls seemed to indicate that the chief of all horrors had taken place: Henry Vincent had been dragged into the cave and there was feebly struggling with the beast.

Could he not hear the sound of blows, as though human hands were beating the supple body of the slayer?

Even with that motive driving him forward, he hesitated for a moment, as he reached the narrow darkness of the entrance. For in there all would be as the thick darkness of night, to eyes accustomed to the brilliance of this daylight.

Then he mastered himself and crawled through the narrow gap, rubbed his eyes and thrust forward his rifle, cautiously seeking for a target.

But all was a wall of black before him, a wall that pressed close up to his face.

And silence had come.

He knew what that meant.

She had finished her work with one man, the feline monster, and now she was stalking forward to make her spring at the second. He dared not back up again through the entrance; as he struggled through, she would find him helpless and would strike with fatal effect.

He could only wait, and pray that his eyes would be able to strain through the murk and make out the target.

And then he heard other sounds, not the growling of the beast, nor the groaning of a stricken man, but a plaintive mewing.

Now, as the brain clears after sleep, his eyes cleared, and he saw the limp, sleek body of the mountain lion stretched on her back on the floor, and the form of the boy rising.

In that posture and that light, it looked like the shadow

of a giant. Then he made out the features of young Henry Vincent and the dull gleam of the hunting knife in his hand.

As one who slams the shutters of his window when he has looked out on some prodigious horror, so Durfee blinded his eyes and closed his mind against the thought which came home to him: with a hunting knife, alone, the boy had faced the charge of a savage mountain lion and killed the beast.

By the time his brain cleared a little, the boy was walking toward him again, out of the gloom and the sound of mewing approached with him.

They came close to the light that filtered through the narrow entrance, and Durfee saw the little tawny beasts, huddled in the arms of the man, mewing piteously.

He saw them only dimly, for with his mind he was seeing more than with his eyes.

"We'd better get her out of here, if we're to skin her," said the boy, in the most matter-of-fact tone.

Durfee said nothing. He simply laid hold on a forepaw, and helped to drag the weight. The head of the monster fell limply down. Under the grip of his hands, the curved, back-edged scimitars of the claws thrust out and gouged into the flesh of his palms. It was like pulling at a thorn tree.

But when they brought the loose weight into the open, then Durfee saw the story more vividly, far, than words could tell it.

The hide of the mountain lioness was worthless. One great knife stroke had ripped her from shoulder to midflank. And there were savage thrusts that had driven into her breast and throat. There was, particularly, one great gash that cut across the throat itself. From that, perhaps, death had followed, with the loss of quantities of blood.

What had she been doing, this finely made thing of destruction, as she died?

Well, young Henry Vincent's body told the tale.

A score of gashes appeared on him, and the blood ran freely from him, yet he was paying no attention to his wounds.

He was a crimson figure, a form dripping red. But he smiled as he looked down at the dead animal.

There was this difference. It was not the dull, blank smile which Durfee had seen in his face and eyes before; rather it was a light that overspread his entire being. The whole recognition and joy of existence were there. He was like a man who has been crowned.

Durfee was amazed.

It made the boy seem older, stronger, swifter, more powerful even, although wounded.

And now, as he looked at Henry Vincent, he remembered a great many things that Bunce had said and done. They seemed more comprehensible.

Whereas, before, it had seemed that Bunce was striving to keep the boy from the dangers of the world, it now appeared that perhaps Bunce was striving to keep the world from the dangers of the boy.

The idea was a mad one; Durfee strove to drive it away from his mind. But the thought was lodged in him.

CHAPTER 7

The care of the wounds was not easy. He got young Vincent to the nearest gush of spring water, made him strip, and then bathed the wounds. They were not deep, and the flow of blood was already ebbing. It was as though, to return to an earlier comparison he had made, Henry Vincent were made of bloodless iron, with a fleshing of human skin above.

He tore up a great part of his clothes, made them in strips, and used the white dust of the trail as a first dressing. In this way the flow of the blood had finally been stopped.

As he worked, he wondered what Vincent would look like ten years from today, his body covered with those long scars, entangling here and there, like the crossing of many trails.

He said: "The horse threw me on my head, Henry. What really happened in this turn-out?"

"The lioness came at me, and she came very fast."

"I know," answered Durfee. "I've seen 'em charge. They take about twenty yards at a jump."

"She was almost on top of me," went on the boy, "when she saw you fall from the horse."

He paused. The brightness, the new brightness of his eyes, was obscured with reflection.

"D'you know, Durfee," said he, "I think that cats are not made of very honest stuff?"

"Why?" asked Durfee.

"Because the puma turned aside. She saw you were lying sprawled out, and she veered off from me and went to find easier meat."

Durfee half closed his eyes. He was wondering, in fact, what he would have been doing, had he stood in the shoes of the boy. Even though a comrade had fallen, if the weapon in his hand had been no more than a knife, he would have taken to his heels, he thought. Perhaps he would have tried to throw stones from a distance, to frighten the beast off as it mangled the body of his comrade. A man cannot tell what he will do in a pinch.

"Well," he said, "what did you do, son?"

"What did I do?" answered Vincent, opening his eyes a little, as though it were perfectly clear what a man should and would do, under such circumstances.

He added, laughing: "Oh, at first I wanted to run; and then I wished that I had a gun, but finally, because there wasn't much time to think things over, I made a reach for her, as she whizzed by, and got my knife into her shoulder. It made quite a rip. I felt the blood spurt and she howled like a demon."

He smiled gently, on Durfee.

The latter felt, suddenly, that words were very silly things. Then he said: "She turned at you, then, I suppose?"

"Oh, she twisted right around," said the boy. "You know how a snake twists, when you stumble on it? She turned that way, and made a jump for me."

"Well?" said Durfee.

"It was just luck," said the boy. "I ducked, and she sailed right over my head. It was a strange thing. Her snarl, as she whizzed by me, sounded like tearing cloth. Doesn't that seem strange to you?"

Durfee was sweating. He took out a handkerchief and rubbed his face.

"Yeah, that's strange," said he.

"I turned around," said Vincent, "hoping that she'd been pretty badly hurt by the knife, and wouldn't want to fight any more. And it seemed that I was right. Because when she landed after her jump at me, she went right on inside the cave."

Durfee stared at him. "Then?" said he.

"Then what?" asked the boy, mildly.

"I mean," said Durfee, "how did you happen to get inside the cave?"

"I?" asked Vincent.

He regarded Durfee for a moment, his brow puckered, his expression one of clear bewilderment.

"Well, I walked, you see," said he. "Of course, that was the only way for me to get inside. Oh, I had to crawl to get into the cave. Is that what you wanted me to answer?"

Said Durfee slowly: "What made you want to get into the cave at all?"

The other hesitated, as one upon uncertain ground.

Then he answered: "Well, she'd come out here and charged us, hadn't she?"

"Yes," said Durfee. "What's that got to do with it?"

"What has it to do with it?" asked the boy. He smiled, puzzled and still very uncertain, as one waiting for the point of an obscure joke.

Then he added: "I didn't know how else to play the game with her. I had to get inside."

"You knew she wasn't killed; you knew that it was dark inside there?"

"Oh, yes."

"But you simply went on in?"

"Well, I didn't simply go in," qualified the boy. "I kneeled at the entrance of the cave and waited there until my eyes got used to the darkness. It was pitch dark, at the first, but afterward, it was like a dull twilight. I could see her clearly. Her eyes were phosphorescent and green. So were the eyes of her cubs, but not so bright."

Durfee cleared his throat. Finally he was able to say: "Why didn't you go over and pick up my rifle?"

The boy nodded.

"Yes, I thought of that. I see you're trying to test me. But I'm ashamed to say that I did think of getting the rifle to use on her!"

"Ashamed?" queried Durfee.

"You know," said the boy, "that wouldn't have been a fair fight. I mean to say, she was already wounded. And I was not hunting to find food. It's a little different, don't you think, when a person is shooting for meat to fill his stomach?"

Durfee cleared his throat, and again he said nothing. His blood was colder than ever.

"After I could see in the gloom," said the boy, "the rifle would have settled everything unfairly, too easily for me. And then—there would have been no game!"

He smiled, remembering.

"Game?" said Durfee hoarsely.

"Well, you think it was very simple, and I suppose that it would have been, for you," remarked Henry Vincent candidly. "I suppose that an old hunter like you would know just how to kill a puma at a stroke. But I had no idea, except to keep firing away at the throat and breast, cutting and slashing and stabbing."

Durfee scrubbed his face again with the handkerchief. "What was the mountain lion doing all that time?" he asked.

"She fought," said the boy. "She was wonderfully quick, and once she knocked me flat. You see how my coat's torn? That's where her claws struck. I tell you, I saw stars."

Again, he laughed cheerfully, merrily.

Durfee did not laugh. On his face was a seasick expression.

"That must have been a lot of fun," said he.

The shining eyes of the boy gleamed still brighter, glancing across at the older man.

"Yes, of course, it was. It was like playing tag, you know."

"Yes, of course it was," groaned Durfee. "You must have thought that you were it, eh?"

"I thought she'd have her teeth in my throat the next half second," said the boy. "The knife was in my right hand. I felt her, rather than saw her, coming through the air at me. But my left hand luckily had fallen on a good big stone, and I threw that directly in her face as she was still in the air."

He looked down at his left hand and moved the fingers.

"See how the stone took the skin off the ends of my fingers?" he said, with his bright, childish, new-found smile.

"Yea. That's a funny thing," muttered Durfee.

"It had an odd effect on her," said the boy. "It hit her fairly in the head and jerked it back and up, so that she missed her spring. I felt the fur of her brushing past me. And I got on my knees in time to meet her next jump. She was growling a good deal, but I saw the base of her throat and tried a straight thrust at that, as a target. She tumbled straight on over me and I felt her claws. They were like knives. You've no idea!"

"No," said Durfee. "I've no idea!"

He was breathing hard. He looked no longer at the face of the boy, but down at the ground.

"I stabbed at her a few more times, and then she was still," said young Vincent.

He laughed again softly, broodingly.

"I must have been pretty badly frightened," said he. "I know that when I stood up, and saw you there, all ready in the door of the cave, I was very relieved. I could see, then, that I had been excited about nothing, and that you could have finished the fight any time, except that you wanted me to kill my first puma. Thanks a lot for that. I suppose it's an old story, to you; but it was the first one, for me!"

CHAPTER 8

Durfee cut off the claws of the killer. While he was doing that, young Vincent got hold of the cubs. He insisted on taking them back with him to the house.

"Why not drown them in the creek?" demanded Durfee. "They ain't gunna grow up to be no good. They're wild, and wild things will always go bad when their time comes and they get the taste of blood."

But Henry Vincent was firm. He said: "You know how it is. I wouldn't feel like a decent man, knowing that the mother was dead, and the little things wiped out at the same time."

So they were stowed in a nest of dead grass, in a saddle bag, and the return journey was made.

"Are you feeling stiff? Are you cold in the wounds?" asked Durfee, on the way.

"No, not a bit," said the boy.

He added: "I'm rather happy, Durfee, I don't know why I should be. I suppose I ought to be ashamed."

"Ashamed, eh?" snapped Durfee. "After you've killed a puma in a fair fight?"

"Oh, if it had been a fair fight, without odds, that would be different," admitted the boy. "But she was as God made her, and I had a long knife in my hand. That's why I'm rather ashamed. But, as I said before, I can't help being rather happy, too. I don't know why."

He sighed, and fell into a streak of moralizing, which Durfee long remembered.

"I wish that I were a great deal more like you, Durfee," said the boy. "You're quiet and calm, and you bear no malice, and you're always gentle and steady."

"Leaving me out of it, so are you," said Durfee.

"I? Oh, no! You've no idea how irritated I grow sometimes. I mean to say," Vincent explained, "that when people have smiled at me, aside, it sometimes makes me angry. I try to swallow it, but it seems that I never can forget. That's not very good to admit, but it's the truth."

Durfee looked straight ahead of him.

"Just for a minute, back there in the cave," went on the boy, "it was as if I were driving that knife into every man who ever had laughed at me!"

He sighed again.

"Well, it was only a mountain lion," said Durfee, gruffly.

"Yes, I know," said the boy. "Only—"

His voice trailed off, as though he were unable to find the proper words.

"It was only a little bit of a mountain lion, able to kill a grown horse in three seconds. That's all it was," said Durfee. "Don't you let a killing like that get on your conscience. You're all right."

"Thanks," said the boy, with solemnity. "I'm rather glad to hear you say that!"

Somehow, Durfee knew that he was smiling again, and he studiously avoided that smile. It was impossible, for

a long time, for him to look at the youngster, for his
thoughts occupied all of his mind. He could not make out
this strange creature. He had lived with the lad for a long
time, and yet he realized, now, that this was the first day
he ever had come close to Henry Vincent. Never before
had he heard the lad speak from the heart, as he had spoken
about the fight with the mountain lion.

Finally, Durfee said, though he still looked straight before him down the trail: "Look here, Henry!"

"Yes?" said the boy.

"Suppose that fight were to come your way again."

"Yes?" said the boy.

"Would you fight with a knife again?"

"I've been thinking about that," said Vincent. "I don't
know. If I had to fight, I don't see how I could manage
with my bare hands, do you?"

"I ain't asking a question to be answered with one!" said
the preceptor.

"I don't know," said the lad. "I should think that just
to start in and, then, to use anything that came handy, a
stone or a stick—that might be a great deal fairer than
simply to step in and do a outright murder with bare hands,
you know."

"I *don't* know," said Durfee.

And he was silent again for a long time, thinking of the
little, twisted body of Bunce, and the strange attitude which,
from the beginning, the rancher had taken toward the ed-
ucation of his nephew.

He was still thinking of that; he was wondering if, on
this day, he had been enabled to take a close view of the
reasons behind the attitude of Bunce, when he heard a
strong, clear voice break into song.

There were no words in the thing. It was no popular
tune which Durfee could recognize. It was simply a stream
of sound such as might have flowed from a violin; from an
organ, rather. It ran and flowed through the grove of pine
trees in which they were riding, and Durfee, turning in the
saddle, saw Henry Vincent well behind him, his hands hanging loosely from the pommel of the saddle his head thrown
back, while, regardless of the wounds that raked his body,
a stream of song poured out from his big throat.

Oh, yes, if nothing else was clear, it was very apparent that young Henry Vincent was a very happy lad.

But it was a gloomy Durfee who finally arrived at the ranch.

He got the boy to bed. He was glad, very glad, that Bunce was away from the house, out riding the range.

But when he went out to the bunk house, a little later, after seeing that the lad had had his wounds properly cleansed and freshly bandaged, he met Red, who said: "How many rabbits has the kid killed today?"

"No rabbit," said Durfee. "Just a little mountain lion."

"Good for the kid. Long shot?"

"It wasn't a shot," said Durfee. "He just used a knife on it."

Red looked hard at him. "Are you kidding me, Durfee?" he asked.

"You darned fool," said Durfee savagely, "do I look like I was kidding?"

This did not irritate Red. He was too interested to be insulted.

"Say, whacha mean?" he asked.

"Oh, nothing," replied Durfee. "There was just a puma that come rompin' out of her cave and took a charge at me, and my fool mustang dumped me on my head. Then the cat come for me; and the kid, he knifed her as she went by and drove her into her cave, where she had a pair of cubs. Then he followed her into the dark and fought her, and she knocked him down. He socked her dizzy with a stone and then he closed in and stabbed her to death."

He enjoyed piling up the impossible, the silly details of that unearthly fight.

"Is he cut to pieces?" asked Red, when he saw that it was not a matter to smile at.

"Him? He's kind of grazed, here and there. Cat claws, they don't make much impression on wrought iron," said Durfee.

Red looked him over. "This here day was kind of hard on you," he remarked.

"Oh, you can go to blazes!" answered Durfee.

He went on into the bunk house, and there he turned into his bunk, though he had not eaten any supper, and fell asleep.

He was awakened in the dusk; Mr. Bunce wanted him at once.

He raised himself on one elbow.

"You tell Mr. Bunce he can go to blazes, and take my job along with him!" he told the Chinese.

CHAPTER 9

Perhaps that message was not accurately relayed. At any rate, word came out again and this time it was Bunce himself who brought it. The rest of the punchers were out in the open, for the night was still and close and hot.

Bunce went inside, and found the bunk house deserted, except for the one mound of blankets and the snoring Durfee.

He sat down on a stool near the bed and awoke the ex-Ranger.

"Well, whacha want?" asked Durfee.

"You're sleeping in early tonight," said the rancher.

"Yeah, I got a long ride and an early start to make, to-morrow morning," said Durfee.

"I gave you no orders for tomorrow," said Bunce.

"You ain't giving me orders no more," announced the other.

"Are you quitting, you think?" asked Bunce.

"I don't think. I know," said Durfee.

"You're going to lay down on the job, are you?" demanded Bunce.

"I sure am."

"What's the matter?"

"Too many spooks."

"What sort of spooks?" asked Bunce. "You mean, Spot Lester?"

"Lester?" said Durfee in violent tones. "I mean the kid himself."

"What d'you mean about him?"

"You know what I mean," said Durfee grimly. "You know that he's a nut. And that's why you didn't want him crossed by a bucking horse, or his hand filled with a gun. Ain't I right?"

"Never heard of such an idea," said Bunce.

"Well, you hear it now, and you know that I'm right."

"Open up, Durfee," said the rancher.

"I mean," said Durfee solemnly, "that I've had hard jobs all my life, and small pay. But the big pay on this job ain't worth the nerves that I gotta spend on it from now on."

"Why?"

"Because I'm scared of the kid, if you want me to tell you!"

"What, scared of Henry Vincent?"

"Yes."

"Why, he loves you, man."

"Does he?" said Durfee, with a sneer. "Well, he loves mountain lions, too. Loves 'em old, and loves 'em young. I'm gunna get out of this. I've said my say. I don't make speeches."

"What happened?" asked Bunce.

"You know that. I've already told enough people, and you've heard your kid nephew talk about it."

"He's mostly interested in how he can train the two cubs," said Bunce.

"You never seen him dancing with a long, sleek, evil-eyed mountain lion for a partner," said Durfee. "But I have, and I'm through. He ain't gunna dance with me that way."

He closed his eyes with a faint groan. He began to feel that this day had been a nightmare.

"The boy loves you," said Bunce.

"Well," began Durfee, and stuck there.

"He loves you," said Bunce, "and I think that you love him."

"I don't," began Durfee, and stuck once more. In the pause he could hear the hard, rapid breathing of the other. And he was glad, for some reason, that the quiet voice of the rancher had merely served as an insufficient mask to cover the real intensity of his feeling.

Said Bunce: "I've got to have you. The time has come when I have to bank on you or nothing."

"You bank on nothing," said Durfee. "You've paid me

cash. You can have it back. I'm paid out already. I want to get back to real men. I've had enough ghosts. You paid me cash. You never gave me no confidence. You knew that he was this way!"

"What way?" asked Bunce, his whining voice sharper and higher than ever.

Durfee considered. Then he said: "There ain't no words for it, but you know what I mean."

"Well," said Bunce, still more slowly, "maybe I know what you mean, too!"

"Come clean with me and I'll go the whole way with you, if I can. I like the kid. That is, I wanta like him. If only he's human. You come clean and tell me what's what!"

And he heard Bunce saying: "I can't come clean because I don't know what's what. And the little part that I know, or guess, my teeth are locked on. It isn't honorable for me to talk it out, even to you. And I think a lot of you, Durfee. I'm mighty sorry for what you saw today."

"You knew that I'd see it sooner or later?" asked Durfee.

"No, but I was afraid."

"You ain't in the open with me," remarked Durfee.

"I'm as close to the open as I dare to come."

"Tell me, has the kid got something wrong with his brain?"

Said Bunce, half in a groan and half in a sigh: "If I had as good a brain as his, I'd tear the world in two; I'd crack it like a nut, and take out all the meat that I wanted!"

"I hear you say that," answered Durfee. "Go on."

"There's nothing more to go on to. I've told you all that I can."

"It's a big pile," said Durfee sneeringly. "Tomorrow I leave."

"You can't," said Bunce.

"Why can't I?"

"Because the time's too late for me to get a man to take your place. That's why."

"You don't need a man for my place. You need an army."

Bunce sighed again. "My friend, he's due to appear very soon," said he.

"Who?"

"The cap for the dynamite. And then—"

"What dynamite?"

"Henry."

"Yeah, he's dynamite, all right, and I saw him explode today!"

"No, you didn't. That was nothing to what could happen!"

Durfee, considering, finally muttered: "Maybe you're right. I don't want to be around when the crash comes, then!"

He felt the light, cold, trembling hand of the little man fall upon his shoulder. The voice of Bunce was only a whisper.

"You've got to stay," said Bunce. "Lester is going to arrive inside of twenty-four hours."

This brought Durfee to his feet, reaching for a gun.

"You sure tempt me," said he. "You make it a pretty picture, if I stay on."

"Oh, you'll stay, all right," said Bunce. "You stay—and God help you and me!"

They were silent. The heat, and the darkness suddenly stifled Durfee.

"Let's get outside," he muttered.

"Yes, let's get out into the air!" said Bunce.

They went together. When they got to the side of the house, the pair paused and Durfee looked gloomily across the dark hills.

Finally he said: "Well, old-timer, I dunno."

"I'm waiting," said Bunce.

"Well, then," muttered Durfee, "I'll tell you. If I stay, it ain't for cash."

"I'll raise the price," said Bunce.

"Dog-gone the price," said Durfee. "I ain't superstitious, exactly, but I won't sell my blood for hard cash. But I'll take the job and keep it, till Lester's bullets put out my light."

He heard a sobbing breath from Bunce.

"Thank God!" said the rancher.

They went into the house together and, as they walked on, Durfee was realizing that he had changed his mind and decided to stay on, though never before had he felt death so near him and never before had he found his heart so small and so cold in the presence of danger.

Furthermore, from Bunce he had gained not one single additional fact—only one more thing to chill his blood, that Bunce felt, and long had felt about the lad exactly what he, Durfee, had felt on this day.

They said good-by at the door of the library, into which the rancher was turning, and he reached up, like a child, and put his scrawny hand on the shoulder of the Ranger.

"Thanks are not what I give you," said Bunce. "Cash, neither. Neither thanks nor money."

Then he went hurriedly, with his grim, sidelong, lurching step, into the library.

As for Durfee, he went on, more slowly, through the dimly lighted old house to his room, next to that of the boy. His place in the bunk house was only occupied now and then, when he wanted to mix with his fellows, and to hear the yarns of the punchers at the end of the day; but nearly every night he slept in the house.

Before he went into his room, he stepped softly into that of young Henry Vincent and saw him by the light of a lamp in the corner of the room, the wick of which was turned down in the circular burner.

Nevertheless, a sufficient light was cast, and it showed the fine profile of the lad and the white streak of the bandage that crossed his forehead, for one of the scratches of the great cat had torn the skin of the head.

That was not all. It showed, also, the smile of one who sleeps with sweet dreams!

Hastily, Durfee backed out through the door and closed it soundlessly after him.

How many men in this world were able to fight a mountain lion hand to hand and then sleep like a child, afterward, forgetful of nerve shock, forgetful of pain?

But perhaps there never had been a nerve shock. Even in the beginning, even during the battle, there must have been little real fear, as other men know it.

He went slowly on into his own room, down-headed, fumbling.

So he found the light, struck the match, raised the chimney a little, and saw the blue-yellow flame run off the end of the match and circle the oily wick.

He settled the chimney down again, and as he stepped back from the table, he halted suddenly, with liquid ice flowing through his spinal marrow.

For he knew, suddenly, that a man and a gun were present, though unannounced, in the newly broken dark of the room.

CHAPTER 10

It was not in haste, but slowly, that Durfee turned his head and saw the gleam of the leveled revolver and then above that, the long, lean dark face of Spot Lester, large and brutal about the jaws.

And he, Durfee, had been the one to light the lamp by which he would be killed!

There was no use, he knew, in trying to reach back and dash the lamp from the table. His hand was fast; but he knew the superior speed of Lester, in deadly adroitness. It was, besides, almost better to die in the light than to be hunted to death in darkness by that great cat.

The hand of the man fascinated him, as always, even more than the face. It was long and pale; the fingers were square-tipped and seemed larger at the ends than at the base. And there was a growth of hair to the knuckles, almost like a black fur.

He saw these things, he thought of these things, as he slowly continued to turn head and body until he was facing the criminal.

Lester sat at ease in the best chair, lolling, his head well back. He looked like a man sinking asleep; but what little of his eyes was unveiled, burned steadily at the ex-Ranger.

"So!" said Durfee.

"Yeah. So," said Lester.

He lounged to the left. He covered a slight yawn. He considered Durfee lazily, but in detail, as though even the fashion of his boots was new and interesting. Plainly, as he allowed the muzzle of the Colt to sag down, he was tempting his victim to make a sudden move. But Durfee knew his man too well for that.

"I've been kind of expecting you for quite a while," said Durfee.

"Yeah. I've been around watching," said the other.

"What for?"

"To take a hand when the time came."

"What time, Lester?"

The other grinned slowly, until the stretch of his mouth was no longer a smile, but a great grimace.

"The time I was waiting for," he answered. "You were doing my job for me. You were doing it better than I could've done it. You were doing it slick."

"Was I?" said Durfee.

"Yeah. You was."

"Tell me what I've been doing, except teaching the kid, there?"

"That was what I meant. That was my job for me. You made a pretty good teacher, Durfee."

"I dunno what you mean," the ex-Ranger said.

"It ain't time for you to know," answered Spot Lester. "But tell me something."

"What?"

"You knew that I was on this here job?"

"I dunno what you mean."

"Bunce, he didn't tell you that he was expecting me?"

"Yes, he told me that."

"And still you wanted the place?"

"I wanted the place," said Durfee.

The other considered him, without passion, as though he were looking at a dumb beast. "Why?" he asked.

"There was big money," said Durfee.

"But what chance?" asked Lester.

Durfee shrugged his shoulders. "About one in ten," he admitted.

"That was about all," said Lester.

"Yeah. That was about all."

"You thought it was worth a play, though?" went on the criminal.

"Why all the questions?" said Durfee. "I know what this here means, well enough. You've got the drop on me, and I'm a dead man. Why all the talk? I ain't interested in anything that comes from you, except bullets, Lester."

"You will be, though. I got a thrilling surprise for you up my sleeve."

"You're full of surprises. I've had some of 'em from you before."

"Nothing to stack up with this one, though. I got a new sensation for you, Durfee."

"All right," said the Ranger.

"It's righter than you think," said Lester. "But I wanta find out about you, Durfee. You interest me a lot. I ain't gunna get any bullets from you, but I'm interested."

"Thanks," said Durfee. "Interested about what?"

"I don't understand you," said Lester. "You ain't a hero, but you don't look very white. You look as though you didn't expect to die."

"I ain't a hero," said Durfee, "but I'm kind of tired. That's all."

"Tired of what?"

"Life," said Durfee.

"Ah?" murmured Lester. "I dunno that I follow that. What you say is just words, to me. I never was tired of life, and I never could get tired. You mean that you're ready to lie down and die?"

"I'm sort of ready," said Durfee.

"Why?" asked Lester.

He was so drawn by his interest that he budged forward in his chair and sat up. His black eyes glistened like the eyes of an animal.

"Why?" he repeated. "You're young enough. You're strong enough. You got plenty of people that admire Durfee, the dead shot, the swell rider, the hero, the policeman."

He stopped himself with laughter. In his laughter he let his head fall back, but well enough the other understood that he was simply being tempted to make a movement to draw a gun.

He did not draw it!

"You got a lot before you," said Lester. "Why should you be ready to die?"

"Because I'm beat," said Durfee. "That's why."

"Because I've beat you?"

"No, not you. You don't have much to do with it. Raw meat without salt, it don't have much taste. I'm a bust.

I'm a failure. That's why I don't care so much, even when it's a yegg like you that puts me down, Lester."

"I don't mean much to you, eh?"

"No, not much," said Durfee. "You'd mean plenty if you was shoved behind the bars, if I had the taking of you. It'd mean a lot of glory, and all that. But you don't mean much."

"I've got you licked," said the criminal. "But it don't mean much, eh?"

"Put a wild cat against a house cat, and let 'em fight. Who'd be fool enough to bet on the house cat? And who'd even go to see the fight?" suggested the other.

"I see what's troubling you," remarked Lester. "I ain't like the rest?"

"No, you ain't like the rest."

"Well," said Lester, "the point is that you're beat. But I dunno about sinking a slug through you, Durfee."

"No," said Durfee, with a faint smile. "I guess that that is about too much for you."

"I'm not gunna put a bullet into you," repeated Lester. "One way of looking at it, we're old friends. We know each other too well. I ain't gunna plug you, for that reason."

"No?" murmured the other.

"No. I mean what I say. Put your hands behind your back and turn around."

Durfee frowned. He did not like the idea of a bullet tearing through his spine. He preferred to take his death facing it, as a man should. And he said so.

"You won't believe me, but I mean what I say," said Lester. "Turn around, and stick your hands out behind your back."

Durfee shrugged his shoulders. After all, it was not a matter of great importance how death should come to him.

At last, he turned, and held his hands back obediently. Strangely enough, he found himself thinking, not of his own sad end, but of the boy.

A double noose of twine or small cord was slipped over his wrists, and drawn tight. If he were to fight for his life, his time had passed. He wondered what sort of hypnosis had worked on him, to keep him from drawing a weapon and fighting, as a human being should do.

But in a moment, hands and feet were tied. He was

lifted in the arms of the other, and laid on the table and lashed to it.

"I've got to make sure that you'll be quiet. There's something else for me to do in the house, here," said Lester, reassuringly. "You see, I ain't so bad. I wouldn't just stand off and murder you with a gun, after I've got the drop on you, Durfee. We've fought too many times before; we're old friends."

He took out a large bandanna, rolled it, and suddenly crammed it between the teeth of Durfee. Then he passed another cord around the mouth that gaped open. Durfee could breathe, but only with difficulty.

Lester straightened.

"Yeah. We're old friends," said he. "I wouldn't want you to die no ordinary death, like a bullet just bashing through the middle of your brains. It ain't good enough for an honest man like you, partner. You need to have a chance to taste what's coming. You need salt on the meat, to get the taste of it. I'm gunna give you salt, too. Yeah, I'm gunna season you so you'll taste the death that's coming to you!"

He leaned over Durfee, laughing. Then he stepped back and drew from his pocket a small box, and from the box he produced two small glass bottles and a hypodermic needle.

CHAPTER 11

He laid the bottles on the edge of the table. One of them he uncorked, then filled the needle from it. As he worked, he talked. "This ain't fast stuff," said Lester. "This is slow-acting. Take a fellow like you, it's likely to use up about a half hour to drive the knife home and twist it and tear the heart out of you. It ain't no ordinary poison, son. No, no! This here has got everything that man would need to make him miserable. It works on the brain, and the nerves, and the blood. It rots you all at once. I tell you, it begins with a kind of warm flush. You sweat, is what you do. I know all about it and I'll tell you how I know. You're gunna be the only fellow in the world that I've told this here story to, son!"

He laid his hand upon the shoulder of Durfee and smiled down on him kindly. "You see, I was kind of chums with a lad, once, some years back. And he had an idea that I had a lot of money cached away. He had an idea that I'd made a lot of coin and that I didn't have no vices. Wine and women and gambling, they don't attract me none, and he knew it.

"So he says to himself that I must have a lot of hard cash stowed away, one place or another, and maybe he could find out where it was. And one day, when I was spread out sleeping, like a fool, he picked the lock of my door, soft as a cat's foot on a wet floor, and he come in and dropped a lariat over me and, as I sat up, he jerked that lariat's noose tight around my arms. In a minute he had rolled me tighter than the best-made cigarette in a wheat straw paper. That's what he done. Fast and neat was his motto, and he lived right up to it.

"He rolled me tight in ropes, and he says that he would like to know where I'd hidden my money.

"I said that I didn't have no money laid by, but he went ahead and he mentioned some bank safes I had cracked, and particularly one train I had robbed. And he says that I can't have spent that money, because I ain't got no way of spending, except to buy dynamite to boil down and make soup, and guns, and what feeds 'em, and enough bacon and eggs to keep me going. So he aims to say that I got money staked out, and he would like to know where it was.

"Well, I didn't know nothing, and I says so, and he lays out a couple of bottles, these same bottles, if you ask me. And he says: 'This here one, when I shoot the juice into you, it'll torment and it'll kill you, slow and gradual. You'll suffer plenty and, while you're suffering, you'll finally feel that there's a band put around your heart, and it's contracting, and when you feel that, you ain't more'n a minute or two from dying.

"'And when you feel that way you're likely to say that you'll talk. Then what do I do? Why, then I take this here second bottle, and I shoot a load of it into you, and in ten seconds that stuff hits the blood stream and the brain and the heart, and percolates all down through the nerves. Then you're as strong and healthy as you ever were! Just a few seconds, and you can talk clear and fine!'

"That's what he said to me, but still I didn't have anything to say, because you know, Durfee, that's only a pipe dream of his. Come easy, go easy. That's always been my motto, and I've lived up to it. So I didn't say anything and he shot the first dose into me.

"It was agony—what I went through. And he sat down, he did, and read a newspaper. Some of the items, they interested him a lot, and he clucked and shook his head over them, and one of them was about a man who had murdered his wife, and he read that out to me.

"'Some people are pretty doggone mean, Spot,' says he.

"I could kind of agree with him, and then I felt something take hold of my heart, like a rope takes hold of a bull's neck, when the horse sits down against the rope and braces its feet. And I knew that what he'd told me was right, and that I was about to die.

"Well, then I talked. Sudden and free I talked, and that dope gave me a grand idea, and I told him a terrible lie about the place where I had hid that coin. I staged it high up in the mountains, and I told him that, at timber line, there was three mountains standing, high and bald and scalped, and there was a ravine running up between the two on the north and the one on the south.

"You come to the edge of the timber line, and there's a big pile of rocks, like the wreck of a whole city. There, a sort of tunnel runs through those rocks, like the one that you and the kid found the mountain lioness in today. And down there, in the bottom of the tunnel, that's the place I'd cached my money.

"Well, he listened to that fairy tale, and he believed it, but he didn't croak me, because I'd made out where that place was it was pretty hard to find, and he thought that he'd need a guide. So he gives me the second injection, out of the other bottle, this one here, and before you could count twenty I was all right.

"Then he untied me, all except the hands, and got me on a horse, and I started off, guiding him to the place, and him riding behind with a gun.

"But my hands was tied in front of me, and the steel frame of the pommel, it had worked through the leather and it showed a nice sharp edge. So, as we rode along, I chafed and chafed away at the rope on my hands until one strand parted, and then another, and finally I was able to break the last strand of all, dead easy.

"Well, when that happened, I give the mustang I'm on a knee pinch, and he swerves over to the side of the trail and stumbles in some bad rocks. When he stumbled, my friend rides up beside me. You tell me, then, how long it takes me to reach over and take the gun out of his hand? Not long, Durfee! No, not very long!

"I didn't hurry none. I didn't want to have it over none too quick. No, I took my time, and I managed to make him think that I wasn't gunna kill him, after all, and I let him get down on his knees and beg a lot and tell me how much he really thought of me, how he respected me, how he'd never intended to let the poison work, but was gunna save me at the last minute, whether I talked or not. It was kind of touching, to hear the way that he talked.

"Finally, I told him that he's yelled long enough and I told him what I thought of him. Then I put a bullet through his leg and brought him down. And then I smashed his shoulder for him. And I loaded up the old Colt twice and, with the last slug, I finished off what was left of him, which wasn't much. He didn't have no endurance, like an Indian that I once handled. That Indian, he lasted pretty good. He had stamina. He was a man. I got an idea that you are too, old son, and I'd like to take the time off and watch the stuff work on you and talk to you a little. But I ain't gunna do that. Because I'm a little pinched for time and must be on my way.

"Tell me, first, if you're resting dead easy and comfortable. No, you don't seem able to talk. You got a big mouth, and you've used it a lot telling folks what a hound I am, Durfee. But you don't seem to have no lip room left to talk around that gag. That's a rough old table, and full of splinters, whole ones and ones that are broke off. I dunno that you'll be dead comfortable, there. I might've tied you on a bed, instead, but a bed, it'll give out squeaks, when a fellow begins to wriggle around, the way that you're going to wriggle, pretty soon. Now, just you lie easy, and I'll soon have you fixed."

With that, he turned back the shirt of his captive and, taking the syringe, buried the needle deep in the flesh.

The eyes of Durfee haunted the face of Lester. And he saw in it a look that he thought he could recognize, not the look of a human being, but the look of a hunting beast when the prey is in its claws.

The pain of the needle's thrust was followed by a duller ache as the fluid entered his veins.

But still his glance was fastened upon the face of his persecutor. For the joy, the savage and brooding joy that filled the face of Lester, was a thing of vicious animalism, not human at all.

After this, he felt a gradual warmth spreading through his body. Fear, perhaps it was, that made the beat of his heart leap for a moment and then gradually slow down.

"I've left you before, Durfee, my lad, thinking that you'd die. But this time it's sure. You won't live after this, Durfee. You're a dead man. Lie there and say to yourself: 'When the rope begins to pull on my heart, I'm a dead man.' Think about that. It'll do you a lot of good. You—and I wish I had twenty more to lay there besides you, all dirty, sneaking Rangers and their like.

"Durfee, I've thought a lot more about you than you're worth thinking of. Don't doubt that! I've thought and thought about you. I dunno why. Maybe because you ain't my kind. You do your job, and you put more into it than you're paid for. Take the kid. There was no call for you to work on him, the way that you did. You gave him everything you had; and what's the result? Why, you've just ripened him. He's all ripe, I tell you, and ready for my hand. I can work on him, now. I can do something with him. I can make him into a tool that'll cut tool-proof steel. And all because you've broken the ground for me."

He paused, laughing softly. There was only the pulse and the rush of his breath, no resonance whatever.

Finally he said: "Here's the antidote, my son. Here's the needle, too. You can crane your head around and see 'em. All you need is ten seconds to feed this into your system, and you'd be all right. Think of that. Think that all over, will you? Because I'll be thinking about you, too.

"I'm gunna leave the door of your room ajar a little. I want you to hear what I say to the kid in there. I want you to hear me work on him. That'll please you a lot. That'll make you see what I'm after, maybe, and I hope that it breaks your blasted heart! But, first, I'll put the lamp out, because pain is always double in the dark!"

CHAPTER 12

The silence, the blackness closed over Durfee like a sea; he heard and felt the racing of his heart; he heard the light sound of the footfalls of the murderer crossing the hall; he heard a tapping at the door of the next room.

Then he made a vast effort but the most that he could manage was a wave of muscular energy that merely made the table tremble. He shrugged his strong shoulders until the cords sank into the flesh and ached against the shoulder bones; but his hands, bound beneath his back, crushed by his weight, he could stir only far enough to make the cord that bound them fast chafe against one of those broken splinter ends to which Lester had referred. The cord stuck on this, and came free again with a tearing sound no larger than a whisper.

But that was enough to make hope rush back into the heart of Durfee. He needed only that glimmer to quiet the tremor of his heartbeat and to comfort him. Thereafter, patiently, he worked his arms up and down, chafing the imprisoning cords and assuring himself that he could not die as the murderer had planned. God would not let such a thing be.

In the meantime, he could feel a slight pressure around his head, just above the eyes, a weight that constantly increased.

It appeared to him now as a hideous irony that he should have to struggle for life so violently and so soundlessly, whereas the least whisper, the least suggestion of his true condition would bring the boy rushing to his rescue.

The door to Henry Vincent's room opened; he could hear the faint, faint creaking of the hinges and the soft whistling of the draft of air. Also, the lamplight from the other room moved feebly into his own, across the hall.

He heard the boy ask: "Who's there?"

"I'm Spot Lester," said the criminal.

"This is an odd time to come to see a person," said Henry Vincent.

"How could I come any other time?" answered Lester. "God knows that there's enough of them that would like to get their hands onto me and have the breaking of my neck! Oh, I know all about that! They ain't put a price on my head for nothing!"

Durfee listened, amazed.

What was the work to which Lester was about to put his hand, since it was not merely the desire for murder that brought him there in the middle of the night? No, it was not the will to murder, only. It was more than that—some design he had in mind against the boy—and now it was introduced by a confession of his real name and state!

But all the ways and methods of Lester were, to say the least, original and strange!

"Is there a price on your head?" asked the boy.

"A price? Twenty thousand dollars, adding up one thing and another," answered Spot Lester.

"For what?" asked Henry Vincent.

"Robbery, arson, and murder, chiefly," said Lester.

"Tell me," said Vincent, "do you admit that you've done those things?"

"Well, you know how it is," said Lester.

"No, I don't know."

"I've lived by robbery, and you find murder right down the road, next door."

"I suppose this is a joke you're telling me," said Vincent, with patience, "and that in the end you will have a chance to laugh at me. But I don't see anything funny about it. If you don't mind, I'll hear the rest of the story tomorrow and go to sleep again, now."

"You think that it's a joke, eh?" murmured Lester. "Tell me, young feller, if I look like a joker?"

"No, you really don't," said the boy.

"Well, just what do I look like, then?"

"Like a big cat, a black cat," said Vincent.

Durfee held his breath.

Then he heard Lester saying: "Like a cat that's eaten its share of raw mice and rats, eh?"

"Yes, exactly that way," said the boy.

"You don't like the look of me, eh?"

"No, I don't."

"I didn't think that you would," said Lester. "There ain't many that have liked the looks of me, but there was a time when your father thought more of me than he did of anything in the world, barring his wife that was dead, and his kid that was away from him."

"You know my father?" asked Vincent.

"Do I know myself?" answered the criminal.

"You knew my father?" repeated Vincent. "Why, that changes everything. I'm glad to see you. Sit down, here. I'll get up. Just close the door into the hall, will you?"

"If I close the door into the hall," answered Lester, "I'll begin to hear whispers and steps stealing up and down it. Even in an open plain, I'm hunted; danger is always sneaking up across the sky line for me. I'm gunna leave the door open, if you don't mind, kid."

"Leave it open, then," answered the gentle voice of the boy.

There was a slight creaking sound, and then the unmistakable noise of bare feet upon the floor, the heel thumping, the ball of the foot spatting against the boards.

So keen were the ears of Durfee that could even hear the swish of the bathrobe which Henry Vincent now threw around his shoulders.

He was saying: "You knew my father. You were my father's friend?"

"Yes," said Lester.

"I want to shake hands with you," said the boy. Durfee winced, as he heard this.

"I don't shake hands with anybody," said the criminal.

"Why not?"

"Because that right hand of mine is my life to me," said Lester. "I ain't gunna take no chance with it. It's my signature; it's my bank account and the blood inside my heart. No, I don't never shake hands with nobody."

It was a peculiarity in the notorious man of which Durfee had not heard before.

Said Henry Vincent: "You say that you were a friend of my father. But you won't shake hands. And I have no proof about what you say."

Amazement took hold of Durfee, when he heard the lad speaking with so much precision and so to the point. It was as though another man were over there in the darkness, speaking in the accents of the boy.

"I dunno," Lester answered. "It seems kind of funny to me to have to prove to Jack St. Clair's son that I knew his father. Dog-gone funny, it seems to me!"

The name struck somewhere upon the mind of Durfee, listening, and raised an echo, a sense of old familiarity. But he could not be sure of it. He could not tell in what degree he had known that name before.

Young Henry Vincent answered, with a distinct air of relief finding expression in his voice: "You've made a mistake, Mr. Lester. I'm not the son of a St. Clair. My name is Vincent."

"Your name is Vincent, is it?" said Lester.

"Yes."

"It's no more Vincent than mine is," replied Lester. "And lemme tell you here and now, I ain't a man that makes mistakes, young feller. I don't make 'em because I can't afford to make 'em. One stumble, and my neck is broke!"

"You call me St. Clair," said the boy, amazed.

"Yeah. That's what I call you. And that's what you are. Unless you're the kind of a hound that changes your name!"

"Change my name? Give up my father's name?" exclaimed the boy. He said no more. The ring in his voice had more meaning than many words.

"You got some of the right spirit, anyway," said Lester. "All you want is to make sure that your father was St. Clair. Ain't I right about that?

"Well, there's proof for you," said Lester.

Paper rustled. "It's the same face," said the boy. "It's exactly a picture of me!"

"No, it ain't the same," said Lester. "It ain't quite as broad across the forehead, and it's made a little finer all over. He was a handsome gent, was your father. I've seen the time when there wasn't nobody in the whole country that was a finer-looking man than him."

"And you say that his name was St. Clair?"

"Say? Look at his name here on the picture. Ain't that his handwriting?"

"I've never seen any of his handwriting before," said the boy. He added slowly: "Yours as ever, Jack St. Clair!"

"Yeah. That's wrote out in his own style," said Lester. "Even his handwriting was a thing that stood out all by itself."

"He looks very like me," said the boy. "It can't be a mistake. I'm sure of that. There's something that speaks to me out of the picture."

"Yeah. If he ain't your father, nobody's your father. How did I know that you was his son, except that I recognized the look? How come you to be wearing the wrong name? No, that ain't a hard riddle to guess, either. But just what have they told you about your father?"

"My uncle tells me that my father was a prospector and miner, and that he died young in Nevada."

"A prospector and miner, was he?" said Lester. "Yeah, he was a prospector, all right; and he was a miner, too. He done his prospecting and his mining in the pockets of other people. He used dynamite to break ground, too, just like a miner, but what he opened up wasn't veins in rock; it was hard cash in bank safes."

"You say that my father was a criminal?" asked the boy.

"Wasn't him and me pals?" said Lester. "Where else did I learn the game except from Gentleman Jack, Handsome Jack, Daredevil Jack St. Clair?"

CHAPTER 13

The boy spoke with deep feeling in his voice: "I ought to be able to say that you lie. If there were another person in the room, I would say it. But we're alone, and I have to find out the truth if I can—if the truth is in you!"

The answer of Lester came in a growling tone: "Say, kid, what would I get out of this? What would I be gaining, eh? Nothing at all, and you know it for yourself. All that I get out of this here call on you is a chance to look at the spitting image of my old partner, and to get pinched and throwed into jail, maybe, before the finish."

The boy sighed. Durfee heard the sound plainly.

For his own part, as he worked on steadily at the chafing of the twine that tied his wrists, he was occupied with the increasing force of the pain that gripped his head. He was, furthermore, pondering what plan could be in the mind of Lester. What would he gain from either revealing the boy's past to him, or from lying to him about it and trying to foist on the lad a false paternity?

Whatever the scheme, there could be no good in it. Otherwise it would not have originated in Spot Lester.

Said young Henry Vincent: "I've never met anyone who found me so very like my father.

"How many people d'you know who knew your old man when he was a kid?" asked Lester.

"My uncle—" began the boy.

"Oh, your uncle!" sneered Lester. "Your uncle, eh? A fine uncle! Yeah, he's a sweet uncle, he is! He never told you that you looked like your old man, eh? And I don't suppose that he ever told you about listening to your father make his death speech—him, Bunce, standing there under the tree while they fitted the rope around Jack St. Clair's neck; him, Bunce, not lifting a hand to help the husband of his sister!"

Henry Vincent groaned. "They hanged my father?"

"Yeah. Under a tree in a vacant lot of Ulma, up there in Montana. I went by the place about six months back, and the vacant lot is still there, and the tree's still standing there in the middle of the lot. I noticed particular the way that the big lower branch was bent in the center, like it was made to order for a lynching party."

"It was a lynching, then?" said the boy. "Not the law, but just a mob?"

"Yeah. That was it," said Lester.

"What did they have against my father?"

"Robbery, murder, and a few like things," said Lester.

"I'm trying to believe what you say," said Henry Vincent, his voice stifled as if he spoke through set teeth. "You say that the crowd went out and hunted him down because he was a murderer and a thief?"

"I didn't say that they went out and hunted him down," said Lester. "No, sir! They didn't have to, because they just set a trap, and baited it, and he walked into the trap. That was all that there was to it! There wasn't no effort, and there wasn't no heat nor no dust raised. They just baited the trap, and in he come, and a sad day that was for me. You can believe that!"

"I'm listening and trying to believe," said the boy.

Then, after a moment during which Durfee could almost see the silent struggle in the face of Henry Vincent, the lad asked: "They charged him with murder, but how did they bait the trap?"

"With poor Jack St. Clair's wife," said Lester.

"Wait a moment," said Vincent. "You're speaking of my mother!"

It startled and amazed Durfee to hear the rising, full sound of the boy's voice.

"I know that I'm speakin' of your mother," said Lester. "And I ain't speaking no harm of her, neither. It wasn't no fault of hers that Bunce, here, dragged her in and used her for the bait. It wasn't no fault of hers at all. But she was the bait. Knowing that, she didn't live long afterward. The shock of it finished her off. Yes, in a way of talking, you might say that the rope that hanged your father, choked your mother, too."

Henry Vincent gasped. "When you talk of setting a trap, what do you mean?" he said.

"What do I mean?" said Lester. "I mean just that. There was a fellow by name of Dolf Cramer that was sheriff, up there, and he—"

"Dolf Cramer? Dolf Cramer?" broke in the boy.

"Yeah. A big fellow with a dark skin and a half-breed look about him."

"I know that man," said Henry Vincent. "He lives just across the range, and he's a friend of my uncle's. What did he have to do with the setting of the trap?"

"Why, he got the idea, him and your uncle together. It was Cramer that planned the thing, and it was Bunce that brought your ma into the picture and made bait of her. It was Cramer, the sheriff, that sat inside the window of his house and looked at the mob busting into the jail. He just laughed and let the crowd come out and hang your father. Somebody bawled out to him that the law was being broke, and that he had oughta protect the lives of his prisoners with his own life, but he answered 'em back

that he'd be darned if he'd spend State ammunition to save
the hide of a crook!"

"Did he say that?" said the boy softly.

"Yeah. He said that," replied the other. "That ain't all
he said, though. No, it ain't half all that he said, and you
can take that from me!"

"Were you there?"

"I wasn't there. But I had friends that were there, and
they told me every word, because they knew what me and
St. Clair was. They knew that we was pals and partners.
When I heard about the letter that had come to your pa
from your mother, I sort of suspected that something was
wrong. There didn't seem no call for her to go up and
visit her brother just then, up there in Ulma. But there
she was. And I got me a hoss and rode like blazes for two
days, but all I found was the body of your pa swinging
from the arm of the tree, with his neck broke, and the
wind turning him and a dog setting on the ground under
him, howling."

He put a good deal of warmth into this grim narrative.

There was a pause. And then Durfee heard the whispering of the bare feet of the boy, as he strode rapidly up and
down the floor of his room.

"And then?" said Vincent.

"It was night," said Lester. "I wasn't as well known as
I am now, but if they had reason for hanging your father,
they had ten reasons for hanging me. But there in the
night, I managed to cut the rope and get him down, and I
carried him over the pommel of my saddle off into the
hills behind the town, and I blasted away some rock and
made him a grave. I blew a hundred-ton pinnacle of stone
off its base and leaned it nice and neat across the grave."

"Thank you," said Vincent. "I want to say more than
that, but I'm rather choked. I don't seem to have words."

"Words don't amount to nothin' in this world," said
Lester with a profound conviction. "What matters is the
things you do, and not the things that you say!"

"I believe you," said the boy. "But now it seems to me
that you've made my uncle into a villain?"

"Him? Oh, he wasn't no villain. He was just a kid, and
he couldn't stand up agin' the smart ideas of a fellow like

that Cramer. Dolf Cramer, he could always take an ordinary man and twist him around his finger."

"He's the biggest of the ranchers on this range," said
the boy. "And I suppose that he's the most respected man,
also."

"Him? Yeah, he was always respected, too. Never been
anything but respected. That's the way with the smart
people, like Dolf Cramer. If he's gunna have a man killed,
he goes and has the law do it for him. That's his way.
That's the way that he murdered your father!"

"You said," repeated the boy hoarsely, "that my father
was wanted for robbery and murder!"

"I said that he was wanted for 'em and he was. But he
wasn't a murderer. He'd killed his man. Yeah, and he'd
killed half a dozen of 'em. But so had others, and stayed
right inside of the law. There wasn't no murder in the
heart of old Jack St. Clair. I know him too well for that.
I know every move that he ever made in his whole life.
And he never was such a fool as all that. No, I done enough
mean killings in my time. I've had my hands dirty, all right,
but Jack St. Clair was a gentleman. He was clean all the
way to the heart!"

"I want to believe you," said the boy.

"You better believe me. It was never proved against him
that he really killed young Tucker, but that was the crime
that Dolf Cramer, our fine sheriff, had him run into out-
lawry for. But, even that way, it wasn't for murder that
the crowd lynched him. It was only for the horse he was
riding, which was a horse that he had bought off of Dolf
Cramer, and Cramer, he swore that he never had sold the
beast. So there you be!"

"Yes," said the boy. "I begin to understand. But will
you tell me, Lester, why that demon, that Cramer, should
have hated my father so terribly?"

"I'll tell you," said the other. "Simply the old story. He
loved your ma. Loved her before she accepted Handsome
Jack. And the result was that from the marriage day, Dolf
Cramer was working to let her see her husband hanging
on a tree!"

"And my uncle, you say that he wanted to see my father
die?"

"Sure, he did. Why not? He wanted to save his sister

from the hands of an outlaw. It was bad business for a Bunce to have an outlaw for a brother-in-law, and the Bunces, they've always been great on business."

He paused. A groan, tearing the throat of Henry Vincent, had drowned the voice of the speaker.

CHAPTER 14

Now, it seemed to the suffering Durfee, a band closed around his heart, stifling him within. And he knew that his last moments had come. He did not need the description of Lester to convince him; the sense of death was in his very blood; the poison was working in its last phase. And he thought, now, of the little vial of the antidote and the hypodermic needle which Lester had left beside him, as an added wretchedness, letting him die with help only inches away and a cure waiting!

Then he heard a footfall coming down the hall; a vague glimmer of hope reached his mind. That footfall might be destined for his room.

"Who's that?" he heard Lester ask.

"My uncle, my—murdering—uncle!" said Henry Vincent St. Clair.

"Well, let him come. This makes it all perfect," said Lester.

There was a sudden exclamation, in the high, snarling voice of Bunce.

"Who's this? What! Lester, by the eternal!"

"Don't look at him," answered the voice of the boy. But it was so altered that Durfee could hardly recognize it. There was a strain of animal fury that muffled and closed up the human sound. "Don't look at him. But look at me. Look at Henry St. Clair, you murdering demon!"

There was a breathless sound of scuffling feet and the exceedingly horrible, new voice of the boy went on: "Now I have your throat in my fingers, why don't I wring your neck? It's because I'm going to do the killing in the right order. I'm going to get Mr. Murderer Cramer first of all, and then I'm going to come back for you. You can taste your death in the meantime. I don't care how many men you gather around you. Don't care how far you go away. I'll find a way to come to you; and every minute that I'm away, think about the way you betrayed my father! And may God torture your rotten heart! Get down from my sight."

There followed the noise of a heavy fall.

Durfee, in the pangs of death itself, almost forgot his own agony, as he heard the boy rushing down the hall and leaving the house. Bunce was there, behind him—Bunce in the same room with Lester—at the tender mercy of Spot Lester! There was little doubt that Spot would finish what the stroke of the boy might be said to have begun.

In the excess of his agony, Durfee writhed once more. Suddenly the cords parted on his wrist; the long and patient chafing had broken through the hard little strands of one round of the cords.

But still he was not free.

He was held at the elbow, and at the shoulders.

Now his right arm was free and the gag was torn from his mouth, but, though he drank down the air in deep gulps, it did not alter the rapid tightening of the pressure about his heart. He was dying fast, and he knew it; with shaking hands, as he sat up, now, free at last, he reached for the vial of the antidote, only to strike it from the table's edge to the floor.

He heard it burst; the shivering sound of the breaking glass went through the ear and the very soul of Durfee. It was the end for him, was it not?

He might get his revolver out and try to finish Lester, however, before his own death.

But, first, slipping to the floor, he fumbled and felt for the fragments. He found what he had dared to hope for—a rounded section, half filled with the fluid. Might it be enough?

He dipped the end of the needle into it and drew it full. He was blind, now, and roaring waves burst like tides of the sea against his eardrums.

Far off, drowned in these sounds, he heard Bunce exclaiming: "Who's here? What's this that—"

"That?" answered Lester. "Don't move, Bunce, or I'll put the knife through your throat. That in there is the sound of a little bottle falling to the floor. Durfee has shaken it loose—Durfee in his death agony. Indeed, a most horrible death, my old friend."

"Durfee dead, and my boy gone," said Bunce. "There is no justice when such a beast as you is allowed to wander free!"

"You talk the rot of a schoolboy, like I used to study it when I was a kid," answered Spot Lester. "Sure, there ain't any justice. Fools like you—"

"What have you done to my boy? What have you done to my lad?" asked Bunce.

"Told him a little fairy tale, that's all," said Lester. "Filled him up with the bunk. Turned his father into a mankiller, for him, made you a sneak and a murderer, and drove him more'n half crazy. He's gone to murder another one of you 'good' men—Cramer."

"Cramer?" groaned Bunce. "What under the blue sky could he have against a decent man like Cramer?"

"Nothin' in the world," said the other, "till I pointed out to him that Cramer and you was the ones that had killed his father, throwed him into the hands of the mob and got him hanged on a tree!"

"We? Cramer and I?" cried the rancher.

"Softer," said Lester. "I'm tellin' you the truth about what he believes right now. That's all right!"

"Is it?" said Bunce. "Lester, I've known for years that there was danger from you. I guessed that your black-hearted malice would follow me and the blood of my poor brother-in-law. That's why I moved so far to a new section of the country. That's why I shortened the name of young Henry. But you've followed us and hunted us down again. I know why you hate me—because I opened the eyes of the boy's father to your villainy. Well, you paid Jack St. Clair off by engineering his death. You are wholly evil! But why do you want to ruin the boy?"

"Because he wears his father's handsome face," said the other. "I don't mind telling you that, if it's any comfort for you before you die. I've tripped him up tonight. I've started him on the murder trail and, no matter what you do, he'll get there and take his man. But he won't have to worry about you. He'll find that you've already been killed.

"Honest Spot Lester, that loved St. Clair so well, he

took accounting with Mr. Bunce and put him out of the
way. But what will the world think? Why, that the old man-
killing streak that was in the kid's father has come out
again. That he turned around and killed his friend, Durfee,
murdered him like a fiend; and murdered his kind old uncle,
too, and then rode across the range and slaughtered Mr.
Cramer, eh? Oh, they will get up their posses now. They'll
hunt down St. Clair's son just the way that they hunted down
his precious father. And Spot Lester, that pulled the wires,
will watch the honest men killing one another."

"God of heaven!" gasped Bunce, choked by what he
heard. "What made you hate poor Jack St. Clair, in the
first place? He never hurt a soul in the world, except himself. As for the bullies and scoundrels whom he put out of
the world, he deserved the world's thanks for his work!
He befriended you, too. What made you hate him?"

"I'll tell you," said Lester. "It was because he could stand
to me. When the spirit came up in him and into his eyes, he
could stand to me, the only man that ever stepped and
breathed that could do that! He could handle me. He had
a faster eye, a quicker hand, and a stronger arm. Besides,
he was something to look at, like his brat of a son. No,
curse 'em—I hate the blood and the breed. The boy ain't a
patch on the father, but let him go down the same way.
I'll take the stamp of that face out of the world, before I
leave it."

Now, Durfee, sitting on the floor, his back against the
wall, felt the injection that he had thrust into his arm begin to work. It seemed to him that, first, it reached the
brain and removed the band of red-hot steel that was pressing into his skull and, in the second place, it reached the
agony that closed about his heart.

He came, as it were, through darkness into light. Then,
suddenly, it was as though he was completely himself.

And he heard Spot Lester saying: "This here job is a
good clean-up, because it's complete. There ain't a soul of
you is gunna be alive to know that I done it!

"They'll trail the kid back from the Cramer place to
this. They'll call it the crazy spirit of his father. There won't
be any blame reserved for poor Spot Lester. No they'll
not even know that I had my hand in the job. They'll simply

hunt down the kid, and they'll have a lot of satisfaction when they hang him. I hope they hang him soon, too."

He added: "Excuse me for takin' you by the hair of the head, Mr. Bunce, but that way, I get a better chance to stick the knife down into the hollow of your throat, the way that I used to stick pigs in the slaughter time in the fall. And I enjoyed that job, but I'm gunna enjoy this one a whole lot more."

It was now that Durfee stepped softly into the doorway with his revolver held level before him, just a hand's breadth higher than the hip.

In his coming, he made no more than a whisper of sound; but that was enough to catch the more than humanly sensitive ear of big Spot Lester.

With his left hand wound into the hair of Bunce, he had crushed the little man down to the floor and jammed back his head until the mouth of Bunce was jerked open, though no sound came from the white lips, and his feeble little hands helplessly gripped at the iron arm of the murderer.

Then, turning his head, Spot Lester saw on the threshold the man and the gun that checked his plans and put an end to his hopes.

He did not surrender. He turned and hurled the hunting knife at Durfee with one hand, while with the other he whipped out a revolver.

So much he accomplished before Durfee, stepping a trifle aside to avoid the swift, true aim of the knife, knocked Spot Lester against the wall with the impact of a half-inch bullet.

CHAPTER 15

Bunce fell backward on the floor. It seemed to Durfee that he had seen the knife of the slayer strike into the little rancher before Spot Lester turned on him, and now, with a rush, he got to Bunce and half raised him from the floor.

But the glassy eyes of Bunce cleared and a desperate light filled them as he stared past his rescuer.

"Watch him! Watch him!" he gasped.

And Durfee, turning, saw the lean form of Lester running silently across the room, leaning to scoop up his fallen revolver as he came.

The bullet of Durfee stopped him.

He felt that he had not struck his target with this shot, but the big man swerved far aside, leaping from the flash of the gun, and the next instant, bounding like a cat, he was through the doorway.

Durfee went after him.

But he knew that he ran in vain. As well set a short-legged bull terrier after a panther in the woods or the rocks, as to expect him to overtake Lester, when the latter had a reason for running for his life.

The servants of the house were up now. Their tardy wakening only served to create noises that masked the sounds of the fugitive's escape. Durfee stood out under the stars, gun in hand, looking wildly around him, but with neither sight nor sound of Lester to guide him.

Bunce came out on the run, and stood beside him.

"We've got to get to Cramer," he said. "Dolf Cramer may die on account of this, and a finer man never lived on the range. Dolf Cramer, and my lad, Henry, to be the killer!"

He gasped and groaned as he spoke.

And Durfee, without a word, ran on toward the corral. It was a twenty-mile ride to get to the house of Cramer, and there were hills and dales to be covered.

He picked out a strongly built mustang for himself and, while he was roping it, he heard Bunce snapping orders to a puncher who had been roused and was on hand.

The gray was no sooner saddled, than Bunce was already mounted on one of his own special string, picked for speed, for a smooth gait and gentle behavior. He was not a rider, but he was capable of covering miles in the course of a day in his own fashion.

Durfee said to him, almost fiercely: "You stay here. You won't keep up with me all the way to the Cramer place."

"Won't I?" said Bunce. "And what'll you do to manage Henry, even supposing that you get there in time? I'm going to come along!"

And he came. It was a bitter ride, over a trail not very familiar to Durfee, and the stars, that were so bright in the sky, very poorly lighted the mountains.

Twice the rancher caught up with him, and twice he left Bunce behind him again. He hardly cared about the patter of hoofs that pursued him, for always the picture of Henry Vincent St. Clair was filling his mind—the clean lad, so strong and gentle! With that picture, he tried to fit in the snarling, animal voice which he had heard speaking, almost unrecognizably, from the same throat.

The two things would not go together. He could not fit them in. But he knew that they belonged, and that it would be a new human entity with which he had to deal.

They came to a rising slope of ground at the top of the range of hills. On the farther side the broad valley sloped down, the valley in which the house of Dolf Cramer was situated. At this point the horse of the rancher came up beside him, and Durfee reined in long enough to bark: "What sort of a man did you give me? Clean goods, or a rat? What sort of a man is Henry Vincent St. Clair?"

"The finest lad in the world," said Bunce, "except that you blooded him today. And God forgive you for it."

The ex-Ranger spurred on, away from Bunce, after this, but as he rode, he looked back and saw the crippled, slanting body of Bunce following him as best he might, looking always as though he were about to topple to the ground. And he wondered what Bunce meant. Well, that was not so difficult to find out, because obviously he was referring to the hand-to-hand battle with the mountain lion.

Had that been his fault?

He began to see that, from the first, Bunce had feared that something might break from Henry Vincent. He had held his knowledge and his fear. That knowledge must have been based upon what the cripple knew of the boy's father. And what did he know?

There was a double picture of poor Jack St. Clair. On the one hand, he had appeared in the talk of Spot Lester as a plain criminal, one who shed blood for the love of the slaying, and on the other hand, to Bunce he had been plainly a man who held his hand until it was forced.

Which was true? He felt that he could trust Bunce against Lester. It simply meant that in Jack St. Clair, the dead man, there had been great and surging forces which had mastered him; and in the boy, Bunce feared the same things. Perhaps, after all, Jack St. Clair had been the same sort of a lad as his son, in his younger days, gentle, easily disciplined, until temptation and the friction of life had loosed hidden forces.

He, too, perhaps, was capable of facing a mountain lion with no more than a hunting knife in his hand. Of him, had not Spot Lester said that he was the only man whom he ever had had to consider an equal?

Durfee knew what that meant. He was still tasting that thought as he urged the tired gray mustang down the slope of the trail toward the ranch of Dolf Cramer.

Fast he rode, and once or twice he was almost thrown from the saddle, as the horse stumbled, but when he looked back, against the stars, here and there, the silhouette of Bunce was always sure to bob up.

Then he made out the dark cluster of the trees around the ranch house, and next the gleam of a light inside the trees. Just as he reached the entrance gate, he saw the multiplication of the lights, until every window in the rambling old house seemed to blaze, and he heard voices shouting loudly, only partly muffled by the thin walls as he ran up the path from the gate.

The clatter of hoofs came up behind and stopped at the gate. That was Bunce, still on the trail! He felt a half-sneering admiration of the little man.

Then he rushed into the house.

The noise of the voices drew him, as a chip is drawn into the vortex of a whirlpool, until he ran into a room where many men stood around a bleeding body on the floor. And the wounded man raised himself on one elbow, his hand pressed against his breast.

It was Dolf Cramer, and his voice arose, steady and booming, the voice which the whole range knew.

"I'm not dead. I'm gunna live. This here bullet, it glanced off my ribs. That's the kind of ribs I'm framed with. Don't you start gasping. Just ride out and get that Vincent kid, that thought he was gunna kill me. Get him, but don't kill him. It was a fair fight. He give a gun to fill my hand, and then he beat me. He's faster and straighter. Get him, and bring him back here, because the look in his face tonight, it plumb reminded me of another man that was my partner!"

That was enough for Durfee to hear. He turned and ran down the stairs and passed little Bunce at the front door. The rancher called to him, but he ran on to his horse and mounted. The way was clear in his mind. He knew that young Henry Vincent St. Clair now considered himself a murderer, pursued by the law, and he knew where the boy would hide—where but in the mountains which he, Durfee, had taught him to know so well?

Steadily he rode. The moon came up and, turning, he saw behind him the silhouette of a little, broken man, canted to one side in the saddle.

Greater respect for him welled up in Durfee. He was tired. The after-effect of the drug weighed down upon his brain, upon his eyelids. And he fought it back. Death was in him, the echo of death.

And the night waned; the gray dawn came and found him on a ridge with a dark valley falling beneath him; and before him, a single rider on a tall horse, a rider with a rifle balanced across the pommel of his saddle appeared as if by magic.

It was Henry St. Clair. Riding up, he saw that the face was no longer that of a boy, but of a man, stern, set, lined. The hard, cold voice of a man was asking him: "You've come to take me to jail, eh? I'm not going to jail, Durfee. You'll go west before you take me to the law!"

Durfee dismounted and sat on a rock. He threw down his hat. Terrible weariness ate at his heart. He said: "You've based everything on what Spot Lester, the gunman, crook, yegg, murderer, told you. He made out your father a murderer. He lied. He said that Bunce and Cramer set the trap for him. He lied again. I lay and heard it from my room. He'd tied me and gagged me, poisoned me and left me there to die in the dark, but I managed to get free. Look! Look at my face, because I reckon it's changed since you last saw me. Here's the place where the cords rubbed my wrists raw to the bone. Here's where he injected the poison into my arm. You see how black the skin is around it."

The boy dismounted in turn. He came and stood over Durfee, solemn, silent, tall.

Who could ever have called him a half-wit? He had the shifting, keen eyes of a hunting cat. He had the same cruel, inhuman ferocity.

He said: "If this is a game, Durfee, you've played it well. But it makes no very great difference. Whether I had a reason or not, I've left a dead man behind me. I'm wanted for murder!"

Said Durfee: "I've been to the house of Cramer. He's not dead. You hit him over the heart, but there are ribs over the heart and the bullet glanced. You're no more a murderer than your father was before you. Cramer doesn't want you hounded. The first thing he said is that he wants you brought in—as a friend! You've wanted to kill Bunce and Cramer, the straightest men on the range. You trusted the word of a cur and a poisonous dog against them. I've told you how Lester tried to kill me before he went in and talked you out of your faith in two of the best men in the world. Now tell me, Henry, d'you still trust what Lester told you?"

He waited a long time for an answer. He looked up and saw that the boy was pale in the light of the dawn, but no less grim than before.

"It seems that I have to believe you, Durfee," said he. "It seems that I've been a fool as always. I'm going to begin trusting nobody. But here's my uncle to repeat everything that you've said. I've simply galloped all night and thought that I'd ridden as far as freedom, but I see that I'm wrong!"

As he spoke, Durfee heard the clatter of hoofs, and knew that Bunce was coming up rapidly.

CHAPTER 16

They went down slowly together, taking the road toward the house of Bunce. On the way, a few words were spoken. Perhaps it was because of the cold, since they were very high above timber line and the wind was iced. Then there was the strangeness of demeanor of the boy and his uncle.

Henry had said. "You're my mother's brother. Nothing else ought to matter. I'm trying to unthink everything that I've already thought about you tonight."

And Bunce answered: "I'm not thinking about tonight at all. Evil has come to life in you, and it's going to carry on a long time. Lester didn't waste his work! He's changed you. Evil was only in your father now and then; but it's wakened up in you today, and it'll never down again."

A very strange speech, and to it the boy made no answer.

They dropped down to timber line. The sun was up, and some of the chill left the air at the same instant that the level ray of the sun struck the heights. Durfee, looking to the side, saw a canyon that ran up between two bald mountains on the one side and one on the other—a sight that he seemed to have seen before, though he could not be sure. And then he remembered the odd tale which Lester had told to his murdered man.

Had there been some truth in it?

He said simply: "We turn this way. Henry, you may need to use that rifle on Spot Lester, if my idea is right. Would you hesitate much?"

"Much?" said the boy.

There was a sneer in his voice. It satisfied Durfee for the moment. Bunce said nothing. His crippled body must have suffered terribly during the long, hard ride through the mountains. Now, though he did not complain, he kept hold on the pommel of his saddle with both hands.

And so they came to the place. The canyon ended, and on a shelving plateau, they saw a heap of broken rocks, like the debris of a city wrecked by earthquake. At the base of the debris, a man was struggling out of a hole, carrying what looked like a saddlebag. He dumped the contents on the ground, to add them to a considerable pile that was already there. And something in his posture, in the form of his long body, struck Durfee.

"It's Lester!" he exclaimed.

At the same instant the rifle spoke from the hands of the boy.

He had recognized the enemy before even Durfee's eye, so practiced in distances, so filled with thoughts of Lester himself.

And the criminal stooped, cast one glance behind him, and then dived back into the mouth of the tunnel among the broken rocks.

"Scatter! Get cover!" yelled Durfee.

But the boy was already spurring toward the cave like a madman.

To the side of it he dismounted, and, picking up big rocks,

he began to throw them into the entrance of the cave until it was quite blocked.

Then Durfee understood. In this way the biting dog was muzzled. He and Bunce came up, panting, not with exhaustion, but sheer terror.

They dismounted. Beside them was the pile of packages. Durfee ripped one open and saw a thick sheaf of greenbacks. Bunce broke another. A stream of jewels spilled out on the ground; a fine gold watch shattered its face against a rock.

Then a voice came out to them.

It was the voice of Lester, saying: "Boys, you've beat me. But what you got there ain't all. There's a lot more. There's enough to buy me a chance for a fair trial at the hands of the law. Let me out, and I'll come with my back to you, and my hands over my head."

Neither of the older men answered, but Henry St. Clair said: "Do you hear? A dog can speak with a human tongue!"

Durfee looked at him. Pale and set was the face of Henry St. Clair, and he sneered as he spoke, but then his laughter rang long and loud.

"Do you see?" he asked.

They looked, and Durfee felt a chill strike inward toward his heart, for the youngster had found a heavy tarpaulin which, unwrapped, showed a number of sticks of dynamite and a length of fuse.

He laughed again and began to insert them under the rocks at the entrance to the tunnel among the broken debris. Then Durfee understood. Such a charge would blast the rocks from the face of the mountain; or if not, the shock of such an explosion would destroy all life within, unless a miracle intervened.

But neither he nor Bunce intervened. The time had come for death. They were not dealing with a human being, but with Spot Lester. He himself seemed to know that the end was there, for not a whisper came from him, hidden within the tunnel. So they carried the pile of loot to a safe distance; they had hardly reached it when the explosion staggered them and filled the air with flying fragments. The boy had taken shelter behind a boulder as large as a cottage.

When they could look again, they saw that the very

ribs of the mountain seemed to have been laid bare. They did not look for the body of Lester, simply because a hundred tons of rock were piled over it. But they looked at one another, as the lad came back.

He could be called a lad no longer. His step, his voice, his eye had changed. He laid a hand on the shoulder of Durfee.

"You know, Durfee," he said, "I thought all this night that I was riding free. But now I can go back there—down to the other men, and I suppose that I ought to be glad. I suppose that I ought to thank you, first of all, and my uncle, next. You've been my friends, and God knows that I'll never forget."

But Durfee hardly heard him or the rancher saying: "You've got more than ten thousand dollars, Durfee. You're rich; even if this stuff is shared, you're rich! Even if part of it is claimed by the people it was stolen from, you're still rich."

But Durfee, staring at the cold, grim face of the boy, wondered if it might not have been better, in the end, if the explosion had taken from this world both Spot Lester and young Henry St. Clair. He had worked to save a dullwitted boy. And he had found what? A monster or a hero, or both together in one skin?

Part Two

CHAPTER 17

Twisting his small, meager body to the side, after the way that he had, Bunce remarked: "Things are not right."

Durfee looked up from the bridle which he was mending. Life on his newly acquired ranch had meant hard work and lots of it. He looked thinner and older. But he looked happier, also, as a man always will look when he is laboring to the full extent of mind and body.

"What's wrong?" he said.

He knew, beforehand, but he preferred to hear it afresh from the other.

"You're a considerably long shot from a fool," answered Bunce. "You ought to know where the trouble lies. Where else could I have trouble, except—"

He paused, after the fashion of one who takes himself sharply in hand. "You tell me about yourself, first," said he. "How are things going with you, man? How does the place pan out?"

"It's panning out pretty well," said Durfee. "I've got land enough to keep cattle enough to support me, and a good deal more. That's all that I can ask. I'm having my chance, thanks to you, and it's turning out."

"No thanks to me," said the other. "Thanks to your own self. You fired the bullet that kept Spot Lester from killing me. Except for you, my nephew would have run wild. I know that, and you know it."

Durfee shrugged his shoulders. He agreed, and he did not agree. Modesty closed his mouth.

"Well, you're planted here," observed Bunce. "You've got the land and you've got the cattle to start with; and this house is good enough for a beginning."

Durfee looked around him at the one-room shack. The sun glittered beyond the cracks. It would never do for the winter weather but, for that matter, he had not expected that it would do. It was a makeshift. He said nothing about his plans, however.

"You've even got a hired man," suggested Bunce.

"There's enough work for three or four, but the two of us manage," said Durfee.

Bunce went on: "That's a sign of prosperity and good brains, when there's more work than a man can really get through. It starts him earlier in the morning, and it gets him to bed a little later at night but—well, he lives just as many years, and the last half of his life is fat and easy!"

"Maybe," said Durfee.

He knew so little about fat and easy living that he did not feel free to comment.

"Better than riding with the Rangers, eh?" suggested Bunce.

"It's easier than that," said Durfee, "if you look at my time of life!"

"No matter what time of life, you've got a good layout," insisted the other.

"Yes, it's a good layout."

And Durfee meant what he said. From where he sat, he looked through the front door, which was partially open, and down the easy slope to the creek, and across the creek to the grove of trees, and the sharp edge of the hill beyond. All of that land was his.

"It's a good layout," agreed Bunce. "I didn't have half as good when I started out. And you've got to say that I did by you as well as my promise."

"You promised me ten thousand dollars in cash," said Durfee, solemnly. "You gave me twenty thousand; no, pretty near thirty thousand, in kind!"

Bunce nodded his head with a jerk. "The point is that you're fixed for life!" said he.

"Yeah. I'm fixed," said Durfee, "unless I hit a flock of bad luck and bad prices. I'm pretty well fixed, I guess."

Said Bunce: "You'd be fixed three times as well if you'd taken a share of the loot that we got from Spot Lester."

Durfee shook his head. His face darkened.

"I took a share," said Bunce, "and I don't regret it."

"Maybe you will later," suggested Durfee. "Every bean that Spot Lester had was stolen money."

"What of that?" asked Bunce. "All the jewels and the money that could be traced down to rightful owners went back to 'em. We only kept the rest. We waited to find out, too! But everybody that could prove a right got his hard cash."

"I know that," said Durfee, "but still I'm as glad not to have a share of that stuff."

Bunce tried to laugh, but his voice cracked, high and sharp.

"You're not logical," said he. "You did the lion's share of running down Spot Lester. By rights, you ought to have the profits out of it. I don't care how you figure the thing. I'm glad to have that extra cash. But half of it, I'm holding in trust for you, and the other half for Henry. You two finished off Lester."

"Yes, if he's dead."

"If?"

"Yes. If he's dead."

Bunce scowled. "You saw the amount of dynamite that Henry shoved into the mouth of that tunnel among the rocks. You heard the explosion. You must have felt it, too. It ripped a hole in the mountain. Now you tell me how that Spot Lester could have lived through the thing?"

The other considered. "He might've turned himself into a ground squirrel and run down a hole," he suggested.

At this Bunce grunted. "He might've turned himself into an invisible bird, too, and flown away," he said sarcastically. "But I'll tell you what, he died on that mountainside! Did you refuse to share in the loot because you had an idea that Lester might be alive?"

"No, I didn't mind that. That mattered, but not so much.

With me, the main thing was that I wanted to have nothing to do with dirty money. There was blood on that money of Lester's. I've got an idea that you'll pay for handling it, one day or the other!"

"Thanks," said Bunce. "But I don't agree."

"All right," said Durfee. "It's only a hunch of mine. But I wish that you'd tell me what you're after today, Bunce. I oughta get out there on a mustang and do some riding, pretty quick."

"I want you to go home with me," said Bunce.

He struck out his twisted jaw. Durfee stared and said nothing.

"Go on," he said, after a long pause, in which each considered the other.

"Can't you guess?" asked Bunce.

"It's Henry St. Clair," said the ex-Ranger.

"You could have guessed that?" said Bunce.

"Yes, with one hand tied behind me."

"He's been different ever since Spot Lester told him his real name."

"I know that."

"And cursed different!" insisted Bunce.

"Well," said Durfee, "what's he been doing particularly strange, lately?"

"Ever since that day when Lester came, ever since that day, he's never been like other normal boys of his age."

"He never was like 'em before!" declared Durfee.

"What d'you mean by that?"

"You know. When I taught him to ride and hunt and fish, and trail game in the mountains, all that time he was different. You knew that. That is why you hired me partly. You wanted him to do what other young fellers of his age on the range would have been doing. But all the time, you knew that he was different! Admit that!"

"I know," sighed Bunce. "Because I knew his father before him. He was just such a half sleepy lad; and when he grew up, he grew in an hour and turned into—well, a fellow that other men were afraid of. Just looking at him, they were afraid. One day he was twenty-five. The next day he was—well, thirty-five. He looked mean and hard! I was afraid that the same thing might happen to Henry. And

I was right. The same thing has happened. Now he lives to himself. He sleeps in the day. He rides out at night. That's what I wanted to tell you."

"It's plenty to tell," said Durfee, dropping the repaired bridle. "Rides at night, eh? Where does he ride?"

"If I knew, I most likely wouldn't be here. I came here to ask you to trail him and try to find out."

"How long has he been disappearing at night?"

"Two or three weeks."

Durfee drew a breath.

Then he said: "The ranch can go hang. I'll tail him to-night!"

CHAPTER 18

They rode out onto the range and found Durfee's hired man, Gregory. He was the type of his employer, iron-gray, middle-aged, sloppy in dress, straight of eye.

Said Durfee: "Do what you can for a day or two. You're going to be alone."

"That's all right," said Gregory. "There's grass and there's water. If the cows can't get along on that, they can go hang themselves!"

There were no other directions; and the pair rode off together.

Bunce simply said: "You give your man a free rein."

And Durfee answered: "He's the kind, if you didn't give him a free rein, he'd take a bit in his teeth. He's as good a man as I am. He likes the place as well as I do. He knows the cows a lot better. What would I be doing, giving him advice?"

"Maybe not," agreed Bunce.

They talked more of Henry St. Clair, on the way to the ranch, and Bunce vented his own theory freely.

"When my nephew found out that his father had been a gun fighter, he began to look for the same thing in himself. And that was the foundation of all of the trouble. I'm sure of that!"

"Are you?"

"Yes. Besides, there was the seed of the trouble in him. He'd been too quiet, and when he waked up he grew too rough."

Durfee made no comment.

But his thoughts were all the more engrossing. And the picture of the tall, handsome lad grew more and more bright in his mind. Often, it seemed to Durfee that the weeks he had spent hunting and fishing in the mountains with young Henry St. Clair were the happiest in his life, a brief moment of content, set in amongst years of distress.

It was nearing evening when they reached the old ranch house of Bunce and, as they dismounted at the corral, Bunce pointed. "There he comes now!" he said.

Durfee turning, saw the silhouette of a horseman come over the nearest hill at a dead gallop, and so sweep down the slope toward the hollow in which the house stood.

A group of trees presently obscured him. But it seemed to Durfee that he had already recognized the broad shoulders and the narrow hips, the straight, easy seat of the boy in the saddle.

"Ride very much like that?" he asked.

"Always," said Bunce, gloomily. "He can't ride without getting his spurs red. He takes the air line. He thinks that a horse is a pair of wings to lift over mountains, across ditches, no matter what comes in his way."

"Take any interest in the ranch?"

"Just as a place to ride over. No, not even that. The faster he gets off it, the better he enjoys his riding. Sometimes he goes off and is gone for a couple of days. He may come back with a string of fish, or with a pelt; wolf, coyote, bear, mountain lion, deer. He doesn't care a whit about curing them or caring for them. But he always brings back something."

"He's got Indian in him, it looks like," commented the ex-Ranger.

"Indian or demon," said Bunce, "I don't know which. It's a pretty good-sized range that we live on, but it seems like a mere corral to Henry!"

They were washing their hands at the pump when young Henry St. Clair joined them.

He seemed leaner to Durfee and, therefore, taller than

he had been when last seen. Yet his shoulders, if anything, were heavier. The strength of a man full grown was rapidly settling around them. He was as brown as a berry.

He threw down a tawny fur and clasped the hand of Durfee. For an instant a smile flashed on his face, softening his eyes. Then it was irrecoverably gone.

"That looks like the skin of a mountain lion," said Durfee.

"Yes," answered Henry St. Clair. "And in the same old cave, Durfee. That's too good a place for the cats to overlook."

The glance of Durfee lifted to a scar that crossed the forehead of the lad, in a thin stripe.

"Kill it with a knife this time?" he asked, rather dryly.

"No, I took a revolver in with me," replied St. Clair. "It was a male. The cowardly brute just crouched in a corner and let my eyes get used to the dark. I had a couple of bullets in him before he jumped."

"And?"

"He missed. He was stunned, I think. Both the shots had glanced between his eyes. He got one through the heart as he jumped past me. Pretty good size, but not much spirit in him."

He kicked the pelt. It unrolled as though possessed of life, and Durfee measured its length. He filled up the hide, in imagination, with the sinewy body that it once had covered. A mere touch of those great paws would have been enough to let the life out of even a more stalwart body than that of the young hunter.

And yet the lad looked down at it with a careless glance and then gave his attention to washing for dinner.

At the table, he was abstracted and silent, as usual. He asked a few perfunctory questions about Durfee's ranch. He wanted to ride over and see it, he said. But Durfee knew well enough that the boy did not intend to come. It would take a keener interest that this to rouse him!

It was not that he lacked affection for his old companion, but simply that his heart seemed elsewhere.

After dinner, he excused himself almost at once; Durfee for his part spent only a few minutes with Bunce.

The rancher said: "What d'you make out of him?"

"He's changed," said Durfee. "I dunno what to make of

him. He ain't what he used to be; he's the same, but a lot more of him. That's all."

"What are you going to do?"

"Go to bed in my old room; keep one eye open; and if he rides out tonight, I'll follow him. That's all."

Bunce nodded, and Durfee went at once to find his former room. He was rather touched to find that everything remained as he had left it. In addition, Bunce or the boy had framed a photograph of Durfee and hung it on the wall. It was his room for life, his place on the ranch, so to speak.

But when he lay down on the bed he did not close his eyes. His body rested, but his attention was focused sharply on the room across the hall, the room of young Henry St. Clair.

He had hardly been quiet for half an hour when he heard what he more than half expected. The sound went down the hall, almost more like the step of a cat than that of a grown man, and a heavy one, at that.

Durfee, however, did not bother with the hallway; instead, he slipped through his window to the ground, and there he waited until he saw the dim silhouette pass out from the front of the house toward the corral.

He followed and got behind a corner of the barn, where he was able to see a horse roped and saddled. He noted the size of the animal and, furthermore, saw it buck furiously when the rider jumped lightly into the saddle.

But it bucked in vain.

With a sort of grim pleasure, not at all unmixed, Durfee observed the skill with which his pupil kept his seat. Then, beyond the gate of the corral, the youngster started off at a canter on a straight line toward the south pass.

That, apparently, was his first goal.

And Durfee, hastily throwing a saddle on a second mustang, a tough roan well known to him, followed at a round pace. He was a rider, perhaps, without the brilliance of the boy. But his weight was much less. Twenty-five pounds on the back of a horse, no matter how good, tells a long tale.

He was almost at the south pass, however, before he came close enough to catch sight of his quarry, and then, beyond the dark gully of the canyon, he saw Henry St. Clair take the trail to the right, the trail toward the newly born mining town of Flinders.

A year ago, there had been nothing in this little valley except a scattering of cattle. Now the gleam of a thousand lights looked Durfee in the eye.

But, of all the places in the world, what had Henry St. Clair to do with a rough mining camp, so late in the night? What associates were waiting for him there? What friends?

Such problems would have to wait.

Now that he was fairly sure of the destination of the boy, he did not risk detection in his pursuit by pressing too close, but remained well behind. Flinders was a farstrung constellation, to be sure, but it was not so large that a man would be easily able to melt from view within it!

He pushed on eagerly, but with his horse well in hand, and before him he saw Henry St. Clair rush down the slope, the horse bounding like a flung stone as the spur and the inclination of the surface of the valley side urged it along.

Inside the town, Durfee found that the place was divided into two distinct sections, the main street, along which there seemed to be little other than saloons and gambling places and dance halls, and back of the main street a town wrapped in darkness where miners were striving to sleep, no doubt, in spite of the caterwauling of music, hysterical laughter, shouts of rage, barking of dogs, and a score of other sounds which went to make up the midnight voice of Flinders.

Durfee tied the roan mustang at one of the long hitching racks. He could be sure of one thing, that the horse was safe. Men, a dozen men, would be killed in that town more lightly than a single horse stolen.

This was a faint comfort to him. But he tightened around his hips the belt that contained his money. Half a second might pick pockets in the town of Flinders.

Then he stepped into the sidewalk gang and leisurely drifted along with it.

He had been in identical places. Therefore the crowd did not interest him greatly. Neither did the flaring display of jewelry in the lighted windows; or the spread of weapons there. But where would Henry St. Clair be?

Durfee followed along into a dance hall and stood grimly in a shadow for a few moments, but his quarry was not there.

He tried three saloons, large and small, with similar lack of success. He followed the crowd into a gambling place, the most pretentious in Flinders.

And there he found what he sought.

CHAPTER 19

There is an old saying in the West that it takes more than a faro box to win money at the game; there needs to be a man behind the box.

And that man was young Henry St. Clair.

He handled the layout with perfect calm, with icy surety and a sort of disdain, true to the proper type of gambler. He wore a wide brimmed hat of black felt, a coat with tails, a sort of white stock that gave him the look of another century, and that made his bronzed face darker.

No, he was not lost in the crowd. There was not the air of the tenderfoot about him, but rather the total impression of the seasoned adventurer. And adventurers are seasoned by experience, not by mere time!

It amazed Durfee more than anything that ever had happened to him in his life!

It was not part of his plan to make himself known to St. Clair. Instead, he moved to a corner and got a chair that was not occupied. A man, with a face cheerful on one side and horribly scarred on the other, came across and shook hands with him.

"Hello, Scar-face," said Durfee. "What are you up to here?"

"Me? I'm running the show," said Scar-face. "How do you like it?"

"Pretty good. You're making money."

"Ain't I? I never knew what money was before. I used to try to dig gold with a Colt, but that way is pretty slow, and dog-gone insecure, when there's Rangers in the world."

He grinned and winked at Durfee.

"You've done your time," said Durfee. "If your games ain't straight, you're likely to do time again."

"Straight?" said the other. "I tell you what, they're as

straight as a string. And I mean what I say. Every game here is straight. I ain't got a crooked roulette wheel even, and a roulette wheel than ain't crooked is a curiosity, ain't it?"

"Yeah, maybe it is," agreed Durfee. "You like this game?"

"Yeah. I like it. It's kind of amusin' to see the hunches that the boys back. It kind of makes you laugh, I tell you. What they call their luck is always a fool break; and 'luck' is what costs them their pay roll in the wind-up." He added: "You're on a ranch, I hear?"

"Yeah. On a ranch. Ain't you robbing the cradle to get your dealers, Scar-face?"

"Whacha mean?"

"That kid behind the faro layout. He ain't twenty-two, or much more."

"He looks twenty-eight to me, but it ain't the years in a man that counts," said Scar-face. "It's the man himself. And that one is a bird."

"Oh, he's an old hand with you, eh?"

"Ain't been working with me a month, but he can stay the rest of his life, if he wants to. When that kid turns up, the faro table is always sure to get a crowd and that crowd will play big. Well, the bigger you play that game, the more you fatten the dealer. And that's the way with the game here."

"Just walked in and got a place, did he?" asked Durfee.

"No. I had a wild man, name of Mike Bray. He was handling the faro layout and doing pretty good, except that now and then he got boiled and thought that somebody had a hand in his pocket. He made a play at a gent in here one night. Just reached over and playfully tried to bash in his head with the butt end of a gun. But the kid, there, was standing handy. And he picked that revolver out of the air like a fish hawk picks a fish out of still water. Mike Bray, he made a mistake, and tried to fetch out his other gun, because he's got a left hand as good as his right, or a little mite better.

"But the kid, he reaches over and takes Mike by the throat —Mike not weighing quite a couple of hundred pounds— and picks him up and slams him down again. And the way that he fell, he didn't want to jump up and do a dance the next minute. He stayed down and took a long count, and we threw water over him. But the fool, when the liquor cooled off in him, got cold mean. He figgered that he'd been shamed, and he came back with a new gun and barked out at the kid, that was talking to me. Simply tried to kill the kid out of hand, but he didn't quite make it, because the youngster made as slick a draw as you ever seen, and shot Bray right through the hips.

"Bray's still talking to the doctor every day.

"When I see that gun play and the quiet, kind of a bored way that the kid had about him, I say to myself that it's an ill wind that don't blow nobody no good. I asks him if he hankers to handle a faro layout, and he says that he don't mind. And there he is. And a funny thing about him, too!"

"What?"

"Well, when I asked him what pay or commission he wanted, he said that we could settle that later on, an' he ain't said a word about it ever since. Maybe he aims to hold me up in the finish; I dunno. But he's made a clean break of everything that he's done in here so far."

"He handles the crowd, does he?"

"Handles 'em? Like nothin' at all. Sometimes the boys get rambunctious. But when they start arguin' there's a cold, mean look that climbs into the eyes of the kid, and the arguments, they stop real pronto. He's got what you might call a kind of a way that sand or water has on a fire. I don't need to carry no insurance while I got that kid in this here room."

And Durfee nodded. It was plain that the crowd liked the young dealer, and respected him. Now and again his steady voice, clear cut, but never loud, could be heard among the exclamations of the players.

Scar-face went on: "Another funny thing about him, he don't start early in the evening, but always late. Only blew in here this evening just a few minutes ago. And sometimes it's later. But I don't mind. I work a second string, to start with, and after the kid starts he gets the money out of the crowd fast enough."

"What's his name?" asked Durfee.

"Jones," said Scar-face.

Durfee smiled faintly. The lad might have chosen a more elusive *nom de plume* than this!

"Harry Jones," said the gambler. "And the crowd that knows him calls him Handsome Harry. I reckon that the name fits, eh?"

But a chill went through the blood of Durfee, for he was looking back into the story of the boy's father. He, too, had borne the same nickname, "Handsome Jack" St. Clair! And now the son was following closely in the footsteps of the other!

"No wonder he took your eye, though," said Scar-face, "because young is what he looks, and young he is. But not young when it comes to a gun or a pair of hands in any sort of a fight. He socked a big Irishman in here the other day, so hard that he won't be able to look straight ahead for a year and a day. But by the way, Durfee, folks have been kind of heated up about the way that you finished up Spot Lester; and what's the new yarn that I ben hearing?"

"What new yarn?" asked Durfee.

"Why, what I found in the paper, and the paper's three days old, at that!"

He crossed the room and came back. The journal was fluttering in his hand.

"I guess it's only somebody stepping into the shoes too big for 'em," said the gambler. "Some fool has gone and got ambitious. Only, it's kind of funny that anybody should want to call attention to himself, using Spot's old methods that way!"

Durfee snatched the paper hastily and read: "Brutal murder and robbery in the Farmers and Merchants Bank at Denver."

He started at the article. The words came slowly, one by one, into his brain. Hammer strokes that could not be the mere pulsing of his blood beat in his ears.

It was, said the article, as though the famous criminal, Spot Lester, said to have been killed in the mountains months before, had returned to continue his old ways.

There had been the same uncanny ability to pick the locks of the outer doors. There had been the same marvelous dexterity in blowing the door of the safe itself, with sufficient "soup" to spring it open and yet not enough to wreck the room, or to call attention from the outside because of so great a noise. There was the same singular passion for neatness, in the rearrangement of everything after the safe had been cleaned out of its contents.

Above all, the night watchman had been found dead. It was death by strangulation. Who would have strangled a man of that size? Who would have preferred such a means rather than using a knife, a bullet, or a club? Who, above all, would have worn gloves while performing the murder? And who, in the end, would have laid his victim on his back, closed the straining, popping eyes, crossed the hands on the breast, straightened the legs?

It was all as though the ghost of Spot Lester had returned to take up his trail of crime and blood, so long successful! Or, could it be, Spot Lester had not actually been killed? Had he escaped, after all? For no trace of the body had been found!

Durfee closed his eyes.

The same thought was tearing at his own brain. After all, they had taken the thing for granted, after the explosion of the dynamite. It had seemed utterly impossible that even a snake could have survived in that tunnel!

And yet all the days of Spot Lester had been filled by achievement of the impossible. Might not this be another case, now so very much more marvelous than certain other of his escapes?

Durfee rose with a sigh. He looked toward the faro lay-out, and the calm, clear eyes of the boy lifted and looked straight across and fixed him with a strange intensity.

CHAPTER 20

After a moment, he saw young St. Clair hand the management of the faro outfit to another man; then the lad came straight across and sat at his table.

He gave no greeting. He simply said. "You followed me here?"

"Yes," said Durfee.

"What d'you want?"

"I want you to go home."

"I'm not going home."

"Why not, Henry?"

"Because I prefer life away from home."

"Gambling, eh?"

"I'm not gambling."

"What do you call it, then?"

"I'm handling the cards for another man," said Henry St. Clair. "I'm making nothing out of the fools who come to bet."

"Your uncle," said Durfee, "he's gonna have a bad time of it, when he thinks that you've stepped out of the picture for him!"

"My uncle has his own life to run," said the boy, "and I have mine. That's all that I can say."

"It's a short saying," replied Durfee. "Your uncle Bunce has given up a good many years to the raising of you."

"My uncle Bunce," said the boy, "made his start on my father's money. The account is squared with him."

"It's squared with me, too," said Durfee. "I've had my fee."

"Yes," said the boy, as coldly as before, "I think that it is."

"Nobody but a young fool could be as big a fool as you are!" exclaimed Durfee. "You think that money can pay for anything."

"Aye, just about anything," said St. Clair.

And he looked at Durfee without blinking. There was neither anger nor scorn in him. He seemed to be looking mere facts in the face.

Said Durfee: "The fact is that you've been spoiled. A lot of people have tried to do too much for you. Been the center of too much attention. You been spoiled!"

"What's anybody done for me?" asked the boy. "I was sent to school. My father's money paid for that. You taught me riding and shooting, and such things. Well, you were paid for that, and overpaid. You got ten thousand cash, or twenty thousand in kind."

Logic annoys any ordinary man, and Durfee was distinctly ordinary. He said: "There ain't any gratitude in you, I see! You got blood that even a snake would be ashamed to have. You hear me?"

"I hear you," said St. Clair, grimly, "and I'm hearing about the last that I'll take from you."

His voice was still quiet, but a grim fear arose in the throat of Durfee and almost choked him.

He exclaimed, snarling: "I ran Spot Lester to the ground for you and your uncle!"

"You ran him partly for your own sake," said the boy.

"You knew that your own skin was not safe so long as Spot Lester was loose. But you ran him down and he wasn't killed."

"Not killed?" said Durfee. "Oh I know. You've been reading the fool account in this paper!"

"No, I haven't been reading the paper," said the boy.

"Who told you that Lester is alive?" asked the other, his scalp prickling with goose flesh.

"Nobody. I saw him."

Durfee sank back in his chair, gripping the arms of it. His eyes started out so far that they were painful.

"You—saw—him!"

"Yes."

"Where?"

"On the trail."

"What trail?"

"I was riding out by myself one night. I had no gun with me and, as I sat on the back of my horse in a poplar grove, I saw a man ride up from the ranch toward the pass. There was something familiar about the length of him and the stoop of his head from the neck. After he'd gone by, I realized that it was Spot Lester. He was too far away for me to see his face clearly. It was only after I saw his back disappearing that I realized who it was."

"What did you do?" breathed Durfee.

"I took out after him. I had glimpses of him far away, now and then. But he rode hard, and my horse was already blown. I got here to Flinders and here I lost the trail of him, naturally."

"Well?" queried Durfee.

"So I decided to stay here."

"What?"

"I walked in here and managed to get a job. I've come back here every night, ever since."

"What's your idea, Henry?"

"I lost his trail here. I may pick it up again."

Durfee stared, for this implied a foresight which he could not follow.

"What made you think that he would come back here?" he asked.

"He may never come back. But I think he will. He hasn't forgotten my uncle, and me, and you. He wants our blood.

I know that. And, since he came south through Flinders, some day he'll ride north again on the same trail and I'll try to pick him up."

Durfee drew a breath. "You've seen no sign of him?" he asked.

"No. Not a sign."

"Tell me, Henry," asked the older man, "what d'you intend to do? If you spot him, will you call for help, or just tackle him?"

"I'll have to see when the time comes," said the boy.

But there was a gleam in his eye that told Durfee his mind was already made up.

Young Henry St. Clair went on: "I've got to ask you to go back to see the ranch and say that you haven't seen me here."

"You think that I'll do that?"

"You'd better," said the boy.

"Had I?"

"Yes. My uncle is full of nerves. He'd get excited if he knew that I were here."

"He'll have to find it out," said Durfee. "I'm working for him and not for you."

"Durfee," said young St. Clair, "I'm holding myself hard. I'm saying good night to you. Go back and tell my uncle what I say. If you tell him the truth, there'll be trouble and a lot of it!"

With that he stood up and left the table, but Durfee, in a great burst of passion, broke out: "And I tell you that you're a young, fat-headed, bone-brained fool!"

The youth turned partially, but immediately went on back toward the faro table, leaving Durfee staring after him with a set jaw and with glaring eyes that saw only vague forms looking through a dark mist. And a pressure, like pain, seized his brain above the eyes and held him in its grip.

Afterward, as his mind cleared, he realized that silence had fallen upon the room and that the gamblers were staring curiously at him.

He realized, then, that he had shouted his final defiance at young St. Clair in a great voice. Everyone must have heard him; no doubt, everyone wondered why the young faro dealer had endured such insults delivered in such a

ringing tone. At any rate, there was respect in their eyes as
Durfee came to himself, finally, and left the place in haste.

He went into the next saloon and there leaned in a corner
against the bar. He asked for a whisky and tossed it off.

It had no more effect upon him than water. Gradually he
could realize the tension under which he was moving. The
calmness of Henry St. Clair and the odd coldness in his eyes
haunted him still.

He could not help telling himself that only a pull of a
spider's thread had prevented young St. Clair from violence,
when he had endured those insults in the gaming house. And
now, what should he, Durfee, do? Could he go back to the
ranch and face Bunce, without telling him what he had discovered?

On the other hand, did there not appear to be in St. Clair
something that commanded trust and confidence?

There might be more formidable men in the world; but,
outside of Spot Lester himself, the ex-Ranger could not
name one.

He thought of Lester, too. There was nothing conclusive,
perhaps, about a newspaper guess plus the guess of a young
fellow in the dark. And yet Durfee was convinced.

St. Clair had been convinced enough to take up his strange
line of conduct, acting as the faro handler in the gaming
house of Scar-face. He must have seen with instinct, if not
with eyes. And Durfee was a profound believer in instinct.

He felt that he had passed the last few months in a happy
dream, getting the ranch, working on it, building the founda-
tions of a full and solid existence. But now it seemed,
Spot Lester was alive. In addition, an evil spirit was plainly
breaking loose in Henry St. Clair.

Just then some one touched his shoulder in brushing past.
Looking hastily about, Durfee saw a swarthy fellow going
by. The latter jerked his head significantly to one side, and
then passed through a rear door.

Durfee followed.

CHAPTER 21

He could hardly believe that he was actually following a casual signal in this fashion. But, for some reason, he simply wanted something to occupy his mind.

In the rear room, he found two men playing seven-up at a dingy little corner table. One lantern lighted the place. It sufficed to show the twists and swirls of the tobacco smoke rather than the human faces in the place.

The swarthy fellow who had guided Durfee into the place now turned about and cornered him. He had a yellow-stained eye and a sneering smile that lifted one corner of his mouth.

"Look here," he said, "you ain't much of a friend of that brat at the faro outfit in Scar-face's, are you?"

Durfee shrugged his shoulders. He could see how such an implication might be abroad.

"I been fonder of a couple of other people," said he.

He meant just that. There were perhaps two other human beings who ever had meant more to him than the boy.

But the other chuckled.

"Yeah, I listened at how fond you was of him," said he. "I reckon that you belong to sit in on our little game here. Wanta take a hand?"

"Maybe," said Durfee. "What's it all about??"

"All about Handsome Harry. That's all! Who takes the first whack at him, and is it a gun or a bomb? I'm for a bomb myself. Bombs, they don't miss, and Colts do!"

Durfee nodded. He was glad of the dimness of the light, for it was plain that in this dingy little room they were organizing foul play against Henry St. Clair. His only plan was to step as far as he could into the plans of these other men.

He simply said: "I dunno, partner. It sounds to me like you were a mind reader."

"Yeah, and I am," said the other. "I'm a lot better at mind reading than a poker hand. Here, you blokes, here's somebody that I want you to meet!"

"Aw, shut up," said one of the pair, a pale, almost white-haired boy of nineteen or twenty. "We ain't meeting nobody tonight. This skunk, this Chuck here, he's just shot the moon four times running, and I'm gonna have his scalp."

"Keep your face to yourself, Blondy," said the swarthy man. "What's your name, stranger? I'm Tony Perez."

"Glad to know you, Tony," said Durfee. "Dinner Bell, is what most of the boys call me, because I can spot twelve o'clock so exact."

Tony Perez laughed. He enjoyed a joke of that caliber.

He said: "Blondy and Chuck, meet my friend Dinner Bell. A handy kind of name to have along, that is. All you'd need would be the grub and the cook, and he'd tell you the hour to eat! Sit down, Dinner Bell. Sit down, Dinner, old son. Blondy, break out a new pack, will you?"

"Say, are you crazy?" asked Blondy, glaring.

Perez smiled with the blandness of superior information. "You dunno nothing, kid," said he. "I just been in and heard this bozo giving it to Handsome Hal to his face. Does that sound to you?"

"If he cursed Handsome Harry, then only his ghost is in here with us now," suggested Chuck.

He was a mere stump of a man, with a look of forty about the eyes and mouth, although the rest of his face declared him to be no further along than the early twenties. On the whole, this was as hardy an aggregation of thugs as Durfee, ex-Ranger though he was, ever had seen.

"No, he handed it to Harry, and that kid took it!" declared Perez, with enthusiasm.

"Maybe Handsome Harry is only a bluff," said the pale youth. "I never thought he was so handsome, either, between you and me!!"

And he leaned back in his chair a little and passed his fingers through his hair.

Perez came to the point with a crash.

"Look here," he said to Durfee. "We're after Handsome Harry. You ain't no blood brother of his, it looks like. Do you want a split?"

"Sure," said Durfee. Then he added: "I ain't living on air, though."

"Dinner Bell says that he ain't living on air," repeated Perez, who seemed pleased by all the remarks of this promising recruit. "He won't have to live on air, if we pull off this here job."

"Not for a month or two. Mr. Faro will cop a lot of small change after this job is pulled off," declared Blondy.

"You boys wanta get the kid. Well, I'm with you," said Durfee. "I came into town primed for a go at him. But he wouldn't fight. Maybe he was too proud to take on a runt like me. I couldn't go and take a crack at him unless he was gonna fight back. But I've given him his chance. Now he can take it in the back, for all I care. But what's the coin in it?"

"Twenty-five hundred for him that shoots the right bullet," said Blondy. "And. one grand for everybody else that helps. Four is the right number. And we've got four now. Ain't that what the Old Man told you to have, Tony?"

"Yeah. Four men is what the Old Man wanted us to have together," said Tony Perez.

"Who's the Old Man?" asked Durfee.

Perez grinned, sourly.

"You'll find that out soon enough," said he. "Won't he?"

"He'll find that out soon enough," said Chuck, with a scowl, and he gazed grimly down toward the floor.

Said Perez: "You're in?"

"I'm in," said Durfee.

"You sling a gun pretty good?"

Durfee's hand flashed inside his coat; came out for the hundredth part of a second and disappeared again. They all had seen the gleam of a Colt.

"I'm pretty well known to this friend," said he.

Perez, his eyes narrowed, nodded. "Yeah, I guess that you know," he said. "You been around a little."

"Yeah, I been around," said Durfee. "I'm gonna play for that twenty-five hundred, boys! What's the game? We mob him?"

"The Old Man, maybe, will have something to say about the plan. My idea," said Blondy, "is that one of us holds the horses and that a couple of us cut through the back of the tent in Scar-face's joint. Then, the man that's been picked for the first crack, he puts the bullet through friend Harry's back. Or else, he leaves a bomb, if you vote a bomb is better. Chuck, here, he knows all about bombs."

"I could make a bomb," said Chuck, with relish, "that would be no bigger than a cream puff and that would be as easy to handle, and that would squash as dead certain, but it would blow Pikes Peak right in two. That's the kind of a bomb that I could make."

"That would finish off Handsome Harry," said Durfee.

"Yeah," put in Tony Perez, "but it would be kind of rough on the other rats."

"What do you care?" asked Blondy. "We're gonna get paid for Harry. The rest don't count. And the more that we sock at the same time, the less of 'em will be left to come riding after us."

"You got a brain in your head, kid," agreed Chuck. "I like the idea pretty good. There's a dozen or so that are generally in there at Scar-face's that I would just as soon see pushing the daisies."

"All right, all right," said Tony Perez. "I ain't a man to argue about the little fine points, because it's the main lines that I wanta lay down and foller out. That's what the Old Man is interested in, too. I claim the plan to be all right. One for the horses. One to chuck the bomb or do the first shooting. Two to back him up, and cover up the rear. The boys ain't apt to run so fast toward three Colts all singing one song."

He laughed cheerfully.

"Well, we play a hand or we cut?" asked Chuck, brusquely.

"Cut? That would be neat for you," said Tony Perez. "But we'll have a cold poker hand. The highest man gets the first crack at the twenty-five hundred, and the lowest man, he holds the horses. Anybody object?

"It's the right idea," said Durfee.

The new pack was properly broken open and mixed, and presently from the lean, limber, accurate fingers of Blondy the cards went spinning and glimmering out upon the air and fell side by side, each hand in front of its owner.

Durfee was fairly content when he took a king and a nine for his first two cards, and still happier when a deuce was his third draw, a little, modest deuce of clubs. Then the fourth card was another deuce; and the fifth was a third of the same denomination.

He had won, if a victory it could be called.

Chuck was cursing brutally. He swore that Blondy had cooked the deck.

"Shut up, Chuck," said Tony Perez. "We're gonna go and

see the Old Man now. We're gonna see him and let him
look over our ideas. But there's one thing more. What do
we stand for? Bomb or guns?"

"Bomb," said Chuck and Blondy in a breath.

"An old Colt is what I'm mostly familiar with," said Tony
Perez. "I never was much of a hand at baseball!"

"Make it guns for me," said Durfee.

If the thing were attempted quickly, he was beginning to
wonder how he would be able to pass the warning to St. Clair.

"Have the guns, then, and be blowed," exclaimed Chuck.
"You don't know your opportunities when they come a-
knocking at your door. Guns it is, then. And now let's go
and see the Old Man!"

CHAPTER 22

They went to see the Old Man, Durfee feeling somewhat
like a youngster who has fallen in with older and bolder
companions, ashamed to stay with them, ashamed to aban-
don the enterprise to which they have given their hands.

They massed along a narrow alley, and from this they
came to a dingy doorway, where Tony Perez, who was the
leader throughout, knocked.

"Who's there?" muttered a voice.

"Tony."

"What do you want?"

"Tell the Old Man that I've got three more with me. He
can look 'em over and listen to our plan."

"Wait a minute," came the growling answer.

A little later, the man inside was saying: "The chief says
that he's seen the three of you. He'll take a look at the new
man and hear the plan from him. Send him in."

"It's you," said Perez, stepping willingly back from the
doorway, as though he were glad enough to be far from it.

And he nodded at Durfee.

The latter came slowly up. There was at least the sentry
at the door plus the Old Man inside. But he had two good
revolvers and, if there were a surprise attack, it might be
the rascals within who felt the surprise.

"Here he is," said Perez.

The door opened a little, and a big scowling man, inside, looked down at Durfee.

"This runt?" he asked scornfully.

"Dinner Bell is the fool name that he travels with," said Perez, "but he's better than his name and young enough to make Handsome Harry back down like an old hoss!"

"Is he?" said the man inside. "That sounds, if it ain't just talk."

"It ain't just talk. I seen him do it!" insisted Perez.

"All right, Shorty. Come on in," said the guard to the ex-Ranger, and Durfee stepped into the cabin.

"In there," directed the guard, pointing toward an inner door.

"All right," nodded Durfee.

And he walked to the door, pulled the latch that secured it, entered a place of dimness and shut the door again behind his back.

He could see very little at first. The light was hardly more than that of a cavern, for it came only from a single lantern whose lopsided wick had smoked up one half of the chimney thoroughly. The air was heavy with the acrid, stifling odor of soot.

In the corner farthest from the lantern and, therefore, where the gloom was the deepest, Durfee was now aware of a figure seated, a long, ungraceful form, holding a sawed-off shotgun leveled at the breast of his visitor.

Old Man seemed an appropriate name for him, since his head was silver; and the hair grew long, hanging in white rags, almost to his shoulders.

A short white mustache, a short, unkempt white beard, also, partially concealed the face of the man, but the voice that spoke had in it a deep, animal snarling sound that was terribly familiar to Durfee. It was a voice which, until today, he had never expected to hear again, the voice of Spot Lester!

That voice was saying: "Why, hullo, old-timer. I didn't expect to be seeing you so soon!"

The room was swaying and spinning about the head of Durfee. But he strove to control his voice and make it casual.

"Hullo, Spot," said he. "I heard that you was out."

"Newspaper talk, eh?"

Durfee decided to take a long chance. After all, Lester

was already, it seemed, plotting against the life of young St. Clair.

So he simply said: "Henry St. Clair had an idea that he'd seen you, too."

There was a muffled oath from the other.

"Is this here a truth party?" asked Lester. "Are you gonna try to tell me truth, the whole truth, and nothin' but the truth?"

"Why not, Spot?" asked Durfee.

Lester chuckled. It was a sound that might have come worthily from the throat of a gorilla.

"Why not?" he echoed. "Well, we're such good old friends, son, that I suppose you're right. There ain't much that we can't tell one another, eh?"

"Whatever we been in the past," said Durfee, "there really ain't any reason why we should be hostile now."

"Oh, ain't there?" sneered Lester.

"No, there ain't. Would I've been hanging around this here town, knowing that you was about, if I hadn't seen that there was no call for you to want my scalp, no more?"

There was a pause. He heard the heavy, irregular breathing of the beast with the white head of an old man.

"By all the witches," muttered Lester, "it kind of does me good to listen to you talk. It kind of is a relief to me. We ain't got no reason to be hostile no more, eh?"

"No," insisted Durfee.

He knew that he was walking a tight wire above a gulf a thousand fathoms deep. At any instant the trigger finger might curl a little and launch into his breast a shattering load of buckshot.

And the double mouth of the gun yawned wickedly at him.

"When did we exchange love letters?" asked Lester.

"Well," said Durfee, "what started us agin' one another the first time? The fact that I was a Ranger, and you—was not!"

He actually managed to grin.

"You had plenty of trouble on my trail, I reckon," grinned Spot Lester.

"I had plenty of trouble. That's all right," said Durfee. "I got out of the Rangers. And then I hooked up with old man Bunce, and he had you on his mind as much as the

Rangers had. So we had another fight and"—he ventured on the remark with a cautious boldness—"and I troubled you about as much as you troubled me!"

"You troubled me enough," said the other, gravely and sternly.

"And now," said Durfee, "the scores are tied, and I'm on the loose, with nothing more to do with Bunce and young St. Clair."

"Why not?" asked the criminal. "Why nothing more to do with Bunce and St. Clair, eh?"

"Why should I have?" scowled Durfee.

"Why not?" said the other, insisting on his point. "Once you started, why not?"

"Because they done me dirt," said Durfee.

"What way?"

"They were gonna give me a high price, once you were put out of the way."

"Didn't they do it?"

"Oh, I was a fool," said Durfee. "I might've taken spot cash, ten thousand flat, and made my own start. But that Bunce, he's a business man; that's what he is!"

"Did he trim you?"

"Yeah. He trimmed me, all right."

"How come?"

"He was to give me, instead of dollars, land and cows to put on the land. And he trimmed me proper."

"How come that?"

"How was I to know the land real good? It looked all right to me!" said Durfee.

"I been and seen that bit of range that you have, and it's all right. There's some parts where you could farm it; and it's all good pasture," said the criminal. "You're lying to me. You're putting up a bluff. You're trying to make me think that you're at odds with Bunce and the kid, St. Clair, but I know better! You ain't at odds with 'em. You're still their slave! Why don't you say so?"

The head of Durfee dropped. He considered the other upward from beneath the blackest scowl that he could muster. For he knew that he was hardly a split part of a second from death by buckshot. His bluff had failed, so far, and the great Spot Lester had looked through him.

But he said: "You know your own business, Lester. That

is, you know how to crack a head or a safe! And you know how to cut a throat, or pinch a poke, and all them little tricks. But you start talkin' about good land and bad land, and you're a fool!"

"Am I?" said Lester, with a sneer. "What's the matter with your land?"

There was nothing the matter with that land. It was as sweet a stretch of grass as ever gladdened the heart of a herdsman. But Durfee shouted: "You fool, didn't you see the alkali patches in the low spots?"

"Alkali?" said the other. "No, I didn't see no alkali. There ain't no alkali, there."

"There ain't any eyes in your head!" shouted Durfee. "That's what there ain't! No alkali, eh? Then why's the grass beginnin' to die in spots all over the low places? In two, three years, that there ranch will just be grass on the ridges and every hollow will be baked mud or blowin' dust, and the alkali will be rising, and rising, and poisoning the air, like I always say that alkali does!"

He ended, fairly sweating with the emotion that he had put into his last speech. And then he waited, knowing very well that his fate hung suspended here. All depended on whether or not the crook could be persuaded to believe that he meant what he said.

Finally, Spot Lester said: "You said that they promised you money and give you alkali range instead?"

"If you don't believe me, go out and take a look and use both eyes this time!"

Lester keenly considered him; then he nodded, slowly.

"If that's straight, no wonder that you wanta cut their throats," said he.

CHAPTER 23

The relief of Durfee was more than could be put easily into words; for he saw that at least he had a fighting chance for his life. A talking chance it might better be called.

"I reckon that you're right about alkali poisonin' the air," went on big Spot Lester. "I reckon that it poisons the mind of a man and rots his nerves the way it rots the roots of good grass. If it hadn't been for alkali risin' to the surface, I would've gone and been a rancher myself, when I was a kid. I had some land staked out, and it was good-lookin' land too; only the white spots begun to show, and pretty soon, it was nothin' but dirty blow sand. My acres, they just started to blow away from under my feet; and pretty soon, I throwed a saddle on a mustang and started out to find something better to do than to watch my land disappear. I been having something better to do ever since. But old man Bunce, he trimmed you, did he?"

"I'll have his heart out for the trimming that he gave me," said Durfee. "One of these days, I'll have the heart out of his rotten breast. But he don't know that. I've been and smiled in his face, while I lay for the chance to hit him harder. One time, he's gonna go down and not have nothin' near to pull himself back up; and then I reckon that he'll have a chance to know me!"

Lester grinned; he licked his thin, wide lips, like a beast that thinks of food.

"There ain't nothing sweeter in the world than getting even!" said he.

Again Durfee seemed to have struck a responsive chord.

And then Lester went on: "What put you off the kid? You liked him pretty good when I knew something about your layout."

It was a facer for Durfee. But he tried to rise to it.

He said: "Who was thicker than me and the kid?"

"Not many fools," sneered Lester.

"Did I teach him to ride?"

"Maybe you did."

"Did I teach him to shoot?"

"No, because he shoots a whole sight better than you ever done, Durfee."

"It's a lie!" said Durfee. "Anyway, I taught him, and I gave him his start. I showed him how to read sign and follow a trail; taught him everything that he knows on the range. Well, sir, then along comes the time when I got to see my ground!"

"Maybe he ain't interested in ranches," said the criminal.

"He's a mean ingrate, and you know it!" shouted Durfee.

"Pipe down," replied Lester. "We don't want the whole town droppin' in and listenin' to us, do we?"

"I'm gonna show the whole world the way that a dirty ingrate had oughta be treated," declared Durfee. "I been the world's greatest fool all the way from the start!"

"Yeah?" queried Lester.

"The loot that we got off of you, they beat me out of my share of it!"

"Hold on," said Lester. "Everybody knows that you turned up your nose like a half-wit and said that you wouldn't touch money that had blood on it. You jackass!"

"It's a lie," said Durfee. "That Bunce, he persuaded me that the money was his. He was gonna pay me a whole ranch for my work in running down Lester. But I was a hired man, and the by-products of the deal, what was found on you, had oughta belong to him. It sounded nacheral and logical enough at the time. I believed it all right. But afterwards, I could see how the slick fox had put me behind a wall. And then he goes around and praises me, and he tells folks that I wouldn't touch tainted money. What difference did the kind of money make to me, once I had turned it into good, clean land and good, clean beef?"

Lester licked his lips again.

"Yeah, I understand," said he. "That's all clear enough for me. You were trimmed, all right."

"And the fools, they think that I'm gonna lie down under it!" said Durfee. "I could drink raw blood, when I think of that. But I'm gonna show them that I ain't such a half-wit neither. They're gonna feel what's in my hand!"

Lester made a short gesture. "I guess you're all right," he said. "I guess that we could work together. I could use you on this here kid."

Durfee said: "Only one thing that bothers me is: Why don't you step out and get him for yourself, if you want him?"

Lester looked steadily at him. "Don't you know?" he asked.

"No, I don't know."

"Well, I can move and do a bit of work, now and then," said Lester. "But I ain't the man that I once was, not half! I'm comin' back slow and gradual, but I'm kind of handicapped just now."

"How come?" asked Durfee.

Lester paused. Then he said: "I dunno that I mind telling you. You've had your share of misery. It's pretty near a clean break between us. I'll give you a chance to laugh now. It was the slug that you put into me, that night in the Bunce house, when I had things my own way. Then you busted loose. How did you manage to do that?"

"The top of that old table that you tied me onto in my room was pretty rough. It was all splintered, and the splinters had mostly broke off. And there was a strong bit of the stub of one of 'em sticking out, and I rubbed the cords on my wrists agin' it till it chafed through."

The other nodded.

"Mostly there's a pretty simple explanation for everything," he observed. "Mystery and luck is what the fools and the weaklings believe in—not me! Well, when you slammed that slug into me and I managed to get loose, I thought that I wasn't hurt very bad, and tied myself up. Then I remembered that I'd done a little too much talking about the place where I'd cached my money. That hung heavy on my mind. You might not believe what I had said—that the yarn was just a lie. So I up and started to trek for that spot."

He paused and shook his head.

"I got there, but I was pretty weak, and then you and those other two ran onto me and blasted the side off the mountain. You hadn't planned on a fissure inside of the rocks, that run down like a knife cut into the heart of the mountain, pretty near."

"That was what saved you, eh?"

"Yeah, that was what saved me."

"Well, I ain't so sorry just now," said Durfee, frankly.

"But I was stunned pretty bad," said the other, "and the bandage that I had worked onto my wound, it had come loose while I was crawling down the tunnel, getting out my loot. And while I lay senseless, that wound kept on bleeding. When I got up, I had no more blood in me than a turnip. After that I had to lay out. I was too weak to make a march. I had to lay out there in the wild, and didn't have nobody to take care of me. There was an infection started in the bullet hole and traveled with a lot of poison right through my whole body. Yeah, I was pretty weak and sick, I can tell you.

"How did you live?" asked Durfee, interested, somewhat sympathetic, in spite of all he knew of this manslayer.

"I lived on berries, on roots, like a Digger Indian. And I rigged up a fish line with withes. I didn't have no ammunition. That had been buried in your little explosion. But I made figure-four traps, and such, and snared a rabbit, now and then. It took a good many weeks before I was able to move around, and then I found that above the hips I was all right, but my legs were pretty near gone. They were weak. They buckled under me. I had to crawl most of the time, and even crawling made me shake, I was so weak. I'm comin' back, now, but I still ain't spry enough to step out and plug a gent and trust myself to make a get-away!"

It was strange to hear this recital from the master criminal, who had been for so long a tiger among men!

"Your hair up and changed color on you, eh?" suggested Durfee.

Said the other: "It was laying out there like a sick dog and thinkin' that maybe I would never be able to come back and take a crack at them that had laid me up. That was what took the color out of my hair, old son."

"Well, I believe that," said Durfee.

"We've wasted a lot of time talkin'," said the other. "Only, when I first heard your voice speakin' in the next room, I thought that by this time I'd sure have a handful of slugs drove into the innards of you! But I was wrong, and now I'm glad that I was wrong, because you and me could do some work together, now that we're on the same side of the fence. You hate the kid, do you?"

"St. Clair? He's no good, like they say that his father was no good before him. Wouldn't you hate him, if you was in my boots?"

"Hating is a dead easy job for me, and always was," answered Lester, with amazing truthfulness. "What's the plan that you and Tony Perez has worked out?"

"We got a pair of lads with us," said Durfee. "They ain't first rate, but they might be useful."

"Yeah, the way poison is sometimes," said the other. "Go on."

"We got a simple plan. We're just going to the back of the tent behind the place that Scar-face runs, and there we'll simply slice down a big cut in the canvas and the spot will be right behind the roulette outfit. When the folks inside hear the noise of the knife ripping the canvas and turn around, all they'll see will be the muzzles of a couple of Colts sticking through the gap, and ready to shoot. I'm number one man on the shooting and I aim to split the heart of the kid right in two!"

"That's good," said Lester. "I like a simple plan better than a long one full of words."

"Right," said Durfee.

"Go on out, Durfee. I like the job. Send in Tony Perez, will you? I wanta tell him that you're the chief guy in this job. Did you give him your right name?"

"I ain't a fool. I called myself Jones or something."

And Durfee went outside and found the three waiting.

CHAPTER 24

When Perez was inside the shack, facing his chief, the latter said: "That new gent, you picked him up where?"

"In Scar-face's dump."

"Doing what?"

"Cussing Handsome Harry out of his second growth."

"That takes a good deal of front."

"Yeah, it takes front. This guy, he has front, too."

"Know who he is?"

"He's by name of—lemme see—oh, yeah, he's called—Dinner Bell! That's a funny one, ain't it?"

"You wooden head," said Lester, gently, "don't you know that that's Durfee?"

"Durfee? That was a Texas Ranger, you mean?"

"Yeah. Him that was a Ranger."

"What's his play in this here? The double cross?"

"I dunno. Maybe it is," said Spot Lester. "I'd trust him as long as I could see him and had the drop on him. You hear me?"

"Yeah, I hear you."

"Keep behind him. Pass the wink to the other boys. Don't let him get away. Let him drop the kid. After that, when

you slide out, just sink a knife in the small of his back.
You'll have that many less to split the coin with. Beside, I'll
throw in something extra for you, Tony."

Perez blinked. "Two at a time ain't my motto," he protested.

"Are your mottoes as good as mine?" snarled Lester. "Get
out of here and do as I tell you."

"All right," said Perez. "But I'll prefer a gun to a knife,
thank you. You can't spear a man on a galloping horse very
good with a knife. You stick the point into a bone, likely
as not. I've tried it, and I know."

"Do it any way you please," said Lester. "But get out of
here!"

Perez left. When he had departed from the room, big
Lester threw away the Indian blanket that covered his legs.
Long and scrawny, they extended before him. The muscles
looked like dried and twisted ropes, entangled under the
skin. The limbs were terribly shrunken.

He looked at them with his upper lip writhing, as a wolf
caught in a trap might look down at the imprisoned paw.

Then, propping his right leg on a chair, he began to
massage it, working from the ankle upward to the hip. Patiently, dexterously, he labored, picking out the muscles one
by one with an expert touch, and then bruising and squeez-
ing them with the immense force of his hands. Every day
he was at this work for hours. He could walk now. But at
the same time he knew very well that he was incapable of
a catlike leap or a running stride, such as had taken him out
of innumerable difficulties in the past.

Outside, the four conspirators gathered in a close group
in the shrubbery behind the long, narrow line of the town.
They had made black masks out of sections of the lining of
an old coat. When the masks were in place. Durfee examined them and pronounced them satisfactory.

He said: "You gents know your business, I guess. I don't
have to tell you that when you get into a job like this, you
wanta look at the details and the big things will take care of
themselves. Gents have been identified in a courtroom—and
by a lynching mob, before this—by the color of their hair.
You oughta know that. Keep your hats on and well down
over your eyes. If any of you walk with a slouch, straighten

up, and them that go straight, stoop a mite. It don't take so very much to fool an eye in the dark of the night."

"That all sounds to me. Sounds like the first grade," said Blondy.

"You're gonna use the knife that cuts through the back of the tent," said Durfee. "Know how to cut cloth, Blondy?"

"You mean, am I a half-wit?"

"I mean, have you got sense enough to run the knife through and cut a slant, or do you jab it straight in and make a fool rip?"

"Never mind me. I'll make the slash in the tent all right."

"Do it right, when there's some noise inside," said Durfee, "and they won't hear a thing."

"All right, all right," said Chuck. "You're still talkin', when we might've had the job all done by this time!"

"One more thing," said Blondy. "We're all together, I reckon. And the skunk that tries to pull out or double-cross, we sock him full of lead, no matter what happens, eh?"

"No matter what happens!" agreed the others.

Only Durfee did not speak.

He had felt, from the first, that he would be able to draw out of this entanglement before the last moment and give the proper warning to young Henry St. Clair.

Then other things lay ahead and, above all, the vital necessity of retaking that fiend among men, Spot Lester.

He sighed, as he thought of all the possibilities that were ready at his hand. If only he could take advantage of them! But, how was he to withdraw from these three murderers now? They were suspicious enough of every one, including one another, and they would certainly not be blind to any strange maneuvers on his part.

He saw himself forced steadily ahead.

He had made all of the delays that he could afford, in the arrangement of the masks. Now they were irritated by his delays. He could only hope that the faro outfit might have closed down for the night, but there seemed little hope of that!

And now he found himself moving forward with the others; yes, marching in the first place. Behind him, he heard a stealthy whispering among the others. He knew that some word concerning him was being passed. What? Whatever it was, the hissing of the whisper told him that it was no good news.

Before them, big unlighted shacks spilled to the right and to the left, but the tent of Scar-face shone like a moon with a cloud gathered about it. Blondy was already fingering his long hunting knife and feeling the edge of it with his thumb. They stood close behind the tightly stretched canvas.

"Now," said Tony Perez. "There's nobody in sight; cut it open, Blondy. There's noise enough inside to cover up the sound of the ripping."

There was, in fact, a loud outcry of voices that accompanied some exciting turn of play. Some one, perhaps, had made a big winning. And Blondy, setting his teeth, ripped a five foot gap in the tent, turning the knife to the side at the bottom of the rent so as to leave a hanging flap of the cloth. Tony Perez instantly pulled the loose flap out and through a narrow window, as it were, Durfee found himself looking straight in upon the faro outfit, with the tangle of men in front of it. The broad shoulders and back of Henry St. Clair were turned to him.

Not an eye had been taken by the cutting of the tent cloth; no one was looking his way, and the target was one that a child of ten could not possibly have missed.

The section of the tent was not lighted by a number of lamps and lanterns, but from the top of the place hung down a thin chain that supported, above the heads of the gamblers, a great hanging lamp with a triple burner.

That, without the slightest hesitation, Durfee made his target. He saw in a flash what he must do; for, even if he fired off his gun simply to give a general warning, there were two other guns ready at this same loophole to fill Henry Vincent St. Clair full of lead.

So up gleamed the big Colt, exploded, and jerked its muzzle high. A crash of glass followed, and a wave of darkness washed through the gaming room. At the same time, the other three outside of the tent were covered by the very same dark shadow.

Durfee sprang back from between two of the men.

He heard the gasping, incredulous oath of Blondy, and felt the very swish and whisper of the boy's knife arm as he struck at the traitor to the good cause of murder!

But Durfee was back and away from them. A corner of a shed nearby offered him the first cover and he sprinted for it with the uncertain step of a true horseman. At the same time, Tony Perez had opened fire. Once, twice and again his gun boomed. The last bullet crashed through the woodwork of the corner of the shed, as the speeding Durfee got behind it.

But he legged it straight on. There would be an outward boiling of angry men through the back of the big tent to find the cause of the bullet that had been fired.

And Durfee, in the meantime, had a desperate need of finding Henry St. Clair.

By himself, he could not possibly handle the Lester situation. The man himself, though he might be crippled, and the guards he had gathered around himself were more than he, Durfee, could undertake to break through. But if he had St. Clair; well, that might prove a different matter!

So he reached the front of the gambling tent, and hurried through into pandemonium. There were voices crying out. Men were hurrying here and there, and back behind the faro layout the tent had been ripped wide open, a gap as large as a double door, through which men were pouring in and out.

In that direction he went as fast as he could, shouldering through the gathering. And as he got back to the place, where the serene head of Henry St. Clair showed above the crowd, he saw a vicious knot of men coming into the tent carrying with them the struggling form of a man. He saw the face of the fellow, the lean, vicious face of Blondy.

CHAPTER 25

In the meantime, he had come close to St. Clair and saw him standing with a Colt in each powerful hand, while he was saying in the calmest of voices: "Just a little joke, a little practical joke to speed up the game, gentlemen. The cards are still in the box, and there's luck there for the fellow who's meant to have it. Step up, gentlemen, and try your hands."

Durfee stepped behind the table and touched the arm of his former protege.

St. Clair turned an unexcited face toward him, as toward a stranger.

"Henry," said Durfee. "There's an inferno turned loose. I fired the bullet that smashed the lights. It was either that or a pair of slugs through your back. Spot Lester is in town!"

Other lights, lamps and lanterns, were being brought. There was no loss of money, fortunately, because St. Clair's long arms and capable hands had seen to it that certain fumblings in the dark had not reached the cash drawers of the faro game.

St. Clair looked quietly for half a second toward his old friend. Then he said to a man beside him: "Dutch, take over the layout for a while, will you?"

The fellow nodded; St. Clair was instantly on the way out of the tent, beside his friend. As the reached the street, Durfee explained and rapidly.

Spot Lester was in the town. That was enough!

Said Durfee: "There was one man with him, a tough-looking specimen. Lester himself is crippled in the legs, he told me. Perhaps he was lying. But his hair was white, though perhaps that's a wig. I don't know. I only really know that I saw the beast and I know where I saw him."

Then he added: "By this time, two of the other thugs who were with me behind the tent may have gone back to him; but I think that they'll be afraid to show their faces after bungling the business so badly."

St. Clair was walking so rapidly that Durfee had to run, every few steps, to keep ahead.

The boy was saying: "Now, if we have luck and can make our chance, we'll end him. I don't like to tackle a crippled man, Durfee, but Lester isn't a man. He's a spider; he's poison and ought to be stamped on!"

"Of course he should," said Durfee. "There—there's the shack that he was in. No light in it now!"

The big man halted. Then he said: "There's a light, after all. I see a glimmer of it at the back of the place. The fastest way will be the surest. We can break down the front door. It looks as flimsy as the rest of the house!"

With a movement inside his coat, he brought a pair of

revolvers partly into sight and then thrust them away again. And so they strode up, with Durfee saying nothing.

He had a sort of strange, blind confidence that all must go well with him, so long as he had such a companion as this boy.

So they reached the door, and, with a glance at one another through the darkness, they gave the door the combined weight of their shoulders.

It flew open easily before them; there was no crash, hardly more than the swish of the air as the door swung in.

The first room was empty, but in the second room there was the gleam of the same smoky lantern which Durfee had noticed on his first visit. Within the radius of that glow, he saw the shadow of a chair falling upon the floor, a chair with a shrouded figure in it.

Was it possible that the hair-trigger senses of great Lester had been so dimmed that he had not heard?

Durfee, with a frantic arm, pointed and made a signal for silence. His companion nodded his head.

The youth's face had changed. The indifference had left it. Instead his eyes flashed and a strange little smile played about his lips. It reminded Durfee of that other smile which would linger on the face of the boy in the old days, the smile of an unawakened child.

Well, he was awakened now, and even Spot Lester would soon learn what that awakening meant.

So, with the big man leading, they crossed the threshold of the other room, gun in hand.

But St. Clair halted sharply and drew himself up a little. Durfee saw the cause the next instant, for there in the chair was not the form of Spot Lester, but a blanket wrapped around some odds and ends, to give to the shadow on the floor the semblance of a man.

At the same time, the terrible voice of Lester came to them from outside the house, crying:

"St. Clair, Durfee! You've walked like a pair of fools right inside the hollow of my hand. Durfee, you almost tricked me, but no trick works twice on Spot Lester. You're dead, the pair of you; you're sunk without a trace. Bill, touch it off!"

A gun exploded, as the two turned and excitedly rushed for the door.

They got through it, racing, as Lester cried: "You block-head, you've bungled the fuse! The other one, then!"

A second shot, and then the bottom of the world opened for Durfee and hurled him into darkness.

CHAPTER 26

He wakened, stretched flat on the ground, in a pool of water and mud. Lantern light struck across him, and on the rim of it he saw a number of faces; young St. Clair was kneeling beside him.

"He's all right," said some one, carelessly. "His eyes are open."

"Thank God!" muttered Henry St. Clair.

His strong hands took Durfee by the shoulders. "Are you all right, Durfee?" he asked, eagerly. "Don't speak if there's any great effort but, if you can tell me where there's pain, inside, there are no bones broken, so far as I can make out. But the shock—"

Durfee remained silent for a moment, for he was still fumbling with reality, rather vaguely, and what, above all else, amazed him was that he had actually detected human kindness in the voice of this strange lad. It seemed to him the greatest of miracles.

Then, with a slight effort, he pushed himself up on his elbows.

"Stand me up, Henry," he commanded.

The power of a giant lifted him gently to his feet, and he flexed his knees and stretched his arms.

"I've been knocked out, that's all," said Durfee. "A good hard whang on the chin would make a man feel about the same way afterward. That's all there is to it. What happened?"

The curiosity of the crowd was already pacified. They scattered, though Durfee could hear one of them saying loudly that it was time for a vigilance committee to take Flinders in hand. Guns and even knives were to be expected, but dynamite in the middle of the night—that was a little too much!

"Was it dynamite?" asked Durfee. "They blew up the house under us—was that it?"

"It wasn't dynamite, I think," said St. Claire. "It must have been something different—a little bit of nitroglycerin. It was so neatly confined, I mean to say. And the fellow who prepared the charge directed the force of it the wrong way. It blew more of a hole in the ground than it did in the air. Oh, it wrecked the house well enough, but we managed to live through it."

"He played a long chance," said Durfee. "Think of him layin' for us, when he didn't know but what we'd come with the whole dog-gone town behind us! We might've surrounded that house and snagged him and his helpers, but he played the long chance to get me. And he nearly got you, as well!"

"Aye, he's a brave man," said Henry St. Clair. "I hope that he lied about his injury. Sometimes I think that before anything in the world, I'd rather—"

His voice trailed away, but Durfee was able to piece out the unfinished picture. It was above all things, then, the will of the boy to meet the great Spot Lester hand to hand and face to face, when the force of that famous criminal, whether in mind or in body, was unimpaired. A curious wish for any human being to nourish, yet the ex-Ranger could guess that the boy was honest in it.

They stood alone in the darkness while the night voice of Flinders was dying down. And Durfee said: "Now we've got to think ahead, Henry. Lester—what's he likely to try next?"

"I don't know," said the boy. "Is he more hawk or more snake?"

"He's both in one," answered Durfee. "He might dig into the ground and lurk there; or he might take wing and fly to the other end of the world. I dunno what he'd be most likely to do. Does he know that we're alive?"

"I don't see how he could," said St. Clair. "We were buried under a pile of debris. And the crowd was on the run the minute it heard the explosion. It was an angry crowd, too. Gun fights seem to be rather popular, but dynamite and soup—no! No, I don't think that even Spot Lester would have been apt to linger around this place very long after the explosion. They'll take it for granted that the pair of us died. They well might!"

"Where have you learned so much about soup and such things, Henry?" asked Durfee.

"I've known for some time that I'd have to consider Lester," said the boy. "And so I've been working all my spare time on one thing and another. There are some good books on explosives, and their uses. There are some good books on criminal devices, too. And I've been spending every minute getting ready to take an examination, with Spot Lester as the examiner. I hope that he'll be able to give me a passing grade."

The touch of humor, ironic as it was, surprised Durfee. Surely the character of the boy was altering apace!

"Those days," said Durfee, "when you were riding out in the hills, spending your time alone?"

"Generally," said St. Clair, "I had with me a few little trinkets, master keys, skeleton keys, various sketches and pictures, plans of locking devices. Locksmiths are an ingenious lot, and yet it seems that they have to work according to certain systems. Once one has an idea of the systems, well, the rest of it is fairly easy."

"It's a job," said Durfee with emotion, "that has occupied some of the finest brains in the world, but most of them get their leisure for study in prison cells. They need the cool and the quiet, I reckon!"

The boy answered nothing to this. Then Durfee said: "And Lester—what will Lester be doing now?"

"Digging himself in in a new place in Flinders, I suppose," said St. Clair.

"No," answered Durfee. "I don't think that even Lester has the courage to do that. He doesn't want to be caught."

"He's brushed us out of his way," muttered Henry St. Clair. "And then what? What would that lead him to do? What else to finish up one picture? Why there's my uncle, there's Bunce!"

His voice rose a little.

"That's true," said Durfee. "But he's not likely to ride across those hills, not with his legs more than half gone!"

"If he thought he had a free hand, he'd crawl a thousand miles, I think," said the other.

"Yeah, perhaps he would," said Durfee. "D'you think that we ought to line out for the ranch?"

"I think that we should," said St. Clair. "Will you ride with me? Are you too much shaken up, Durfee?"

"I'm never too shaken to sit in a saddle. If we're to go at all, let's start now!"

They went straight for their horses. Durfee's was already waiting, tethered at its hitching rack; St. Clair himself was only slightly delayed, and presently they started out on the trail.

It was one of the strangest rides that Durfee had ever taken, because his companion was silent all the way.

He had made silent rides as long as this before, but that was when, as a Ranger, he was bringing in a criminal to stand trial on some capital charge, with the conviction plainly written beforehand in public prejudice. But St. Clair, a friend and a young man, sat silently in his saddle all the distance.

His mind seemed busy, not with the trail, but with the future and, when the stars gleamed against his handsome face, it appeared to Durfee as hard as a carved rock.

His hands were busied, too. Some little metal trinket or other was constantly in his fingers, being fumbled at. And Durfee asked no questions. He could guess that the eternal mystery of locks and their makers was occupying the hands and the thoughts of the boy. Then another wonder began to grow up in Durfee.

Spot Lester, for many a year, had been taken for granted as an unequaled master in every form of crime. But might it not be that the master of Lester was riding here beside him: a brain as clear and as cold, a heart as stern, a hand as strong, a wit as agile?

If experience was on the side of Lester and animal cunning, the passion of youth and a greater heart were in the boy.

All of these conjectures, these wonderings, were swept at once from the mind of Durfee, when the boy pointed straight ahead. Durfee saw, instantly, a dull, reddish glow above the next hill, beyond which the house of Bunce was standing.

They rushed their horses forward to the brow of that hill, and there saw the scene clearly lighted up by the glow of a fire. The light of its own destruction showed them the house of Bunce in flames.

CHAPTER 27

They came down from the hill with a rush after that. Only once they looked at one another, and then spurred their horses. Durfee was almost born to the saddle; he had ridden all his life; and this night his lighter weight had saved his tough mustang much, and yet Henry St. Clair fairly beat him down the incline to the house of Bunce.

The flames were jumping higher every moment. From both ends of the house the fire was working, and the punchers from the bunk house had formed two carrying lines by which they poured a continual big stream of water on either end of the place.

They were working valiantly, but quite vainly, and when the two riders dashed up, the whole body of men desisted.

As they dismounted, Durfee called to Red Al, the foreman, now soot-covered, his clothes smoking from the nearness with which he had been elbowing the flames: "Al, where's Bunce?"

"Back at the barn, wetting down the roof, I reckon," said Red Al. "This here ain't any accident, Durfee. Some fire bug has started this here—"

"Anybody seen Bunce?" shouted Durfee.

"Must be back at the barn," some one began to answer.

"Who's been in his room to see?" asked Durfee.

"What would he be staying in his room for?" asked the foreman. "He ain't fool enough for that."

"Not if he can walk out," answered St. Clair.

Both the front and the rear door of the house, of course, were totally blocked by red walls of flame. St. Clair and Durfee ran about to the far side of the place and there they saw the window of Bunce, heavily shuttered.

"Why should he have his shutters closed, a warm night like this?" asked St. Clair. "There's something wrong!"

He could reach the shutters from the ground, and now he tugged strongly at them; they were locked on the inside. Durfee joined him, pulling likewise.

And now, behind them, the entire body of the cow-punchers were gathered, but making no attempt to interfere, since it was clear that not more than two could work at the window.

There was a sudden snarl from St. Clair. The thick, heavily nailed slat at which he was tugging came away with a rip and a crackling. He seized on the center of the shutter's frame, to which the aperture now gave his hand access, and, jumping up, he braced his feet against the wall of the house, and thrust his weight out horizontally. Durfee, laboring as well as he could, heard the cracking of the tendon as St. Clair applied all his force. Then, with a groan and a sigh, the shutter pitched open.

St. Clair landed yards away on head and shoulders, yet rolled instantly to his feet.

Durfee, pulling himself up onto the window sill, jerked up the lower pane. Instantly a thick, stifling cloud of white smoke rolled out, entered his nostrils, choked and baffled him. He dropped down from the window sill, gasping, and staggered away from the side of the house.

"Nothing's alive in there!" he said to St. Clair. "I know that much."

"There may be air close against the floor!" said St. Clair, and bounced straight way through the open window.

In the meantime, a running, shouting puncher who had run to the barn returned. He was yelling that it was true— Bunce was not at the barn. The men who were drenching the roof of that building to keep it safe from the shower of sparks reported that the boss never had been with them.

Durfee, resting on one knee against the ground, heard these tidings and looked at the window where St. Clair had disappeared into the boiling white smoke.

Another pair of men had striven to get in to assist the youngster but, incautiously breathing, the acrid gas drove them back, coughing, staggering, beating the air with their hands in their frantic efforts to get clean oxygen inside their lungs once more.

That caution was enough for the rest of the punchers. They gathered together, muttering. Presently, it would be necessary to rush that window and strive to rescue the body of young St. Clair. They shouted to Durfee to keep back, when he stood up and prepared to enter.

But he paid no heed to them. He wet a bandanna in a bucket half full of water that stood near, tied it around his nose and mouth and sprang in through the window.

Even through the cloth protection, he could feel himself choked. He remembered what the boy had said and flung himself down on the floor, lying with face close to the boards.

Those boards were smoking hot to the touch!

The air was better, to be sure, close to the floor, but still he knew perfectly well that a very few minutes would be all that he could possibly hope to endure here.

How long had the boy been inside the room already? A whole sixty seconds, or less?

He strained his eyes; he crawled forward. But tears were blinding him when a mighty crashing shook the house, and red lightnings flickered before his eyes. Then followed a greater, freshening roar of the fire.

He knew what had happened. A great section of the roof had fallen in. In a very short interim, the whole building would be aflame.

Then he thought that he heard a sound of voices behind him; yes, the sounds were not in his own brain alone, but in the night outside, where the punchers were shouting for the rescuers to return before it was too late.

"The whole roof is smashing in! It's caving!" they yelled.

And Durfee, hearing them, already half-choked, no longer fumbled in the white mist, but tried to get back to the window. He could no longer find it!

In frightful panic, he rose to his knees. Instantly the thicker atmosphere of the upper levels of the smoke smote his brain, stifled him.

He crawled forward and felt a wall. It was almost red hot; it took the skin from the fingers that touched it.

No, that was toward the fire; in the other direction must be the window.

If only he could find it before his lungs burst, his lungs which were already lined with consuming flames!

Then, before him, he saw a long, weltering line of fire. The flames were eating up through the flooring! Any instant, now, as the fire increased, or as a draft of air entered, that

whole room might burst into flames; and so would end
Durfee, ex-Ranger!

But the fire showed him two other things, the dull square
of the window, through which the frantic, defeated voices of
the cow-punchers were roaring, urging him to come back;
and, to the side, the form of young Henry St. Clair, on
hands and knees, creeping backward and dragging after him
the loose body of Bunce, whose coat he held gripped in his
teeth.

Durfee wavered.

If he left the boy to drag the body clear to the window,
the room would certainly be aflame before St. Clair succeeded in getting there. If he went to help with the rescue,
he would, nine chances out of ten, perish with the youth.

Fear whipped him one way, but duty gripped him like a
rawhide lariat and dragged him straight forward to join the
rescue work.

He laid hold with one hand; he backed away; and rapidly
they got the unconscious man to the wall, beneath the window. St. Clair, with a last enormous burst of strength, rose
up and flung his uncle through the window into the waiting
arms outside. But the effort seemed to take all that was left
in him. He staggered back, he would have fallen among the
fire snakes that now were working rapidly along the floor;
but Durfee put a shoulder against the small of his back,
urged him forward, toppled him in turn into the freshness
of the outer air.

He himself got onto the sill. He struggled there, feebly. A
splinter had caught him and was sufficient to hold him
pinned and helpless, with the oven heat increasing behind
him, while his eyes almost burst from his head and he knew
that he was strangling.

Then fresh, strong hands gripped him and jerked him out
to safety.

He was flung on his back. Strong men pumped his arms
up and down, pressing his fists against his breast, then jerking out his arms to full length.

He gasped and groaned in protest. It was as though the
air they forced him to breathe were liquid fire. But, very
suddenly, he felt a catch in his throat, and then a sweet,
pure current swept down to the bottom of his heart.

He sat up, bracing himself with his arms.

"He's all right, now," he heard Red Al saying. "But he had a narrow squeak!"

Durfee was biting at the air like a dog at red meat. He never could have enough of it. He swore that never again would he so much as feel the sensation of thirst! Burning deserts would be as green fields to him. Nothing could match the torment of that brief breathlessness!

Before him he saw the house of Bunce turned into a thin shell. Within the shell of the walls, all was upward shooting fire. The heads of the flames wagged in the center of the sky. The roaring flights of sparks put out the stars. And the light, flowing widely all around, brought all the nearer hills close up with the effect of a red sunset. The farther mountains remained in outer night.

It was a strange effect; they seemed to be in the center of the universe, surrounded by horror. The world seemed to be watching them.

Two punchers got Durfee under the shoulders and jerked him to his feet. But he could walk and support his weight. He hardly needed their help in running back to a little distance. Then, as they halted, he saw the wall that faced them bulging at the base. Suddenly the remainder of the roof and the other standing walls crashed, and it seemed as though the building were in that second sublimated into a terrible column of fire that leaped upward and made the leaves glisten on distant trees.

After that, the flames settled at once to a steady hissing and growling.

And Durfee turned for the first time toward St. Clair and Bunce.

Even their human lives had seemed less important, until now, than the fate of the old house. So many hands had wrought to build it, so many steps had fallen, so many voices had sounded within it; it was so filled with ghosts, and all of these seemed to have departed in that last great upward gushing of flame. Yes, in a way it was more than a mortal death.

He felt awed and depressed and shaken as he went, at last, toward the two.

St. Clair was sitting up, braced on trembling arms; his head was down on his chest. But Bunce was still stretched flat on his back, and the work of resuscitation went on methodically.

Red Al had charge of it and seemed to know his business. A faint groan now came from the senseless rancher.

Tom Crocker, a sourdough turned puncher, came up to Durfee.

"What are you gonna say about a beast that ties an old cripple and gags him so he can't yip, and then leaves him there in his room, locked up, and sets fire to the house? Watcha gonna say, Durfee? Is there anybody in the world that would do that?"

"Lester!" said the ex-Ranger.

"Spot Lester? You're crazy. Lester's dead, ain't he?"

"I wish he was," said Durfee. "How does it go, Henry?"

St. Clair rose to his feet. He rested a hand on the shoulder of Durfee to steady himself, but his touch was light, and almost at once he was able to breathe freely.

"I'm well enough," he said.

Then he turned his head, and his eyes looked at Durfee with a gathering light.

"I was glad to see you in there," he said, and pointed at the red ruin of the house.

"That's behind us," answered Durfee.

But he knew that it was not. He knew that it would be in their minds every day of their lives. It was written into them in such characters as time cannot rub out.

"It was Lester," said Durfee. "Of course, it was Lester."

"Aye, of course," said the boy, and turned away.

Durfee squatted at the side of Bunce and watched the older man recovering, saw him sit up; then instantly relax again.

It was at Durfee's suggestion that they carried him on a blanket to the bunk house.

There he lay for two hours, as the gray morning began and brightened and during this time he muttered, from time to time, deliriously. There was no thermometer to take his temperature, but his skin was burning hot to the touch and his face was dry.

Here and there, flakes of fire had burned through his clothes and seared and tormented his poor, withered body; and the punchers bound up his hurts with wonderful skill and gentleness. It was plain that they loved the little man in spite of his many unpleasant mannerisms.

And so, when the sun came up, his eyes opened wide, a slight perspiration came out and made his face gleam. And suddenly he was himself again, except for a continual tremor that shook his entire body.

He asked for Henry St. Clair, first of all.

"Henry's outside," said Red Al, "but here's Durfee. Neither you nor the kid would ever've got clear except for old Durfee, here."

The little man jerked his head to one side.

He measured Durfee up and down with a glance that seemed full of hostile criticism.

"Aye," said he, "there's some that are all made of asbestos. They can't burn! Why isn't Henry here? Is he badly used up?"

"Him? Oh, it was only a breather for him," said Durfee. "He's all right. Might be a few square feet of hide were burned off him, but that ain't anything to a fellow like your nephew."

Bunce closed his eyes and smiled.

"His luck is all gone!" said he.

"Whose? Henry's?" said Durfee, surprised.

"Lester's," answered the rancher, still with his eyes closed.

"If Lester hadn't spent so long after he tied and gagged me—spent so long telling me just how it would feel to lie there on the floor and choke with the smoke, and then be waked up by the fire handling me—if he hadn't wasted that time, I wouldn't be lying here now, laughing at him!"

And his lips actually parted and he laughed in a high, crackling mirthful voice!

CHAPTER 28

Camp coffee and a morsel of roasted venison, served in the bunk house, brought Bunce around amazingly. He kept asking for Henry St. Clair, but had to be told that the boy was not there just then. He had disappeared; he would soon be back.

"Whether he comes back or not," said Bunce, "he's paid me and the world now, for everything that I've done for him and for all the worries that I've had about him. Good blood will out; good blood will tell, eh, Durfee?"

"Yes, it'll tell," agreed the ex-Ranger.

"When I was lying there," went on Bunce, slowly, "I was wondering how long it would take me to strangle, and watching the red of the fire begin to eat through the walls. It meant something to hear that window go crash."

"It was Henry that pulled the shutter out, with his bare hands," said Durfee.

"Yes, he has a pair of hands," said Bunce.

He clasped his bandaged hands above his head and looked up, smiling.

"And then he came at me through the smoke. There wasn't much sense left in me; I was blind; I still don't see very well. But somehow, without any words spoken, I knew that it was Henry. There aren't many others in the world who would have come into that furnace, not for the sake of an uncle, or for a father either. Not many would've come, except Henry and you, Durfee, you worn-out old lobo!"

He turned his head and scowled at Durfee, and the latter scowled back.

"It wasn't you that I was thinking about, no more'n an empty sack," said Durfee. "It was only the kid that I went in to get out."

"You lie," said Bunce, happily.

"So do you," said Durfee.

"Yeah. Of course, I'm lying," said Bunce. "Durfee, I've thought that life didn't mean much to my twisted, wrecked old body. But I'm glad to be living now. And Lester's beaten! He's beaten once again. And I think he won't be long in this world, my lad. When a man's luck is out, his death follows pretty quickly. It can't help but come!"

"Maybe," said Durfee. "But I'll believe that Lester's dead when I see a bullet go through his brain and a couple more in his heart, and then watch his body fed into an incinerator, and see the ashes throwed away. Maybe he's lost two or three of his lives, but he's got plenty more."

"Where's Henry?" asked Bunce. "I want to see him. Not to thank him, though. No, I'm blowed if I'll waste my breath thanking anybody, and that goes for you, too."

"I don't want your blasted thanks," said Durfee. "I wouldn't be weighted down with 'em."

"That's all right, too," said Bunce. "Go and fetch me the boy. I want to tell him that Lester didn't even get any money because I'd cleaned out my safe three days before —papers and everything. As for the house, I'm mighty glad that it's gone. It was well enough for me, but it was never the sort of a house to please my boy. Tell Henry to come in here. He and I will draw up a new plan, straight off!"

Durfee went slowly out into the open. At the door of the bunk house, he paused to roll a cigarette and light it. He looked beyond the trees to the swelling lines of the hills where he could see the groves, the shadows beneath them, the silver streaks where water ran, the little patches of color where the cattle strayed, grazing in the cool of the morning. Other lands might be better to other men, but to him this was as near perfection as could be—except for his own slope of land, his own little shack, his own bit of running creek.

He had fitted into this landscape and he had fitted himself into the life of the people, also. The cow-punchers, still cooking around their breakfast fire, looked over to him with respect and friendliness. He had come among them as a far removed stranger, but now he had opened the door to their hearts.

Then he walked slowly away from the bunk house. He was tied up in half a dozen places where the fire had bitten him and his bandages pinched him a little in walking, made him step short and limp with the right leg.

He strolled on, hardly thinking of his mission to find the boy and to bring him in, hardly thinking of Spot Lester either, for it seemed that under such a sky there could be neither harm nor trouble in the world.

Then he saw a rider, a big man, sweeping up the hills and pausing at the corral.

He knew the man when he dismounted. It was Henry St. Clair, now turning loose his mustang, and adroitly roping another mount out of the angle of shining, sweating horse-flesh in the corral.

Durfee hurried on and reached the gate of the corral as the boy was leading his mustang out, freshly saddled.

"Your uncle wants you, Henry," said Durfee.

"Does he?" said the boy, fitting his foot into the stirrup.

"He wants you right away."

"For what?"

"To plan a new ranch house. He wants to have your ideas."

"You tell him," said Henry St. Clair, "that the foundation has to be made safe and sound before it's worth while building a house."

"What d'you mean by that?"

"Why should we build again? Just to let Lester have the pleasure of burning us out, once more?"

And he swung up into the saddle. "What's the matter?" asked Durfee. "Where are you bound?"

"For Lester," said the boy. And, for the first time, Durfee noticed the long rifle holstered at the side of the saddle.

He could also understand, in one easy jump of the mind, why it was that the boy had not come in before this to see his uncle. In fact, his brain had hardly cleared from the fumes of unconsciousness before he was hunting about the place for the sign of the trail of Spot Lester. It seemed that he must have found it!

Said Durfee: "You've found sign, Henry?"

"I think so," said the boy.

"Wait half a minute till I catch myself a horse," said Durfee. "And I'll ride with you."

"You've done enough, Durfee," said the boy, sternly. "The thing for you now is to stay here and watch my uncle, and take care of him—while I go scouting, and bring back word of whatever I may be able to find."

Half proudly, half sadly, Durfee stared at the youngster. He seemed no longer a mere boy, but the most formidable of experienced warriors.

"You want the glory all for yourself, Henry," said Durfee. "Don't you think that there's enough to fill two pairs of hands, in the hunting of Spot Lester?"

"It's not a question of glory," answered the other, surprisingly. "It's simply that I feel a thing driving me along. Fate—anything you want to call it. If you really have to come, well the same thing is driving you. I'll wait while you get your horse."

There were plenty of young horses in that corral, swift and keen as hawks. As Durfee stood watching the flashing bodies mill in a corner and then spill past him like water running down a chute, he waited until his eye rested on a veteran whose dappled gray was turning more silvery pale. That mustang had a good dozen years behind him and had, no doubt, lost something of his fastest foot.

Nevertheless, Durfee did not hesitate. He had in his mind a picture of the ragged uplands of the timberline and, above, that region where the great outlaw had hidden out before and where he was most likely to hide out again, now that he was fleeing with the feeling that he had committed the murder of Durfee and St. Clair, the destruction of old Bunce, the rancher.

Yes, up there among the rocks, where the hunter of mountain goats and sheep would be most likely to go with his rifle, Spot Lester would have established himself. In that case, the horse for the hunter would not be merely the fast colt, but the cool and seasoned veteran, whose step was very sure.

So the rope fled out of his hand and, as the noose dropped like a shadow over the head of the gray, the gelding pulled up suddenly, and then stood with ears back and hanging lip, the very picture of sullen malice.

Durfee had to sit through some hard pitching before the veteran gave up, and then rode out to the side of Henry St. Clair, who remained at a distance, looking on with an indifferent air.

Durfee said: "Henry, it ain't right for us to go off and leave no word with your uncle."

"We've no time to argue with him," said the boy. "And if we tell him what we intend to do, he'll order a dozen men to go along with us, and I dare say you don't expect to catch a tiger if you go stalking him with a hundred men."

Durfee nodded. "He'll most surely be worried," said he.

"He'll worry, perhaps," said St. Clair. "Of course, I know that, but he'll not be able to find our trail by worrying, and that's why I want to make a start now. Are you ready?"

"I'm ready," said the older man.

He was angered by the grim terseness of St. Clair; his pride was challenged, and so they trotted off down the slope with St. Clair leading and Durfee close behind.

CHAPTER 29

For two miles they went in an almost straight line; by this time the ranch was well sunk behind them, and they were not likely to run into cow-punchers out early for the day's work.

Then, as they came to the mouth of a small valley, where they paused to look around, Durfee said: "You might tell me how you know that this is the trail of Spot Lester and what the signs are like."

"I think it's his trail," said the boy, "because the signs are only a few hours old and because the tracks were certainly made by somebody who started from near the ranch house at a dead run. There's another one of the prints."

Durfee swung low in the saddle and examined the mark. He could tell by the angles at which the grass stood out on the rim of the cut that the animal had stepped here not very many hours before—three, say, or a little more or less.

"That's a mule's hoof mark," he said to St. Clair. "D'you think that he'd ride a mule, actually?"

"If he wants to get up into the mountains, why not a mule?" asked the boy. "A mule will get fat on thistles, it will stand the cold a lot better; and it isn't likely to fall down a crevice and break its neck and its rider's. A man up there among the rocks wouldn't care so much about a fast traveling animal, I take it."

"Perhaps not," agreed Durfee.

"There you are," said St. Clair, a moment later, as they began to ride up the shallow valley.

"What?" asked his companion.

"See where the trail comes in again, right up there close to the tree?"

"I see the same print," said Durfee. "But it could as well be made by a mule running loose. More likely was, because a man in a saddle, passing under this branch, would probably be scraped off the mule's back!"

He felt rather grimly triumphant, as he pointed out this fact.

Henry St. Clair paused and considered the evidence gravely.

"It isn't likely to be the track of a mule running loose. This is still on my uncle's range. His land doesn't stop until we come to that next divide, you see? And he doesn't keep mules. You know how he hates 'em."

"It might be a mule from a neighbor's lot," suggested Durfee.

"Of course, it might. But the chances are against it, though. And why should it have grazed up close to the house, last night, and suddenly started off straight across country? As for the way the sign goes close up under that tree, well, isn't that evidence that a man was riding fast, and by night, so that he didn't see the tree until he was almost on top of it?"

Durfee nodded. He could not help agreeing with the logic of this suggestion. At the same time, he began to think that there was truth in what St. Clair thought; and that they really might have embarked upon the trail of the great outlaw.

It was a thought not absolutely thrilling with joy, but rather with horrible possibilities.

Somehow, all the glory was gone out of the hunt for a man the world believed that they had killed once before. There remained only the brutal necessity of fighting the battle over again, a more dangerous battle than ever before.

However, he could be glad of his companion. More and more he was convinced that all those long lessons in trailing and hunting had not been wasted upon young Henry St. Clair. He himself was never without a good hand glass which would magnify the imprints made by an animal going over rocks. And before an hour was out, they had need of it.

In the meantime, they took every precaution to insure their ability to follow the trail. When they found imprints on soft ground that received the impressions and retained them clearly, they paused to sketch in the sign of the separate feet. They measured the step with which the mule went up a grade and down it, the stretch of its trot and the short pitch of its gallop. No horse would have galloped with a stride like that, though a horse might conceivably have left all the rest of the trail, one with badly pinched hoofs.

They had, finally, sufficient data to unweave the tangle

of sign left by a whole herd of horses. And by prime of
the morning they had just such a task. Fifty or sixty horses
had run up a valley, and the sign of the mule disappeared
in the river of tracks!

They cast straight away to the head of the valley, but
there, after close scrutiny, they made reasonably sure that
the trail of the mule was not worked into the close braid of
the other sign. So they had to work back down the valley,
patiently, until Durfee discovered the point where the tracks
of the mule had diverged from the other and turned up toward the next divide.

They followed on.

"He's gaining hours and hours on us," said the boy.
"And hours mean a lot of miles, when you're following a
rider like him!"

"A lot of miles," agreed Durfee, "but this is the only way
we can go about the job. What else would you suggest?"

"I'd cast ahead to the place where we blasted away his
rock-nest that other time," said the lad.

"You think that he'll go there?"

"I think that he may go into that part of the mountains,
at least. If he remained about that place for a long time, recovering from his hurts, he must know it like a book. Why
wouldn't he go back there to hide?"

"Yes, he might do that. But if we cast ahead as far as
that, we may find out that we've got to come back to this
point and pick up the trail all over again."

"When we're hunting Spot Lester," replied the lad, "we'll
have to make up our minds to take a lot of chances. Don't
you think so?"

At last, Durfee nodded.

And so they planned the shortest route and followed it
industriously.

By noon, they were riding up that narrow gorge that pointed
among the three tall, scalped mountains. They scanned
the scene carefully, but they had hardly expected to find
Spot Lester in view. All that met the eye was the broad
sweep of the upper mountains, the cool promise of many
blue distances, and the blazing heat of the rocks about them.
The stones were fire-hot, and the radiation beat up under
the broad hat brims and into the faces of the men.

"We'll have to cut for sign," said Durfee. "I reckoned

that we would; and sign ain't so easy to find where there's mighty little more than granite for a horse to step on. Mind that broncho of yours, old son, or you'll soon be skidding on your head."

"I'm going on foot," said the boy. "That'll get my eye a bit closer to the ground."

He had dismounted, when he pointed suddenly to a higher shoulder of the mountain: "There's a pair of eyes that may have seen something we'd like to know about," said St. Clair.

Durfee saw a small dump heap on the side of the slope, and a staggering little lean-to close by, made apparently of cloth, canvas, wood and piled stones. By the lean-to a man was tending a fire. Certainly, such an outpost could not be overlooked as a source of information. They rode straight up to the stranger.

He was such a man as Durfee had seen before; a type, rather than an individual. No razor had touched his face for many a month; the hair had been sawed short with a hunting knife. But the dense growth could not conceal the sunken cheeks, and unhealthy sallow color of the skin. Overwork, exposure, bad feeding, all were represented in that picture.

Now he was stewing over the fire what looked like a mess of greens or roots; and he looked up from this work to nod at the strangers. That was his only greeting.

"This is one of them hard-boiled old sourdoughs," whispered Durfee to the boy. "We're lucky if we get more than six words out of him."

It appeared that they would hardly get as much as that. But when they came up and dismounted, the miner removed his stew from the fire, sprinkled some salt in it, and then placed it on three old, battered tin plates.

Durfee, for his own part, looked down at the portion that was offered him and shook his head: "We've ate hearty, already," said he.

The miner shrugged his shoulders.

"Been up here a long time gnawin' the shoulder off the mountain?" asked Durfee.

He did not wait for an answer, but went over to the mouth of the shaft. It was sunk a considerable distance; and the windlass mounted there at the side of the dump heap showed signs of considerable use.

The boy, at the side of Durfee, murmured: "I don't think he has anything to eat except that stewed stuff. No coffee, even; no bacon; no flour. I haven't seen even the sign of a gun or ammunition."

"No," said Durfee, "he's just hangin' on and chewin' away at that hole in the ground, hopin' that he'll make the strike. He's about all in, I reckon. We'll try some food on him to loosen his tongue."

They went back to their saddlebags and brought nearly all of their food supplies. At least, the three standard western necessities were represented, coffee, bacon, flour. And they put down the small sacks in a heap.

Said Durfee, by way of presentation speech: "I know how it is. A gent will run pretty short of supplies, out here on the edge of things. You take this stuff. It'll fill a bad spot for you!"

The miner was sitting cross-legged, filling a pipe. And the boy noticed that the two plates of berries and herbs set out for the guests had not been touched by the gaunt hermit. Perhaps a small portion of that tasteless diet was all that his rebelling stomach would accept, but it seemed more probable that some great precept of mountain hospitality prevented the starving man from eating what his guests had refused.

Now his hollow eyes turned upon the food supply that was being offered.

Then, slowly, he stood up, and the boy saw, or thought he saw, a distinct wavering in the knees of the miner. Once erect, he reached into a trousers pocket and pulled out a single coin, a twenty-five cent piece. This he considered for a moment, shook his head, and then, lifting the little sacks of food, he returned them to the saddlebags.

Durfee interrupted him in the midst of this work, by saying: "You know, brother, it ain't money that we want. The grub is yours. If you'll take it. We ain't up in the mountains for a long stay. We don't need that chuck, and it's all yours. We was just follering after a friend of ours that was riding on a mule, a big, long, lean-looking man. We lost his trail a while back; and he's a pretty hard traveler, and don't wait for them that fall behind."

At this speech, the miner turned, regarded Durfee with a fixed intensity and finally, still in silence, resumed his work and put away the food. After that, he took his place near the fire with a rock to support his back. There he must have sat every day, for the stone was darkened and polished a little. Now he used a coal from the fire to save a match and light his pipe. He half closed his eyes and inhaled the smoke deeply; but as a whiff of the smoke reached the nostrils of the boy, he coughed; there was not the slighest trace of a tobacco smell; apparently the poor fellow was filling his pipe with nothing more than a mixture of acrid barks!

At the scent of that smoke, Durfee muttered to his companion: "I'm going to get him now! Watch!" And, taking out his pipe, he loaded it leisurely from a well-filled pouch, packed the tobacco down hard and then drew on it heavily, until the air was rich with the smoke.

Said Durfee: "You take after a long day's work, or a short one either, there ain't anything half as comforting as a good pipe, brother. Ain't I right?"

The miner stared hollow-eyed at Durfee. His nostrils expanded.

After a moment, he cleared his throat and spoke for the first time.

"That gent on the mule, he took the west pass, there, riding pretty brisk."

Durfee stood up at once.

"Thanks, partner," said he. "By the way, you might keep something to remember us by. Here's all the tobacco that I need out of this pouch, and you keep the rest, will you?"

He offered the rolled up sack that contained the treasure. The miner, his hand half-extended, twice drew back and shook his head, but a third time he received the gift with an eager clutch. He took a deep, quick breath, as though the delicious fragrance of the tobacco smoke were already in his nostrils.

Durfee, in the meantime, went back with St. Clair to the horses, and they quietly replaced on the ground the provisions which they had offered before.

"So long, brother!" called Durfee.

"Good-by!" chimed in St. Clair.

The miner had risen; a brief wave of his hand was his answer. As the two rode down the slope, St. Clair looked back and saw that the starved figure of the miner had already seemed to have melted into the rocks of the mountainside.

"Will he really take that food we left behind?" asked St. Clair.

"Likely he won't," said the other. "Likely he'll just let it lie there and rot in the tin because he didn't have the money to pay us for it. But anyway we'll feel better because we left it behind, and the taste of the tobacco may sharpen up his appetite for food, too."

They came off the shoulder of the mountain, and saw before them the western pass; the walls of it stood in close together on either side. And as they entered that pass, neither the boy nor Durfee spoke; they looked earnestly ahead, for there was a feeling on them that they had crossed a threshold over which neither of them might return!

CHAPTER 30

In the golden evening, they rode down Timber Creek, making their way with difficulty, for they were following it down from the western pass, at that point where it descends through a series of box canyons.

One after another, they wormed their way down the precipitous walls that made the boundaries. From the upper rims of these, they looked up and out upon a region of naked rock; but in the bottoms of the canyons, they found many fine level meadows, and lofty, ancient groves, some of the great pines lifting their dark heads above the top of the valley walls.

But more than mountains or valleys, trees or the great blue road that flowed above them, sunset colored now, was the sound that hung continually in their ears. Near or far, ringing thin and small as bells or a blown horn among the hills, or booming and trampling like a herd, or roaring deafeningly, just at hand, they heard the falls of the upper and lower canyons.

It had grown sufficiently dark, now, to make the following of sign very difficult and, just as they were about to look for a suitable camping place, they came into a fine, spacious canyon full of groves of trees and interspersed with grass lands, with fat cattle grazing over them in the cool of the evening.

"God laid out this canyon for a ranch," said Durfee. "Look here! He even built the fences around it and a dog-gone smart mountain lion or wolf it would take to jump over them stone fences. Where there's cows like this, and land like this, and water and wood, there's gotta be a house, too. Men ain't such fools that they'd ride by this here place and not settle down!"

He had hardly finished speaking when they saw before them the shoulders of a big log cabin in a gap among the trees.

"There you are!" said Durfee.

St. Clair, instead of answering, pointed down at the ground before them. There was no need to speak, for in the soft ground the trail of the mule was plainly visible.

"Yeah," commented Durfee, "I suppose that Lester has gone this way before us."

"Would he have the courage to put up at the house?" asked St. Clair.

"He's done it before, plenty of times," said Durfee. "Sometimes just having danger on his trail and in the air around him ain't enough. He's gotta lie down under the same roof with it! Come on, son. We'll cache the hosses among the trees and go and take a look."

So they did, hiding the horses well back among the trees and then going on most cautiously across the open ground and among the smaller grove that surrounded the house. St. Clair went first, his noiseless feet pressing down the pine needles without so much as a whisper! Durfee needed merely to take care that his own footfall touched the same spots.

So they came out on the clearing where the cabin stood and found that the open space ran straight down to the edge of the river, which broadened here, reflecting the gold of the evening on its more quiet face; but close in shore the force of the current poured on with arrowy speed.

Part of the shore line of the clearing was a clean, pleasant little beach, with a canoe drawn up on it and turned bottom-side up. Close to where the trees began, mounted a pile of shining rocks on the top of which sat the gaunt figure of a man, with a great, broad-brimmed hat on his head and a rifle across his knees.

He surveyed like a guardian statue the upper reaches of the river, the clearing and the cabin itself.

Durfee gripped the arm of the boy and drew him back among the shadows; but the arm he held had turned to iron under his touch and the whole body of St. Clair was trembling slightly, as an animal trembles with eagerness for battle.

"It's Spot Lester!" breathed Durfee. "And we've got him. Spot Lester, at last. I won't shoot him from cover. We'll get the rifles ready, step out from cover, yell to take his eye, and kill him, Henry, before he can get his own gun into action."

And the boy answered, speaking softly and rather thickly, like one whose tongue has been blurred with alcohol: "No, there's a better way than that."

"What better way?" asked Durfee.

"I have a better way!" said the boy.

A pair of lads, ten or twelve years old, came out from the door of the big cabin in evident trepidation.

"Mr. Lester," they called. "Ma says that supper's ready."

And Spot Lester answered. "Tell your ma to keep supper hot till it's dark. And don't speak my name again, you little fools; not even if there ain't no more than the sky to hear you!"

CHAPTER 31

The boys turned back. From within the cabin, Durfee heard a man's deep voice saying: "I ain't gonna stand it, Lester or no Lester."

"Hush! Hush!" said a woman's voice, barely audible. "You're laid up. Don't get on your high hoss when you're just sure to fall off ag'in out of the saddle!"

"They're not friends of Lester, anyway," murmured Durfee. "He won't have them at his back, anyway. Now, Henry, what's your better plan? Because the light is getting a lot dimmer every minute. It ain't the best shooting light in the world, even now."

"I'll show you in a moment," said the boy. "I'll show you what my plan is. But tell me this, Durfee—is Lester really crippled?"

"If his legs are good enough to hold him up on a ride like he's just made, all the way from Flinders," said Durfee, "they're strong enough for most things. And in the arms and the hands, he ain't a man; he's a baboon!"

"He's an ape. Yes, he's an ape," said the boy. "That's why I want to get at him."

"Get at him with a gun," said Durfee. "There's others that have got at him with their hands, but they never lived long enough to tell much about it afterwards. They died fast!"

He took a breath as he thought of the body of one such man as he had last seen it huddled on the floor of an Arizona shack.

"All right," said the lad. "Wait here a minute. I'll be back. I'll show you the plan."

He faded off among the trees to the left, as he spoke, and Durfee looked after him with an odd feeling of admiration and awe commingled; admiration of that stealthy, soundless step, and a ghostly awe of the same quality. It seemed hardly human!

It was not a half a minute when he saw young Henry St. Clair gliding straight across the clearing toward the rocks on which loomed the great form of Lester!

He could not believe his eyes.

Then he remembered, with horror, how the boy had been quivering like a beast of prey about to attack. It was a fair comparison. And now he was out here in the open stalking Spot Lester as a cat stalks a bird.

He, Durfee, would have to end the horrible suspense with a shot from the distance. Ah, if only the shooting light were just a little bit better!

He raised his rifle as the determination came to him, but before he could get Lester in the sights, he saw the tall man leap up with a wild cry, and then drop back out of sight among the rocks of the stone heap.

St. Clair, as though at a signal, sprinted straight forward. Yes, he was attacking Spot Lester in person and he had left his rifle behind him among the trees! He had thrown off his coat, also. There was not a sign of a weapon about his person as he raced toward the outlaw.

Lester's unfailing rifle rang out. Durfee shuddered and half closed his eyes; but when he looked again, he saw that St. Clair had not fallen. Instead, he had sprinted on until he was in the shelter of the steep-sided rocks—in the shelter of them and swarming up them like a sailor, a barehanded man, to attack Lester; Lester armed!

The rifle spoke again. At such a range, it was impossible to miss. It must have been that Lester simply did not have a proper chance to level the rifle.

For there was the boy still working his way upward toward the crest of the rocks.

The boys came to the door of the cabin and their screaming voices went tingling up against the sky.

Durfee himself, maddened, left his cover and rushed straight forward. He knew that it was a madness. When St. Clair was a trifle higher and in fuller view of the outlaw, a bullet through the brain would settle Henry. And one more bullet would snuff out the life of Durfee, ex-Ranger.

He knew this, but he could not resist the impulse to rush in and be at the finish of the long trail.

As for thinking, he dared not think. He dared not even guess what burning passion had mastered the wits of the boy and whipped him forward to such a wild venture as this. Was it not true, that which he had guessed in the very beginning, that Bunce had tried, not to protect the boy from the world, but the world from the boy?

Then he saw a dark-outlined figure rise up on the top of the rocks. He saw the two grappling fiercely, saw them twisting and turning, and out of their throats came a sound like the roaring of a lion and the snarling of a tiger.

He could guess which throats were uttering the different cries.

If only he could get there in time—for it needed few seconds for the terrible, apelike hands of Lester to find a human life and tap it.

Forward and backward the closely entangled bodies

swayed, and then he saw them lean out, stagger, and fall sheer down into the current of the stream!

If only the children would stop their shrieking, paralyzing to his brain! When he rounded the side of the rock, rifle at the ready, he saw to his bewilderment that they had not stopped their struggle, even in the water, but as the swift current swept them down the stream, they still struggled and rolled over and over.

It was as though two jungle animals had gripped one another, and rather than relinquish the hope of murder, both allowed themselves to be carried to perdition.

And death lay straight ahead for the pair.

Not a hundred feet below the rock, the river disappeared over the falls, not very high, but it was a sufficient drop to have ground the life out of bodies ten times greater and stronger than the human frame.

Right on toward that danger the struggling pair were carried. Poor Durfee, rushing ahead to the verge of the falls, looked down with horror on the gleaming arch of the water, felt the beaten spray and spume fly against his face, and heard the roaring pour upward mightily, filling his ears with a death chant.

Just above the brink of the falls, there was a white-rimmed shoal place in the very center of the danger, and there the two struggling men were checked.

They rose out of the water. It boiled and swept about their knees. If they staggered, death was not a step away over the verge of the precipice, and the river was struggling to carry them over. But they fought, heedless of the place. Death was in their hearts, and neither fear nor mercy.

Twice and again, Durfee raised the rifle to fire, and each time the twisting of the fighters brought big Spot Lester within the sights, out of them, and gave Henry St. Clair for a target instead.

In despair he flung the rifle back on the shore and started to wade in deeper, when the end came.

The sight stopped him, freezing his brain, flooding his nerves with an electric fluid that had no sensation except numbness.

For he saw big Spot Lester beginning to bend backward, beginning to sway.

It was not a strangle hold, but the boy was simply bend-ing the other backward as one might bend a thin board. And Durfee saw one hand of the outlaw's wrenched free from the grasp of his enemy, saw that hand flash upward, bearing a gleaming knife, only to be caught by the wrist.

As a child squeezes out a wet seed from its finger tips, so the terrible pressure in the grip of Henry St. Clair forced the knife out of the nerveless fingers of Lester.

And still he was bending backward.

Suddenly he seemed to snap; he fell into the water, side-long, and young St. Clair held him up with one hand, and the force of the current trailed out the loose limbs to the side of the waterfall.

Durfee, reeling, shouted: "Have you killed him, Henry?"

"I don't know," answered the boy.

"Then," screamed Durfee, a frenzy seizing him, "kill him now, and make sure. Let the body slide into the water. If he ain't finished off now, he's gonna live to make more trouble in the world!"

St. Clair shifted his grip.

He took Spot Lester by the long, white hair of the head and held him so; turned up his face and looked into it. Then, he called back the very strangest answer that Dur-fee had ever heard.

"If that fellow were gone for good, wouldn't the world be a sort of an empty place?"

Durfee stared.

He was hardly aware of the two boys, scampering down the river bank, shouting with excitement, and of how they threw the rope out to St. Clair.

Bewilderment seized Durfee. And now he saw the giant come striding in through the ripping current that foamed shoulder high about him, with one hand gripping the rope, and the other hand dragging the body of Spot Lester.

He could not believe that his eyes saw the truth, that Lester was broken, and by the hands of a single man!

CHAPTER 32

Afterward, and forever, Durfee could remember the picture in the house of Tom Williams, for that was the name of the man who had built the cabin and on whose hospitality, however unwilling, Lester had intended to force himself for the night.

Williams himself, stretched on a couch with his right leg in splints—it had been recently broken—talked with great excitement of the capture.

Lester, his wrists and ankles securely tied, was tended by Mrs. Williams with a species of horror and of disgust in her face. The man had recovered consciousness but, though he sat up with eyes opened, all his features sagged. In his eyes, there was no realization of what had happened. His face was blank. Crowned by his white hair, he no longer looked like a youth wearing a wig, but like an old man in truth, haggard and stupefied by time.

There was much to be done for him, for there were a hundred cuts, large and small, where the jagged rocks had torn his flesh.

The boys were busy, too, and their care was the hero, Henry St. Clair.

For a hero he was, now not only in fact but in public esteem forever. Well as Durfee knew him, he regarded the big youth with increased awe. So did the boys. Like true young frontiersmen, they knew all about the care of wounds and for every cut on the body of Spot Lester, mule-tough as he was, there were half a dozen on the body of the boy.

He regarded them not. He permitted them to apply stinging or soothing lotions and wrap up his hurts in strips of bandage, and all the while they were about it, his eyes never left the form of his enemy. It was not a savage, but rather a smiling regard, and Durfee could not help feeling that it was rather like the attitude of one who has been interrupted in what he considers a splendid game and hopes that it may continue again before long, when the other side is rested a trifle.

Whatever his look, Durfee realized the meaning of it; St. Clair was actually sorry that the battle had ended. For once in his life, then, he had been fully extended, fully employed, every faculty bent upon a great end. And only gradually the fire of joy was sinking in him.

Williams said, aside to Durfee: "It kind of looks like the boy's a professional man-catcher, don't it?"

Yes, that was the look of it, beyond a doubt.

With the great Spot Lester out of the way, what would become of St. Clair?

That same thought remained in the mind of Durfee during the prolonged silence of the trip back. They remained for five days with Williams, who was delighted to have such distinguished guests. Then they saddled and rode steadily for two days and nights, forging across country until they came to the county seat. It had not many claims to greatness, but it possessed a good, strong jail, and that was of more interest to Durfee than anything else in the world just now.

A pair of fast-riding punchers, bound for the town to celebrate the end of the month, passed them a mile or so out of town, and recognized them and rushed on with the tiding. The result was that when they made their entrance the entire town had turned out to greet them.

They got out a ten-piece brass band that was the pride of the town. This blocked the street and marched down ahead of returning heroes.

At the jail, on the steps of it, the sheriff met them. He rose to this occasion, not with length but with fervor. He paid a neat tribute to the "ex-Ranger, still devoted to the guardianship of the law," but when he came to the terrible outlaw, he exhausted every bit of his vocabulary, except certain purple passages which remained for the crowning of the principal hero, Henry St. Clair.

For the first time, Spot Lester was brought to the bar of justice to answer for his long career of crime. Well, it ended, finally, by seeing Lester into a steel cell, where he was thoroughly and heavily ironed in the most modern and approved manner. After that, they left him, still sunk in the lethargy which had overwhelmed him since his defeat.

To Durfee it seemed apparent that the heart of the man was already crushed. He, the Achilles, could not realize that he had been defeated by a single man, in combat. Now what happened to his life and limbs hardly mattered.

The town would have kept the two heroes for an indefinite time. Durfee was willing to be lionized, but the boy insisted on returning straightaway to his uncle's ranch.

There they found the news before them. The whole place was in an uproar, and neighbors rode in thirty miles to behold the hero and congratulate him.

There were huge preparations for an outdoor barbecue that night. A hundred cow-punchers and ranchers and their families were to sit under the stars and hear the story of the man-hunt from the lips of those who had performed it.

So, when the sun sank, a great banging on a tin dish pan was the signal for the feasting to begin, and the crowd had gathered when it was found that the chief hero was gone.

Nowhere was young Henry St. Clair to be found, until, looking straight toward the brilliant west, some one saw the silhouette of a tall horseman along the top of a distant hill.

Old Bunce caught the arm of Durfee. "Go after him, Durfee. You're the only man who can bring him back."

But Durfee shook his head. "I've brought him back once," he said, "but there ain't power in me to get him again. He's gonna ride his own trail from now on; and Heaven make it straight! You and me and the rest of the range—there ain't excitement enough in us to fill his hand, Bunce. He's gotta find a bigger world than we know about and another Spot Lester for a playmate!"

Part Three

CHAPTER 33

When Durfee came back over the hills of an evening, he always reined up his horse when he came into the first clear view of his home. Once every day, in this manner, he loved to look at the little house and remind himself of the long homeless years which he had spent wandering.

But this evening he saw something more than the shack itself, green with the climbing vines which he had planted around it. He saw something more than a few cattle, drifting here and there, or the entangled fences of the corrals, or the high-shouldered stacks of hay.

This evening, all was as ever, except that a swift rider came flying toward him up the slope, and he recognized in the distance his niece, Mary. She had been with him a fortnight, seeming to enjoy a taste of range life and finding time to keep house for her uncle; also, to do all that any boy on the range would ever accomplish, from roping a steer to shooting a deer.

She greeted him with a whoop and a halloo from the distance, and presently brought her horse up on its hind legs, in a sort of pitching halt. The wind of the gallop had brightened her eyes and tinted her brown cheeks with rose.

"Hello, Mary," said her uncle. "What's brought you boilin' over the side of the pot this time of day? I reckoned that you was back there fryin' bacon."

"I'm roasting venison," said the girl. "The finest, sweetest saddle that you ever saw."

"Venison?" said he. "You mean you been out and found a deer again, since noon?"

"I mean that Willie Beardley came over and left some meat for you."

"Left some meat for me, eh?" said Durfee.

He took off his wide-brimmed sombrero, ran his fingers through his iron-gray hair and smiled at her.

"It's dog-gone thoughtful of Willie to leave some meat for me!" said he. "It's the first time that he's ever done such a thing!"

"All right, then," said she, with a shrug of her shoulders. "He left it for me, if you want to put it that way. But why don't you ask me why I'm not back there in the kitchen watching the fire?"

"I reckon you'll tell me, when the time comes," said he.

"Not curious?" she asked.

"Whatever happened, you wasn't scared away."

"You're wrong," said she. "I ran out of the house half an hour ago, and I've been fiddling around the corral ever since, with my saddle on the fastest horse in the string. I've been waiting for a look at you."

"What kind of a tomfool idea is this anyway?" said Durfee. "What would've scared you out of my house?"

"A man," said she.

"Shucks," answered Durfee. "You ain't goin' to make me believe anything could scare you; leastways, not a man."

"But I was scared. I had the shakes," said Mary. "Suppose that you saw a fellow about a mile high, riding a whacking big, fine horse, with three more of the same breed prancing along behind him on leads. Suppose that you see he's armed to the teeth, that his clothes are nothing but ragged deer skins and that he looks like a wild Indian with a white skin. Suppose you saw a fellow like that. What would you think?"

Her uncle grinned at her. "What did this here wild man do?" he asked.

"He pulled up and hitched his horses," said the girl, "in front of the house, and then he walked in through the front door, right straight for me. He had an absent-minded smile on his face. I saw that he would have walked me right into the floor under his feet, if I hadn't moved. And I jumped out of the way."

"What did you say?"

"When I got my breath, I asked him who he was and what he wanted, and told him that you were not at home."

"And then?"

"He just didn't seem to hear me. He stalked out to the kitchen, and looked around there, and then he pulled open the door to my room, and looked inside of that! The impertinent puppy!"

Her anger rose at the thought and she added: "You don't seem a bit upset!"

"I ain't," said he. "Not yet I ain't."

"Well, then," said she, "he still didn't say a word. I began to be afraid that he was a crazy man, and I walked over and got my hand on your rifle that was leaning against the wall in the corner."

"What did he do at that?"

"Nothing. He just sighed and frowned. Then he went outside and took big packs off the backs of the three horses that he was leading. He started with one of those packs, marching for the door. But I slammed the door shut and dropped the bolt in place. Then what d'you think happened?"

Her breath quickened; her face grew pale.

"Go on, Mary," said her uncle.

"He rattled at the latch. He didn't ask me to open it. He didn't offer a word of explanation, but all at once I heard the bolt creaking and groaning as he pulled from the outside. That frightened me in earnest, you can imagine. I grabbed up your rifle and told him that if he didn't stop wrenching at that door, I'd shoot through the wood into him."

"Did he stop?"

"Not a bit! The next second, he had that door open. He literally wrenched the bolt away from its staples, and stood there in front of me, picking up the big pack he had put down on the ground. Then he marched in and dumped the pack on the floor. I ran back into the kitchen; I was frightened to death!"

"I kind of don't blame you," said Durfee, but still he was smiling a little.

"He brought in the other two packs," said the girl, "and

then he sat down in your chair and took out the biggest hunting knife that I ever saw and began to sharpen it on a little whetstone that he had in his pocket."

"And that was enough for you?"

"I wasn't going to wait to have my throat cut!" she exclaimed. "On the other hand, I didn't want to have to shoot down a crazy man. So I slid out the back way and pelted for the corral and slammed a saddle on Boots here. I'm still a little jumpy!"

She broke off to exclaim: "Why, you don't care a rap! Who is the man?"

Instead of answering, he said: "D'you think that your Boots, here, could have got you safely away, if he'd wanted to run a horse after you?"

"Boots? Why, Boots is a flash, and you know it. And that wild man weighs two hundred pounds if he weighs an ounce."

"And the horses he keeps can carry his two hundred pounds like a feather," said Durfee, "and they could run down your Boots in two minutes."

"I don't believe it," said she. "But who in the world is he?"

"You've heard about Spot Lester?" said Durfee, now sober enough.

"If you're going to talk about him at last," said the girl, "it's worth the scare I've had, but you know perfectly well that Lester is in prison for life. Besides, I've seen pictures of Lester. I'd know his horrible face a mile away, the long, brutal beast. It gives me the creeps even to think of his photograph!"

"It gives me the creeps, too," said Durfee. "But I've told you that I didn't actually capture Spot Lester. It was another fellow who fairly beat him, hand to hand, for the first time in his life."

"I know," said the girl. "You mean Henry St. Clair."

He nodded. "That's St. Clair who's sitting in the house."

"No, no, no!" she cried. "I know that St. Clair is the nephew of the rich rancher, Bunce; his heir, too. But I'm talking about a wild man, who doesn't know how to use his tongue, it seems!"

"It's Henry St. Clair," he insisted, "but he's gone native, as they say. He's taken to the woods, because life on a ranch was too dull to suit him. He lives like a wild Indian, alone. Shoots and traps, and gives himself only one luxury —horses. He's caught 'em wild and trained 'em himself. And better horses never carried men. He comes in once in a while with some packs of skins and sells 'em to me."

"Why in the world should the man do that?" asked the girl. "You're not a trader."

"It saves him from having to go to town and meet other men. That's what he hates worst in the world—having people around him and listening to their chatter. He brings the stuff to me, and I pay for it. Then I cart it to town. I can price a skin; I don't lose anything by it, and he uses my house like a store."

"Henry St. Clair, or whoever he may be," said the girl, "is crazy!"

CHAPTER 34

They galloped rapidly down the hill together but, in spite of the galloping, she still called out her questions.

"Why won't he speak?" she asked.

"Because he hates words," said the other.

"He's either mad or the rudest man I know!" she exclaimed, angered again by the memory.

Said Durfee, lifting his finger at her: "I'd've been dead long ago, except for him, and him except for me. Don't you forget it, honey. There ain't anything I've got, down to the scalp on my head, that Henry couldn't have for the asking."

She fell back into a sullen silence; and her eyes were still bright and ominous when she reached the house.

As they entered together, Durfee said: "You people need introducing. This here is my niece, Mary Durfee, Henry. And this here is Henry St. Clair."

St. Clair stood up, and he bowed gravely and gracefully to her; but she went straight past him, without a glance, and disappeared into the kitchen.

Durfee merely grinned, and shook the hand of his guest vigorously.

"You're gonna turn plain savage, one of these days, Henry," said he. "Looks like you been lying out, face up, in the sun. Why don't you let me get you some clothes, man?"

"Why not?" said Henry St. Clair.

"I'll be driving into town tomorrow," said Durfee, "and I'll get you whatever you want. What do you say?"

St. Clair shrugged his shoulders.

"Corduroy wears like iron," suggested the rancher. "I'll get you some corduroys for winter, and boots, too. You're all rags and patches, son. Now lemme have a look at what you've brought in and show me what I have around the house that you want."

Two gestures indicated the answers. The first was to point out the heap of pelts; the second was a gesture toward a small heap on the table. It was composed of flour, bacon, salt, and above all, ammunition for rifle and revolver.

This means of communication did not appear to worry Durfee.

"Put up your horses in the pasture, Henry," he said. "Better put 'em in that ten-acre patch. It ain't been grazed for a couple weeks, and the grass is growin' up as thick as hair. Besides, your wild nags will like runnin' water better than trough."

St. Clair, without answering, left the place and went out to the horses.

Durfee, in the meantime, began to go over the pelts; and presently the girl stood in the doorway, looking grimly at the pile as it was being sorted.

"He's an old friend, all right," said Mary Durfee. " 'Why not?' is a whole stack of conversation. He wanted to know all about you, didn't he? Couldn't wait till he found out how the cows were doing, and everything like that."

"He can use his own eyes and find out that the cattle are in good shape," said Durfee. "He sees the hay in the stacks, the horses in the pastures, and the new fences that I've been building. Besides, what he finds out for himself means more than what he learns from talk."

"And what can you learn about him?" she asked, still angry.

"Well," he said, "you can learn quite a little from this here stack of skins."

"You can tell where he's been hunting and what luck he's had," said the girl.

"And something more, here and there," said he. "Take a look at this mountain lion's skin, will you?"

He stretched it out on the floor. It ran almost from wall to wall.

"It's a whopper," said the girl. "What else?"

"Where's the bullet mark?" asked Durfee.

She examined the tawny hide with care.

"He must have brained it while it was in the trap," she said. "There's no bullet hole."

"Where's the mark of the jaws of the trap, then?" he demanded.

"Humph!" said she. "Are you making a mystery out of it? What's the trick?"

"No trick at all," said Durfee. "Find anything funny about that there pelt?"

"No. There's just the place where his knife slipped in getting the skin off the throat."

"Look on the other side of the pelt, the other side of the throat."

She lifted it. There was a deep slash there, also, well below the ear.

"Them two cuts would fit together, wouldn't they, if that hide was mounted?" he asked.

She raised the skin of the throat and rounded it as in nature. Suddenly she cried out: "You mean to say that he killed this beast by cutting its throat?"

"There ain't nothing else that I do mean," said he.

"But how could he get close enough to the brute?"

"By crawling into its cave, most likely. He's done it before."

She exclaimed: "Oh, stuff! You know that no one would dare go into a black hole in the rocks and fight a mountain lion hand to hand."

"No?" said Durfee. "Well, honey, I've seen him do it."

She dropped the pelt as though it burned her hands, and straightened with a shudder.

"You mean, said she, "that he went in there and waited for the beast to spring, then cut its throat as it went by?"

"He carries his knives extra long and extra sharp," said Durfee.

She drew in a long breath. "But suppose that his hand should miss, or that he didn't dodge the paw far enough!"

"Then the cat would eat him, of course," said Durfee. She stared at him. And he expanded: "That'll be the end of him. Some time a wild hoss will savage him, or a catamount'll rip him open."

"And he could live at home with everything that money can buy?" she suggested.

"Yeah. Old Bunce would sell his soul to make that kid happy. But he prefers to stay out in the woods and mountains. He says that nothing happens on the range, nothing except a cattle thief to run down, now and then."

"Hush," said the girl. "I see him coming. He walks like a cat, doesn't he? Well, for my part, I'd rather have a mountain lion in the house than such a man. He gives me the creeps!"

And she shuddered as she turned back into the kitchen. Thereafter, during the evening, as she finished the cookery and laid out the meal on the table, and afterward while she sat with them, she used her eyes more than her tongue. And it was Henry St. Clair whom she watched.

In all that time, she was sure that he did not speak three words. Like a monk with a vow of silence, his air was pleasant enough, and he gave his attention to everything that Durfee said, for the latter was the perfect host, on this occasion and kept up a running fire of talk. But it seemed to the girl that the interest of St. Clair was only on the surface.

When the supper ended, she heard the rattling of hoofs sweeping up to the house. A moment later in the doorway appeared the lean, twisted body of a little man, his face drawn with suffering. She knew, without being told, that it was Bunce, the uncle of Henry St. Clair.

As he stood there, supported under one arm by the hand of a big, red-headed puncher, he gasped: "Durfee and, thank God, here's Henry, too! He's loose! The demon is out again!"

CHAPTER 35

She could not make head nor tail of it for a moment. But then she heard Bunce exclaiming: "Law? There's no sense to such a law! Life imprisonment—as though prisons ever could be made to hold people like Lester! Now I hope that he kills another hundred victims. I hope that he robs the treasury. I hope that he commits a thousand evil deeds. It would serve the fool lawmakers right!"

Durfee sat huddled in his chair. He had not risen to receive these visitors. Now he muttered: "Spot Lester again! It don't seem right or possible."

"It ain't right," said the red-headed cow-puncher, "but it's possible. Possible for Lester, but nobody else, what he done!"

"How did he get away?" asked young Henry St. Clair.

The girl looked at him, amazed by the change that had come in his face and his entire bearing. His eyes shone with such a light as she never had seen before. He was awakened, he was lighted with a fire of joy that was a terrible thing to see.

Suddenly the wild tales which Durfee had been telling of the lad seemed not at all incredible.

"Tell him, Al," said Bunce. "Tell him just what happened. You know as well as I do. And I can't talk. I can't do anything except curse the government that failed to hang him by the neck. Oh, if only that crowd in Flinders had managed to get hands on him!"

"Yeah, I can tell the yarn, the way we got it," said Al the cow-puncher. "They had this gent in solitary confinement, not because he'd been acting up any, but because he had a pretty long reputation when he went to the pen. These here solitary cells was off by themselves, and there was nothing the prisoner seen every day except when the shutter in his steel door was lifted, once a day, and some chuck pushed through. Inside the cell, there was chains, and the chains was hitched to the wall at one end and to the crook at the other.

"Well, along comes the guard, the other day, and opens the shutter and pushes through the food. As he does that, a long arm jumps out and grabs him by the throat, jerks him in close and brains him agin' the steel door. Beg' your pardon, ma'am," he added to the girl, "but that's what happened, and Henry, here, wanted to know."

"Yes," said St. Clair. "And go on, will you? What happened next?"

"Yeah," said Red Al. "The chains was on his legs, but he worked the staples out of the wall."

"Pulled them out?" asked St. Clair, his eyes more keen and brilliant than ever.

"Nope, it seems that these here staples were sunk down deep in the concrete," said Al, "and they was big bolts, too, that the chains was anchored to. But friend Lester, he had lots of time and lots of patience. He just used a rough link to rub on the surface of the concrete, and he wore it down until the concrete was all rubbed away from the head of the bolt and part way down the shaft of it. That give him a sort of leverage, you see. So he begun pulling and hauling at the bolt. And he kept on until the bolt kind of weakened, they say."

"The steel crystallized, of course," snapped Bunce. "Get on, Al. You take a thousand years to turn around once."

"I never wore a fast tongue," drawled Al. "But finally that bolt snapped off, and that was what let Lester get close enough to the door to throttle the guard and then brain him agin' the door.

"After that, he managed to haul the body of the guard around and up till he could reach the coat pocket, and in there he found the keys that he wanted.

"There was a lot of keys, and he had to try 'em one by one in the lock, reaching around through the shutter to the lock from the inside. Them long arms of his must've been pretty useful on that stretch!

"Finally he got the right key, and opened the door of his cell, but by this time, the other prisoners in solitary row, they was beginning to bang on the walls with their chains and make a holler, because they knew that it was time for their chuck to arrive, and they wondered what was keeping the guard from feeding 'em!

"That racket was sure to fetch other guards, before long, and Lester, he had to hurry.

"First, he pulled some of the clothes off the dead guard, and he wadded the cloth around his chains, so that they couldn't rattle so much. And then he hobbled down the corridor.

"What with the shackles on his feet and the heavy chains, he was carrying about forty pounds of steel along with him.

"The door at the end of that corridor was locked, and it was locked on the outside. That there prison, it sure was full of a lot of precautions, wasn't it?"

"Hurry up and get ahead!" loudly shouted Bunce. "Before you're through, we may have Spot Lester with us! He'll have time, at your rate of telling a yarn!"

Red Al went on, unperturbed: "The guards opens the door and, when he does that, Lester socks him over the head with a length of the chain and drops him flat. And then Lester, he takes the gun from the guard that lies with his head pretty near bashed in on the floor, and goes on.

"There's still forty pounds of steel on him, mind you! But now he comes to a window that looks out on a yard, and that window is a forty-foot drop to the ground.

"Well, he tried the window bars, and he managed to get one of 'em loose, and that bar was a lever for him and he pried the rest of the bars away. When he looked out, he seen that forty-foot drop that I was speakin' about.

"It must've pretty near broke his heart to see that. And he turned around and went back to his solitary ward, and the prisoners is making a big row, by this time, but he bawls out and tells 'em that if they don't pipe down, they'll get nothing but water gruel for three days. That shuts them up for a while. Of course, they thought that it was a guard talking.

"What he wanted was the rest of the clothes of the dead guard and the one that lay near as good as dead. He took them clothes off and left 'em naked, and went back and knotted the cloth together to make a rope, and one end he tied around a window bar, and then he squeezed himself through the window. It was such a tight fit that he left blood on both sides of it, but he got through, like a snake, and the line come down far enough to let him drop safe to the ground.

"So there he was, in the middle of the night, with the empty yard around him and the outer wall of the prison dead ahead, and a couple of guards walking up and down on top of it on their beats.

"But how was he to get out, and him still wearing them chains?

"Well, he thought of a way. Mind you, he still had a gun, and he walked straight up to the office of the head night watchman, the officer in charge of everything, and finds him in there alone. And this here Lester, he shoves a gun under the head of the gent and makes him shell out the key that unlocks the shackles and then he takes the coat and pants of the man and steps into 'em and makes him go to the prison gate.

"The gun of Lester was in the small of his back as this gent sings out to open the gate and, by thunder, they done it. The guard, he wants to know who the second man is and why the head of the night watch is wearin' an overcoat on that kind of a hot night. But the gun at his back made the watchman pretty handy with his tongue, and he cussed the gent out hard and strong!

"So the gate opens and Lester walks through and has his friend along with him.

"But just then the alarm bell rings, and there's an uproar that spreads all through the prison, because somebody had found the dead guard and the wounded one in the solitary ward.

"Well, the guards on the wall they start shooting, but the one they drop and nigh kill is the wrong man.

"And Lester runs on, and the machine-gun nests around the prison, they spot him and they start shooting, but he gets down to the lake and dives in.

"There the guard boat spots him, and comes charging, but after he dived in he was never seen to come up again, and they say that he must've turned into a fish and swum away, or else he's lying and rotting at the bottom of the lake. But I say that a gent that got that close to freedom must've gone the rest of the way!"

CHAPTER 36

When that grim story had ended, there was a proper silence through the group. The mind of the girl was harkening back over the words, repainting the horrible pictures of the escape.

She was amazed to hear the voice of Henry St. Clair saying: "There's a man for you! There's a man! Think of turning back from the window and going into the hall of the ward and silencing the prisoners as if he were a guard. There's a man!"

It was not an ironic compliment either. She stared at him as at a strange phenomenon. And so did the other men. His face was shining; his mouth pinched hard together, and the nostrils flared a little.

Bunce continued to look at his nephew, but he spoke to them all, when he said: "You can call Lester a man. I'd rather call him an evil spirit. The point is, that if he lived to get out of the water of that lake, we'll have him about our ears in no time."

Durfee said: "I dunno about that. He's tackled this gang twice, and he ain't had any luck. He was pretty near killed, at the wind-up the first time; it turned his hair white, what he went through. The second time, he was caught and beat and slammed into prison. That time he spent in solitary confinement, it won't seem particular pleasant even to a man like Lester!"

"What d'you think that he'll do?" asked Bunce.

"I think," said Durfee, "that he's learned his lesson from failing with us before and he'll turn his hand to other sorts of jobs. The first thing you know, he'll have cracked a couple of bank safes and laid up some hard cash. That's what he needs, most of all. He ain't gunna tackle the same trail where he's failed twice!"

"I don't know. Perhaps you're right," said Bunce. "I'd like to think so!" He turned to his foreman, Red Al. "Al, what's your opinion?"

"He's had his fingers burned twice—burned to the bone,"

153

said Al. "He ain't gunna come back again to the same fire."

Suddenly Henry St. Clair was laughing. "Oh, you don't know him, you fellows," said he. "You don't know him because you haven't seen him as I have, close up, with his teeth grinding, and Satan in his eyes. He won't forget us, I tell you. All the time that he's been in prison, he's been dreaming about us and how our throats would feel under his thumbs. He had three killings to do and he's hungrier for 'em than ever a mountain lion for meat after a starving winter. He's been tasting the deaths of the three of us, I tell you, for a long time and he's heading across country to get at us now, as steadily as ever a wolf ran, night and day, to get to the familiar old range."

He spoke with such conviction that the others were silenced. The boy went on: "He wants to kill you, uncle, simply because he tried his hand on you before and he doesn't like to leave failures behind him.

"He hates Durfee, of course, the way a wolf hates a dog, after it's felt the dog's teeth.

"But, most of all, he wants to see my blood again and watch the ending of me. No, don't make any mistake. He'll be here before long!"

"He's right," groaned Bunce. "I can feel in my bones that he is."

"Well," muttered Durfee, uneasily, "when he puts it that way, it's kind of like he knew what he was talkin' about."

Said Red Al: "Oh, yeah, Henry oughta know. He's had Lester in his grip. He's smashed him, too. He's the only one that's likely to know all about what's inside of Spot!"

The girl looked with new eyes at Henry St. Clair. He was big and formidable enough, to be sure. But it seemed incredible that this was the engine of savage strength that had run down Lester before and mastered him hand to hand. But, if in his silence, he had seemed formidable, he was more of a giant than ever now. He was kindled with a strange sort of content and anticipation.

Bunce was saying: "We'll have to put our heads together. And we'll have to stay together, too, I take it. Day or night we ought to stay in a close heap, and never lose sight of one another. Because if Lester can run us down one by one, his job will be simpler."

"If he can catch us together," said Henry St. Clair, "he'l

have a still simpler job—one stick of dynamite for the lot of us. He believes in blasting powder, too! That and fire, as well as guns."

He laughed again. The content was so great in him that he stood up now and sauntered back and forth through the room with his noiseless step.

The girl shuddered, overmastered by an irresistible repulsion.

"What do you suggest?" asked Bunce of his nephew. "You may be right—that he'll have a still better chance to bag us all at a stroke, if we stay together. But I, for one, would never close my eyes at night, if I were living alone. I want to have you near by, Henry. And I want Durfee, too. The pair of you have beaten Lester twice. I think that you can manage it again!"

"So do I," said Durfee. "And I'd rather stay in a huddle, the three of us. I say that this is a good place to stay. No woods too close. The ground is more cleared and open than at your new house, Bunce. One of us could stand watch night and day."

"We could do that. We could keep the house like a fort," said Bunce, nodding. "I like the idea."

"Stay here like sheep and wait for him to come?" muttered St. Clair, a frown darkening his face.

"What else, Henry?" asked his uncle, with irritation.

"Why, we could go out and try to cross his trail some way," said Henry.

"We'd be fumbling in the dark and he's a hunting cat that sees in any kind of light!" exclaimed Bunce. "Henry, I want you to stay close to me!"

St. Clair sighed.

"I'll do what you want," he murmured finally. "You've never asked a thing of me before."

"Thank you, my boy," said the uncle. "It's life or death for all three of us now. I think Durfee's idea of staying here is a good one. But not with a woman in the house. Things are apt to happen here—a stray bullet might strike a woman as well as a man, Durfee."

"No, she can't stay here," Durfee agreed.

Mary Durfee sprang up from her chair.

"But I'm not afraid," she said. "I'd rather stay here, a

lot rather. And I'm not a helpless thing. I can use a rifle. My uncle knows that!"

"Sure you can use a rifle," said Durfee. "But you can't stay, Mary. The time's come for you to clear out. It's a four-hour ride from here to Flinders, and you're gonna make that ride tonight. I'll take you over. No matter how fast Lester travels, I reckon he won't be on hand around here, before tomorrow night. Daylight ain't his good hunting time."

Bunce agreed. "Let Henry take her over to Flinders. He can be back tomorrow by noon. We'll be safe enough till then. And we'll have Al, here, with a handy gun in case of a pinch. Al's nerves are steady enough, even when it's a Lester that has to be hunted. Henry," he continued, "will you take her over?"

Henry nodded, rose and left the room.

The girl was very angry. "It's not fair!" she said. "You think that I'll be in the way; but I won't, I promise you!"

Old Bunce soothed her. She had the proper spirit, he said, but it was simply a time when a woman must not be in the way.

Then the hoofs of horses trampled outside and Henry St. Clair strode back into the house.

"The horses are saddled," he said.

He looked at the girl and something about his impatient, indifferent eye annoyed her. Her anger flared.

"I'm not going!" she exclaimed. "I won't be huddled out of the way like this!"

"Mary, do as you're told," ordered her uncle.

She shook her head. "I won't go," she repeated. "I—Henry St. Clair, don't touch me, or—" For, to her bewilderment, he had walked straight up to her. It was an incredible thing, to Mary Durfee. She knew the range and range ways. She knew that a woman could expect courtesy and respect from every man, but now the big hands of the hunter picked her up by arms, holding her just below the shoulders, and so bore her lightly, without effort, out of the house, down the two steps at the door, and placed her beside her horse.

"You shameful bully!" she gasped at him.

He merely answered: "Will you climb onto your horse and sit in the saddle, or do I have to throw you on that pony's back and tie you there?"

He spoke without heat. There was no more regard for her in his eyes than there might have been for a sack of grain.

And she, without answering, gathered the reins on the back of the horse, put her foot into the stirrup and swung up to her place.

She was angrier than she had ever been in her life. Durfee was standing in his doorway, half laughing, half apologetic. "You're safe with Henry," he told her. "Sorry that there was any trouble, Mary, but I—".

"You stood by and let me be handled and bullied by a great oaf!" she cried in answer. "I hope that I never see your face again."

And jerking the head of her horse about, she raced blindly away through the night.

CHAPTER 37

She realized two things, after the first wild heat of her anger. One was that it was her favorite Boots that carried her; the other, that she had her own light rifle in the holster at the side of the saddle.

A plan darted through her mind. She would ride straight away from Henry St. Clair; she would prove for one thing to her uncle that no heavyweight like that could possibly have a chance in a long straight run against Boots and her own burden in the saddle.

When she had dropped all sign and sound of pursuit, she would go off by herself, she would camp in the woods, she would shoot her own game. She would live like an Indian for a while—a thing that her tomboy nature had always craved to do.

In the meantime, they could do a little worrying about her and it would serve them right. The flame of her anger embraced the entire male world.

But the cool air of the night, the slow sweeping of the stars above her head, their slight swaying as the horse rose and fell in the pulse of the gallop, pacified her, little by little. Her uncle might be a little obtuse, a little too simple.

But, after all, he was the kindest of men. He, to be sure, had not ordered Henry St. Clair to manhandle his niece. It was the brutal suggestion of that fellow's own mind.

Well, one day he would pay for it! She gritted her teeth.

Now they fled through a hollow among the hills; and they struck out across a plateau region of gently rolling ground.

It was now that she heard the beat of hoofs well behind her and, looming back, she could see the image of the rider behind her. There was the great Henry St. Clair! Well, she would simply ride away from him. If he had not been able to catch up with her by this time, it was proof that his horse could never match paces with redoubtable Boots!

To drop St. Clair hopelessly to the rear was her greatest ambition now, and she gave Boots his head for a moment.

Like an arrow he flew, straight and hard-running. The hills swept by, the trees whirred beside her and the pounding hoofs of the gelding knocked up the sparks from the rocks, here and there.

At last, when she could feel the heave of his sides and his head began to bobble a bit, sure sign that he was used up, she pulled in the reins once more and turned her head expectantly, triumphantly.

She could hardly believe her ears that caught the rhythmic stride of the horse in the rear. What seemed a giant on a horse loomed close beside her.

Run Boots from that monster? The poor gelding seemed to know the hopelessness of the task better than its rider. It chucked the contest and dropped its head. It fell from a canter to a trot, and now to a walk, with the hand of Henry St. Clair on the rein.

Never had Mary Durfee wanted words so badly. Her slender body quaked with the fullness of her passion. She nearly choked afresh, when she saw St. Clair calmly drawing the reins from her hands, and tying them to one of the strings that dangled from his saddle.

She was to be led on like a helpless prisoner.

To be helpless is perhaps to feel self-pity allied to anger. She felt it now. She dared not speak now, because she realized that if she ventured upon words her voice would tremble frightfully. That weakness, also, she blamed upon Henry St. Clair.

He rode on with never a word to her, a tall form in the saddle on the tall horse.

What an animal it was, high-headed, fresh, eager for the trail, in spite of the run that had exhausted stout little Boots; unexhausted by the toil though with such a ponderous weight of a man on its back.

The horse was like the rider. There was a wild breed, a blood of the wilderness, that ran in both. She told herself that St. Clair was a heartless ruffian, a villain. And some of her hatred for him she transferred to her uncle because he so much as knew this cruel fellow.

She would be safe with Henry St. Clair, he had said, and then had allowed the brute to hunt her through the dark of the night. On the heels of that reproachful thought, she realized suddenly that he was right. Yes, totally right. No danger could come near her while that high head and those broad shoulders forged ahead of her through the night.

Suddenly she made a mental turnabout. "I've been playing the fool, a silly, childish fool. I'm sorry," she said.

Instantly he unknotted the strap that held her reins to his saddle and passed them back to her.

"I know how it is," he said. "You wanted to be in on the fun. I don't blame you. But you know how it is—men in the West who let women get into danger or trouble, well, other people don't forget about it. Their reputations are spoiled forever. I suppose that you simply had to be taken out of the way of trouble."

She thought, on the whole, that it was the pleasantest way in which he could have received her apology. And now she was utterly glad that she had not poured forth her wrath on him when he first overtook her. She might have said things, then, that could not be withdrawn easily now.

But he talked no more. They went on over the long trail in silence, except that once or twice she heard him singing softly, wordless songs that told how utterly he was content.

At last, they came out on the hillside from which they looked down on the gleaming, long street of Flinders. Most of it was lost in darkness and in sleep, but there were enough all-night gambling houses and saloons to make a distinct streak of light along the main front of the amusement world down there.

Here he gradually pulled up his horse and said: "You know Flinders, don't you?"

"No."

"It's a mining town, and a pretty wild one, but not as wild as it was a little while ago. There's a sheriff in that town who has it pretty well in tow. And your uncle is well known there. You won't have any trouble. We'll get your things together and send them over after you in the buckboard tomorrow. Your uncle will know what's best for you to do, whether to stay here till we know definitely about Lester and his game, or whether you ought to go back to your home."

"What do you think?" she asked. "When will Lester come?"

"Before tomorrow night at the latest," said he. "He may be at—" He stopped short.

"At my uncle's house now?" she asked.

"Oh, no, not that," he muttered curtly, and rode on down toward the town.

They stopped at the best and biggest hotel. In the lobby half a dozen men were sitting smoking, talking earnestly. One of them had a whole handful of money which he kept offering to another, only to have it refused on each occasion.

A man with a puckered, scowling brow stood behind the clerk's desk. He turned his scowl deliberately on the two who had just come in.

"We ain't got no rooms, folks," he growled. "Filled up."

Henry St. Clair answered: "You must have a room, somewhere. I don't want the lady to go any other place in Flinders."

"You don't?" answered the clerk. "Who are you, anyway, to—"

He paused. His eyes widened. His jaw fell. "It's St. Clair!" said he.

The name reached the men who were talking over business earnestly in the corner of the room. It lifted them out of their chairs and jerked them around.

"St. Clair," she heard them muttering.

And the clerk was saying: "Didn't recognize you, Mr. St. Clair. Of course, we got rooms for you, sir. Always! Got rooms if we have to throw folks out on the street to make way for you!"

CHAPTER 38

She found that she was receiving her share of attention also. For St. Clair introduced her as the niece of Durfee, and it seemed that that name was almost as well known as St. Clair's. She was led up the stairs like a princess, but not until every man in the lobby had been introduced to her and had bowed and shaken her by the hand. And every one of them had some little compliment to pay, not to her, but to her uncle.

She was revising opinions all the way to her room. She had found her uncle good-natured, genial, but as she thought, the most commonplace fellow in the world. It was very plain, however, that he was something more than this to the men of the range. He was one to be looked up to and revered.

In fact, she was both elated and depressed as she lay, at last, between the sheets of the bed, looking up into the darkness. She was elated because the great man was her uncle; she was depressed because she herself seemed quite an inconspicuous member of society.

The darkness of her room was not complete. The hotel was a ramshackle affair of boards very loosely strung together, and lamps, burning in a room below hers and another to the side, made thin pencil strokes of light across the blackness. Besides, she could hear sound from one end of the building to the other—the creaking of a bed when a man turned over, a pair of voices talking quietly and rapidly and above all, the steady, tuneful note of a mighty snorer.

However, she began to grow sleepy at last, when something like the tick of a watch startled her into wakefulness.

She thought, at first, that the sound came from her own heart; then she realized that she had heard it from the direction of the door. It was as though an unconscious guard, posted near her, had seen what her closed eyes had failed to see.

She was frightened horribly. But she told herself that nothing was wrong, for in a building of this sort there were

161

bound to be all manner of creaks and groans of ill-seasoned timbers. Yet no matter how she argued against her fear, it persisted steadily.

She did not sit up, but raised her head a little, cautiously, from the pillow. As she did so, she saw a form gliding noiselessly through one of those pencil strokes of light, straight toward her bed.

It was the form of a man, looking taller than human, and now an unsheathed ray of light struck full upon her face.

She could neither move nor cry out; her jaws were locked.

There was another metal click, subdued and soft; the light left her face, and above her the intruder leaned. A hand dropped like a mask upon her, a hard, damp hand, that felt like flexible stone, as hard and as cold.

"It's the girl; it's the brat," she heard the stranger mutter.

And still she could not stir; she could not cry out. Yet she knew that there were a hundred men who would come swarming to the sound of a woman's voice in distress. They would come as fiercely as wasps, with .45-caliber six-guns for stings. It was not dread of a mere man, but of a strange beast in the form of a man that controlled her.

"Curse my luck!" she heard the man mutter.

Then a ball of cloth was between between her teeth.

She was not so hysterically excited that she could not instantly understand that murder, at least, was not his intention.

So she continued to lie still.

But now her staring eyes saw the door of her room sway soundlessly open, and against the dull gray of the hallway, lighted from far off, appeared another man in silhouette. He did not close the door, as the first one had done, but came gliding onward with steps more breathlessly still than those of the first intruder.

The latter straightened suddenly; then whirled about and there was light enough to strike upon gleaming steel in his hand.

"St. Clair!" he snarled, like a fighting dog.

"Lester!" cried the second man and leaped in as a cat springs.

She tore the handkerchief from between her teeth and screamed. The madness of fear seemed to pass out of her brain with that wild outcry that pierced through the building from end to end.

She sprang from the bed, as the two combatants, locked together in a writhing ball of humanity, crashed against the wall of the room and threatened to stave it in.

All the while her brain was perfectly clear. It was the monster, Lester, who had come here, not searching for her, it seemed, but perhaps for the very man who was now gripping him on the floor of the room.

Had she not heard men say that Lester, like a beast, could see best in the twilight? He must not have that advantage now. If she could help St. Clair in no other way, she could at least give him light.

With the thought, her hands were on the lamp, the chimney was off, the match struck and the flame jumped readily across the wet wick, lighting the room.

Something, an arm or leg, struck the table away with a crash and the chimney went down, smashing into a million fragments, but she stood with the lamp held high, the smoky flame streaming off in the draft.

Tumult was rising through the hotel and sweeping up toward her room, but all that she saw was the battle that was taking place under her eyes.

She saw St. Clair on the floor and Lester above him, striving to drive downward the knife which he gripped in one hand. She ran a step forward, ready to crash the lamp against the head of Lester. She had no other weapon.

But then she saw the face of the man more clearly, and horror and revolt stopped her. It was not like the face of a man. What the difference was, she could not tell. Perhaps it was the ageless evil of the features.

Once checked, she did not rush in. If she struck with the lamp, perhaps the flaming oil would pour over both the fighters.

Furthermore, she saw that St. Clair was not helpless. He was the under man in position, but not in fact, so to speak. No, for with one hand he gripped the throat of Lester, and the other was locked about the wrist of the knife hand of the criminal. A twist of that hand now caused the knife to fall tingling to the floor from the unnerved fingers of Lester.

He turned that bad touch of fortune into an advantage by catching up the fallen knife with his other hand.

That was answered by a shifting of grips. The throat of Lester was free; they spun over and over across the floor as the hotel men came rushing into the room—a gun in the hand of every man of them, half a dozen, a dozen!

They got in front of her. She lost sight of the battle, but held up the lamp at the full stretch of her arm to give light to her champion.

Disaster came almost at once, though not to St. Clair.

She heard a wild outcry. She heard a thundering voice, the voice of St. Clair, calling out to the others to "Stop him!"

And then two men in the crowded doorway were struck down as by a catapult, and uproar flowed down the hall, down the stairway.

Everyone turned and started struggling for the doorway, but through them, like a bull through a herd of calves, St. Clair crushed his way, his mighty hand hurling men right and left.

He was out before most of the rest and they poured after him.

She heard the exploding of guns far away, the sounds dying out; she heard the pounding of hoofs.

And so, transformed into a statue, she found herself still in the middle of her floor, grasping the lamp in one raised hand, when St. Clair came back into the room.

There was a streak of red across his forehead and down one side of his face. His blood or that of another but he was terrible enough without that added touch of horror. His face was transformed. Both joy and rage were in it, and the gleam of his eye burned her very soul.

He came straight up to her, took the lamp, set it on the table, and then stood close to her.

"Are you hurt?" he asked. "What did the beast do?"

"He started to gag me," she said. "He was going to tie me. There's a cord he must have dropped on the bed when you came in. There's the handkerchief that he stuffed into my mouth. But I'm not hurt."

He looked her over as though he could hardly trust her words.

"If anything had happened to you, Durfee—"

He left the sentence unfinished. It seemed wonderful to

her that this man should have cared for the opinion of any other, especially that gray-headed rancher.

"And Lester?" she asked.

As she mentioned the name, a trembling weakness came over her.

"He got away. A crowd, you can't do anything in a crowd. They have two hundred riders scampering about; and Lester is gone. All that they'll manage will be to dim the trail and confuse it."

He turned on his heel and went back to the doorway.

"I'm riding back now," he said. "I have to be out at the place of your uncle before Lester can get there. Goodbye. Stay quietly here till you have word from us. Trust nothing, believe nobody until you hear directly from one of us three."

So he was gone.

CHAPTER 39

They made a great deal of fuss about Mary Durfee the next day. The hotel changed her room, because the one which had been the scene of the fight was being visited all day long. And the places were marked where spurs had ripped the flooring and where boards of the flimsy wall had been knocked loose by the impact of the spinning, struggling fighters. Knife strokes that had sunk into wood instead of flesh were found. Above all, everyone was shown the chimneyless lamp with which the girl had lighted the battle, as the only small aid she could give to her champion.

For her own part, she kept very still in her room and spent long hours that day lying on her bed, trying to overcome the tremor which had seized upon her body. She could could turn her head and look through the brilliant sunshine at the rolling hills and the blue mountains piled against the sky. And her thoughts were out there.

St. Clair, long before this, must have reached the ranch of her uncle. And what would he find there? Smoking ruins, with the bodies of Bunce and Durfee among them? Well, that was a possibility, also.

If St. Clair found such a thing, then let all the gods be

kind to Lester, for he would need their help. It seemed to the girl that no human power could stand against young St. Clair, for there was no fear in his heart and shattering power was in his hands.

She had trays brought up to her room for lunch and supper. After she had finished supper, the hotel proprietor came up to see her, his third visit of the day. He brought her a letter on which she recognized the crabbed handwriting of her uncle.

The proprietor waited a minute to learn if there was to be a reply. "A red-headed puncher brought it in on the gallop," he said. "He didn't stop, but I reckon I could find him wetting his throat down the street a ways."

She was reading:

Dear Mary:

Henry came back and told us how that demon paid a visit to you in Flinders. We expect him around here before long. In the meantime, Flinders is no place for you to be and, considering the way things are, I don't see why our friend Henry ever left you there, but I reckon that he was in a terrible hurry to get back here and check things up.

I'm going back to Flinders to get you this evening. But I'm not coming into town.

I reckon that you can see why it don't pay for me to show my face in a big town right now. The lonelier I live, the better. Besides, we got to count the minutes and even seconds, when we're sitting in at a game with Lester, confound him.

Around about sunset time, or between that and twilight, I'll be out on the Chester Trail north of Flinders Creek. Meet me up there, any place around the top of the hill. Don't fail, and remember that time counts.

                                          Your Loving Uncle

She raced through the latter part of the letter, rather puzzled and frowning. But she could understand it. Her uncle wanted to remove her to some other and safer harborage; but he did not want to risk being seen in Flinders by Spot Lester or any of his brutal friends. Therefore, she was to meet him on the trail.

She told the proprietor, in answer to his anxious inquiry, that there was no answer. Yes, he could have her horse saddled, if he would.

Five minutes later, she was riding briskly out of Flinders on the north trail. The last ray of the westering sun struck her as she trotted her horse up the slope and she kept it at a good round pace, for her uncle had named in the letter sunset as the earliest moment when he could arrive.

It was just after that crimson and golden moment when she came to the top of divide. At this point there was a gradual slope ahead and back of her. The trail had almost disappeared, and in place of trees she saw about her big, gray-sided rocks, as large as cottages.

The breeze was cool and pleasant, the whole horizon of the sky was a glory, and all nervousness left her.

She heard the trickle of water presently and, going toward it, she found a small stream that pooled itself conveniently in the lap of a sunken boulder. She dismounted, drank, and let Boots drink also.

Then, as she stood there, cold struck through her from behind, like rays of darkness. She turned, and Lester stood close by, his unhuman face smiling at her with joyless satisfaction. She was not benumbed this time.

The simplicity of the ruse was perfectly apparent. Now that she thought back to it, she felt that she could have told that the handwriting in that letter was not exactly similar to other specimens which she had had from her uncle. No, she should have exercised caution. The last thing St. Clair had told her was to trust nothing in the world except the three of them who were sworn allies.

In the tenth part of a second she thought of all this; then she leaped for her horse.

It was a vain effort. Lester picked her out of the air as though she were made of feathers and brought her down to the ground.

She had reached for one of the little revolvers which she always carried in the saddle holster; now he stripped it out of her hand; she felt as though his fingers were steel thongs. "You walk first," said Lester. "I'll come behind and lead the hoss. A right smart little mustang, this here looks to be. And that's a lucky thing, for them that need to ride, to have a hoss that can pack them!"

He talked along smoothly, almost gently, as though he wished to quiet her fears. And she obeyed. It was a blessed thing to be able to turn her face away from the monster and have him behind her for the moment at least.

Her brain struggled desperately. In one way or another she must be able to think of something to do. Other people had been in situations as desperate and they had devised ways. There were signals to be given. There were a thousand things to be done, perhaps, but she could think of nothing.

He, from behind, directed her first to this side and then to that, until in the midst of a copse they came to three magnificent horses, one wearing a saddle, two carrying small packs.

"And here we be," said the outlaw, "arrived at our little traveling home. Don't look so bad, does it?"

Even the beauty of the horses had a sinister look in her eyes. A desperate man might well trust his life to their speed and courage. She leaned an aimless hand against a shoulder of one of these animals, a shoulder rippling and hard with muscle.

"Now, tell me what you want to do with me?" she asked, facing Lester at last. "What earthly thing can you gain, except to torment my uncle a little?"

"Why, honey," said Lester, the softness of his words always commenting oddly on the brutality of his face, "I reckon that you know what a paper chase is?"

"Yes," she answered.

"Well," said he, "I reckon that there's gunna be a chase and you'll be the paper."

He laughed. Then he pointed toward the horizon. "Them three, Bunce and your uncle and St. Clair, they've gone and dug themselves in for the winter, you might say, and bedded themselves down real comfortable. Maybe they think that I'm gunna go and tackle 'em in their own quarters? No, sir, I ain't that much of a fool. I'm getting old, and I aim to save myself considerable. It's a mighty lot easier to be hunted than to be the hunter. Any fool can lay a trail that'll make hard following for a wise man. And I'm gonna be the fool, and you'll help me to lay down the trail that the wise men'll have to follow. That clear?"

She frowned at him. "I'm to be bait in a trap?" she asked.

"Yeah," he nodded. "That's about it."

"They won't come after me," she said. "Only my uncle, perhaps, with hired men. Not St. Clair, not Mr. Bunce. For, you see, I'm nothing to them!"

He only grinned in response. And then he said: "You dunno the folks out here on this range, honey. These here men, they're chivalrous, is what they are. When St. Clair hears that you're gone and the villain Lester has laid hands on you, he's gunna blame himself, partly, that he didn't take better care of you. Oh, he'll come ragin'. And so will Durfee, and so will Bunce, because he'll be afraid to stay behind!"

CHAPTER 40

Like a man who has traveled beyond the seas to an unknown land, inhabited by people strange and barbarous, with savage ways and a savage tongue, so the girl gazed at Lester. And she felt that any criticism would be futile, so vast was his distance from any humanity that she understood.

Perhaps her loathing of him grew less, as she reached this understanding.

She said: "I'm to trail along with you and, when the three of them follow the trail, you'll drop back and pick them off, one by one. Is that it?"

"You're a bright girl," said he.

"It's a wise idea," said she, "but you'll never beat St. Clair that way."

"Not St. Clair? He's a hero, is he?"

"He's been too much for you before," she told him. "He'll be too much again. As sure as fate, you're beaten. You may murder my uncle and Bunce, but the best thing for you to do is to drop this business and clear out. Perhaps St. Clair wouldn't follow you, after that. He's run you into the ground a couple of times, and perhaps he's tired of the business."

So, calmly taunting him, she took note of the lifting of his upper lip and the flash of the teeth behind it.

"He's had luck, twice," said Spot Lester. "But nobody in

the world has luck with me three times. I ain't made that way. Luck ain't made that way. Now we'll drift along, Mary."

She got obediently into the saddle on Boots and rode off with a lead rope running between the pommel of his saddle and the neck of her horse.

"What are the rules of this game of yours?" she asked him.

"They're simple," said he. "You gotta have simple rules to make a good game, don't you?"

"Yes," said she.

"The rules go this way—you just don't make no sudden moves, day or night. You're gunna be safe till you try to make a break. And that would only earn you a lot of pain collected and paid down in a heap, Mary. Realize that?"

She managed to look him in the face for a moment.

"What would it be, Spot? she asked him. "A bullet?"

"No, not likely," said he. "I don't aim to waste ammunition when I can help it."

She looked down at the great hand that controlled the reins on the neck of his horse. She knew the coldness of that hand; it already had touched her face, but the next time it would touch her throat.

She said: "Women are not a weakness with you, Spot?"

"Women are all right," he said, "in their own place. But I never found out what their place is."

Panic was spreading at the roots of her heart. Yet she forced herself to talk on. She had a feeling that utter silence must be avoided, if possible.

"Why," she said, "a woman's place is to be a comforter to you big, strong men. Of course, she can't be a companion. She hasn't enough brains. But how many men come home at night, after they've been kicked in the face, and show how really big and strong they are by beating up their women, sometimes with their fists. But anyway, their women have to pay for what the world has done to the male. You have to admit that we're some use that way. Like the padding in a pair of boxing gloves, we save our men a lot of wear and tear on the knuckles. Sometimes it's rough on the stuffing. But that doesn't matter."

"You got one of these smooth tongues, ain't you?" said he. "Well, I don't appreciate jokes. And what was all that abou' women being like padding? Got a double meaning in that, I suppose?"

"No double meaning," said she. "What I said ought to be clear enough. So how useful I am to you. Henry St. Clair has kicked you about several times, and you didn't like it; so you picked up a woman to kick around in turn."

He halted his horse. Drawn by the tug of the tightened lead rope, Boots turned about, also, and horses and riders faced one another.

Mary Durfee made herself smile; and she learned that the easiest way of facing the monster was when she looked straight into his inhuman eyes.

"One of these bright girls," said he. "Bright and sassy, the pride of her pa and ma, is what she is! She just lacks a few lessons in manners."

She could have fainted with fear; but she had made herself keep on smiling.

"Oh, I expect lessons in manners, before I get back home," said she. "What else would one expect to have from Spot Lester except lessons in manners?"

"One of them wild Western cats, eh?" said he. "But I'd much rather have it that way. Some screamin', howlin', faintin' fool would be worse to travel with."

"Thanks," said she. "I didn't expect to hear you saying such pretty things, Spot."

"Aw, go on up the trail," said he, "and leave me be for a while."

And he actually unfurled an added length of rope from the pommel of his saddle to give her greater freedom of movement.

In this manner, they rode out of the twilight and into the darkness, with Lester in the lead. They crossed the shallow valley; they climbed among the rocks and pines of an upland. And, with the sound of running water nearby, he halted at last in a considerable grove of trees. There he dismounted and told her to follow that example, merely saying: "You wouldn't be fool enough to try to run and hide among the trees and rocks, eh?"

She answered: "No, the moon will be up in a little while, and I know that owls and mountain lions and such things hunt better by moonlight than in the sunshine."

He was not offended. Instead, he laughed, a convulsive pulsing of the breath rather than a vocal sound.

"That's all right," said he. "Maybe we're gunna understand each other. Unsaddle your hoss."

She obeyed, taking off the saddle and the blanket roll behind it, while he performed the same services for his own three animals and hobbled them for grazing. Then he built a little fire, no larger than the cup of a hand and over that he boiled coffee. This and hard tack made up the meal.

"You'll get sort of thin while you travel along with me," he told her. "But you won't starve; if you look at this in the right way, it'll be a sort of vacation outing for you."

"Of course, it will," said she. "I'm looking at it more and more in that way. I'm going to turn in."

"That's right," said he, "and sleep tight; because we start early. A long trail makes any man nervous, and them three are gunna be nervous before they get sight of us." And the pulsing whisper of his laughter reached her ears again.

A moment later, on a sparse bed of pine boughs she rolled out her blanket and lay down. Over her head she saw the arrowy rising of the pines against the stars; and as the sky grew pale with the rising of the moon, she fell asleep.

In the middle of the night she wakened suddenly and sat up. She could not remember what her dream had been, only that it had been horrible. As she sat up, something else rose from the ground not far away. It was Spot Lester, likewise sitting up, watching her. A single move had been enough to waken him, and now he sat there with half his face masked in black shadow and half illumined by the moon.

He said nothing and she, lying down again, was instantly asleep once more. She was not comforted, but the surety of despair told her that she would never be able to escape from this man whom a whisper of blankets could arouse in the middle of the night.

CHAPTER 41

Two days slid into the past of Mary Durfee. At the end of that time she knew her companion no better than at the first meeting.

He treated her with strange consideration that amounted to courtesy; but all the while she knew without question that the first move on her part to escape would mean her murder at his hands.

He was not altogether silent. Sometimes he would even answer the questions she asked of him, and often his answers were long and detailed.

Then a day came when she said to him: "What started you, Spot?"

"Started me doing what?" he asked.

"Oh, robbing, murdering, and your other little diversions."

He stared at her, but he had gradually grown somewhat accustomed to her calmly bantering way.

They were sitting their horses, just then, on the rocky shoulder of a mountain to which they had climbed from the deeps of a valley below them, spread out just like a picture in the crystal clear light of the early afternoon.

And she, dropping her eyes from the mountains to the trail far beneath them, saw three horsemen, one close behind the other. A wisp of dust hung in the air behind and above them.

She started. Then she strove to look unconcernedly away. But she heard the half-whispering, half-whining chuckle of Lester.

"You seen 'em at last, did you?" said Lester.

"Who?" she asked.

"Your uncle, and Bunce, and St. Clair?" said he.

The last hope shot out of her heart.

"Do you think they—" she began.

"Why," said Lester, "I been watching 'em from time to time coming down that valley. I knew that they were following the trail, all right, and I made that trail one that can be read fast. Here they come up the hill, all three of 'em,

but will any of 'em ever see the other side of the mountain?
I reckon not!"

He made her dismount; the horses were led back and
tethered among the trees; then he returned with her to the
ledge of rocks which overlooked the steep pitch of the valley's side.

He said: "You can stay here and look on. Just keep your
face shut all the time."

She regarded him with an always fresh wonder.

"I'm to stay here quietly and watch them ride up to the
mouth of your rifle. Is that it, Spot?"

He only grinned at her, so that she could see his teeth.

"That's about what you'll do," he said. "I've heard such a
lot about the fineness of women. According to the poets and
the cow-punchers, a good woman, she'll up and die to save
her men. A dog-gone heroine is what every good woman
west of the Mississippi is. And here you're gunna have your
chance, honey. You're gunna have lots of time, too. A voice'll
carry pretty far, with this here wall of stone to make it echo.
And I'm gunna wait until they're inside of point-blank range.
Then I'll open up. Because when I shoot, I want to use three
bullets, and make everyone of 'em count."

As he talked, his eyes were on her, but his hands were
softly caressing his rifle.

The slanting sun stood full against her face as she looked
away from her companion, across the deep well of the
valley to the trees that stood on its western rim.

Her uncle was coming up that trail at the head of two
other men. And what was her uncle to her? In this searching blaze of sunlight, he seemed a mere stranger, a man she
had seen a few times and of whom she understood little. As
for Bunce, the little cripple was really a stranger, and St.
Clair was hardly more. But her own life was young and
sweet.

It would not be a rifle bullet, probably; no, but the iron-
shod butt end of the gun would be used to bash in her skull
if she gave the warning.

She peered carefully down through a crevice between two
boulders and saw them appear, one after the other, her uncle,
Bunce, St. Clair last of all. Astonishingly close they seemed,
as though wings had lifted them up through the intervening
space.

She looked over her shoulder with a gasp at her companion, expecting to see the death-dealing rifle already at his shoulder. Instead, he was merely sneering at her, challenging her, it seemed, to live up to the bright picture he had painted of the Western woman!

No, she was incapable of that, she told herself. For people near and dear to her, oh, that would have been a different matter, but not three comparative strangers.

She flung herself face down on the ground, her face buried in her arms.

And she heard the snarling voice of Spot Lester, saying: "Thank God, I never wasted no time on one of you. God give me better brains than He give to other men, and He lets me see through you. Them three, they're out riding, brave and bold and free, up agin' the muzzle of my rifle. Another five minutes, they'll be dead—for you! Why, they could easier catch me in a trap baited with dead fish than in a trap baited with a woman. That's what I think of you and your whole tribe!"

She heard his footfall as he moved away from her. At the same time, the iron-shod hoof of a horse rang against loose rocks, just beneath her hiding place. And the sound lifted her to her feet.

From beneath the boulders, just beneath her, yet, hardly fifty yards away, came the three, with her uncle's grave, ugly face in the lead. She saw the dust gray on their faces, and new dust still was rising from the trail and settling about them again.

Head down, the horses labored, with ears back, pictures of gloomy and unrewarded effort.

Past her uncle she looked to the face of little Bunce, awry in his saddle, riding in pain, pain that was stamped into his features. Durfee would soon be dead; Bunce would soon die.

And last came big St. Clair, his rifle balanced across the pommel of his saddle, the three led horses stringing out behind him. He would die, too, the first to fall.

From the corner of her eye, she saw the gleam of the rifle that was being raised to the shoulder of Spot Lester, slowly, as a man will do when he is sure of his target and wishes to make a dead shot.

Then a voice burst on her ears, wailing hysterically high: "Go back, go back, Spot Lester!"

She saw them all flinging from the backs of their horses to take shelter under the rocks.

She saw the shadow of the blow from Lester looming at her head. Before it fell, she realized in a detached way, that the voice had been her own involuntary scream of warning; her throat ached with the distending force of it.

Then the stroke fell.

She thought her neck was broken. Her head struck heavily against the opposite shoulder, and she dropped, stunned.

But yet it was not utter darkness of mind.

She was able to wonder why he had not started shooting, instead of wasting time to strike her down. One or two shots he surely might have sent home, though at suddenly dodging targets. But now that the three of them were under the rocks—swarming up to attack his higher position, no doubt —he could not consider himself safe.

In fact, he scooped her up lightly in the hollow of a long arm and ran with her to the horse. There he flung her into the saddle with brutal force. He took a handful of her hair and twisted it until it promised to tear from its bedding in her scalp.

Then she roused, and sat up groaning in the saddle, involuntarily feeling for the stirrups with her feet.

"That's better," he told her through his teeth. "And now ride like Satan was inside you, because he certainly is behind you. Do you understand me? You hear?"

She heard and she obeyed.

She was not on Boots now, but one of Lester's own long-legged, powerful brutes, and it whipped her over the ground at an amazing speed.

For two or three miles the boulders and the ragged trees flew by her, and gradually the ache in her neck, the throbbing pain on the side of her head where his fist had fallen subsided. She was half nauseated, fear ate coldly at her heart. Her death sentence, surely, had been passed.

"Pull up," shouted Lester.

She drew obediently on the reins and the horse slowed.

Then she ventured a glance at his face, and saw it distorted with passion. He was pale; his eyes were literally green, like the eyes of a hunting beast. And hastily she jerked her head around and looked again at the ragged pass before them.

CHAPTER 42

"There ain't any call for a grand hurry now," he explained, his voice ringing like an iron bell, hard and flat. "By the time they find that we ain't in that nest among the rocks, and by the time that they get back to their hosses and then hunt up our trail, we'll be a pretty far cry away. Only, I had to get us out of eyeshot pretty sudden."

She was silent.

"You ain't answering back, eh?" he demanded, riding up beside her.

"Why not?" he asked her. "I ought to've brained you, back there, the same as I said that I would. I didn't brain you though. I left you special, because I wanted to hear you wag your tongue. I wanted to see what was inside of your head, if they's anything more than wind and emptiness there!"

She said faintly, "I'll answer all questions."

"Proud. That's what you are now," he said. "You proved me to be a liar, eh?"

"I?" said she. "How?"

"And me—that said there wasn't nothing in women. And there was meanness enough in you to prove me wrong, eh? Even if you had to die for it?"

He added: "But I seen how it was. It was too dog-gone well planted in your head. You thought that nobody out of the West would dare to do it—murder a woman. But women or men, they ain't no difference to me. I never killed a woman before, because I never needed to. But now you think that my hands are tied, eh?"

"No," she said, "I know that I'm dead. You only wanted to take time to find a harder death for men than just a bullet or a knife would pass out. But I know that I'm dead, Spot."

And she looked hopelessly across at him. His eyes were almost lost beneath the profound darkness of his frown.

"Tell me something," he said. "You're smart. You're so smart that you waited till your yell would surprise me and spoil my aim when the gun was at my shoulder. You're smart, so now you tell me why I didn't try to bag one of 'em before I knocked you over?"

She paused.

"You thought that you could get them later on," said she. "It didn't matter to you, really, how long the trail lasted."

"Is that it?"

"Yes. And you wanted to make sure of me. Just killing off-hand wasn't good enough. You wanted to make sure, that I didn't step through the boulders and jump down the cliff to get away from you.

"You would've done that, eh?" he demanded.

"Yes, if I'd had another half second."

'I don't believe it," said he. "If you're so dog-gone set on dying, why didn't you throw yourself off the hoss onto the rocks, when he was running at full speed a while back? Why didn't you do that?"

"Because I wasn't so desperate, then," said she. "I hadn't the courage, any longer."

"Just a kind of nacheral coward?" he asked.

"Yes, I suppose so."

"Tell me something."

"Yes, if I can."

"You planned the whole thing out—lyin' flat on your face, actin' as though you was through, your nerve all gone. That was to throw me off guard, so's you'd get a chance to holler when I didn't suspect nothin' like that out of you. You planned it all, and you planned it real slick. I gotta admit that. What surprises me is that you planned it so quick and early in the game."

"I didn't plan a thing," said she.

He laughed in his ghastly way.

"You're gunna play simple and sweet, now, eh?" said he. "You didn't realize what you was doing, I guess."

"No," she replied. "I was lying on the ground sick and shamed. And all at once, I heard the horse stumble on the trail just under me, and that got me to my feet. Instinct did the rest, not my own planning and wits."

"I'm to believe that, am I?" he said, showing his teeth.

She shook her head. "I can't make you believe anything. I know that," she said.

"What makes me hot," said he, "is that you should think that I'm like the rest of 'em—a kind of halfwit, ready to have the wool pulled over my eyes. Ain't I seen that you're a great liar and a regular smart one? Ain't you fooled me once, and d'you think that you'll ever be able to fool me ag'in?"

"I don't know what to say," she replied.

"You—don't—know—what—to—say!" he echoed.

The bitter disbelief in his voice gave it a grating sound, but he spoke no more to her and she was glad of that.

Through their continued silence, she and Lester rode out of evening into night. The trees closed over them like dark waters, and the shadows flowed thickly about them.

Then, turning sharply to the side, Lester made camp.

He was so secure, that he built up a fire that evening, as though to prove to her that he scorned his pursuers, and he made it larger than usual, although it was well screened behind rocks that he rolled into place for that purpose.

Over that fire he cooked a rabbit, shot earlier in the day, bacon, and made some soft pone, which she baked by twirling lumps of the dough over the flames on the end of sticks. It was a good meal.

Afterward, she made up her bed, but when she was about to lie down in it, he called her back to the fire.

He said: "You've noticed something, eh?"

"Yes," said she.

"What have you noticed?"

"That I'm still alive."

"Sit down here," said he.

She obeyed, sitting close by the small tongue of the fire. It was a pleasant warmth, for they were high in the mountains, and a cold wind found them out.

"I'm gunna make a bargain with you," said he. "The way I promised it to you today you're due for a knife in the throat. But there's a way it could be managed that you wouldn't get either knife or gun. You know how?"

"No," said she.

And she looked with wonder, across the flickering firelight, to his ugly face.

"It's like this. You ain't with the rest of 'em," said he. "You got brains, and you got nerve, too. You kind of beat me. Tell me what you've done in your day. You ain't cracked nobody over the head, maybe, and you ain't robbed no banks. But you've done other things. Nobody as slick as you has wasted her time all these years for nothing! You out with it, and tell me what you've done."

Suddenly, in spite of her weary, aching body, she was able to smile at him frankly.

"I understand what you mean," she said. "You want me to tell you the dark, hidden story of my life."

"Yeah. That's a fancy way of putting it."

"Well," she said, "I've been no better than a lot. I've told my share of lies and done my share of foolish things, I know. But there's no dark story, Spot. Don't try to make me into a strange woman because I've done one thing that seems strange to you."

He regarded her for a time with his twisted grin.

At last he held out his hand. "Will you shake?" said he.

She allowed the cold, iron-hard fingers to close over hers. Then he said: "I've seen some of the finest and the best in the world, but for nacheral talent and smartness, I reckon that you're the greatest freehand liar that I've ever known."

CHAPTER 43

It dawned upon her at last that these remarks did not spring out of any revulsion of feeling against her, but from the deeps of a profound admiration. He felt her to be a consummate actress and expert deceiver. He was speaking to her with the open tribute of a fellow spirit.

She controlled her wonder, trying to keep it out of her eyes, as she looked across the flicker of firelight toward him.

"But the way it is, it's kind of late," said he, in conclusion. "You're dead tired. Go on to bed. I reckon that I would've handled you a mite easier, if I'd known what you was made of before. Good night!"

She said good night and went off to her blankets, where she curled up and lay for a moment looking at the dark shafts of the trees and at the brilliance of the moonlight that gilded the tops of them.

Sleep began to drift over her when the voice of Lester cut

in again: "I reckon that St. Clair is big enough and straight enough to take your eye, Mary. Is that right?"

She answered frankly: "Yes. I like him better than any one I ever knew."

"Ah, ha!" he answered. "You'd marry him, eh?"

"If he asked me to," she answered. "I would in a minute, I suppose."

"Well, but he ain't asked you, is that it?"

"He hasn't asked me," said she.

She had no shame in speaking of her most intimate thoughts to this outlaw. She felt as though she were speaking to the empty mountain air. None of her ideas would ever be echoed by him in the hearing of ears to which they would make any difference.

"Lookin' at it from one way," said Lester, "it's kind of a shame that you couldn't make a match of it. I mean, the size of him, and your looks and your brains. But I reckon that you'd find him too much for you to handle, no matter how smart you are!"

"Why?" she asked.

She grew intensely interested. She forgot her weariness, her aches and pains.

"I'll tell you why," he replied. "I'm kind of a wild man. But I'm only as wild as I wanta be. He's different."

"He's never hurt a soul in the world, I believe," said she.

"Ain't he? Nobody except me," said Lester. "But he's only starting, and when he gets through with me—if he's to win out in this game that we're playing together—then he'll find his hand pretty empty. He'll have to have something to fill up his attention, I tell you. And what will it be?"

"I don't understand that," said she.

"What I mean is this," he went on, "there's some folks in the world that can't be happy unless they're hunting, or being hunted. I'm one of that kind. But I ain't as dead set on it as St. Clair. Because I ain't got so much animal in me!"

She remembered one or two moments in which the glow of almost unearthly, brutal joy had filled the eyes of St. Clair. Was there something in what the outlaw was saying to her?

She listened as though to an inspired seer, saying: "Perhaps you're right, Spot. I have an idea of what you mean. I've seen a look in his face, two or three times."

"You never seen it that way that I did," said the outlaw, "when we were standing chest to chest, and I seen him turn into a demon. I ain't a scary kind, but I was scared then. I seen that he wasn't nacheral or human. It took the nerve out of me. Maybe I would've had a chance with him, in spite of my legs being dead weak. But the look in the face of him sort of done me in. I turned numb, like you do in a nightmare, when you wanta run, but you can't lift a hand. And that was how he beat me."

She closed her eyes, trying to visualize again that battle of giants. Spot Lester frightened by the expression in another man's face! But perhaps the thing was possible. She knew that the tale of it had rung through the length of the range; men were never done talking of the fight.

"Well, what's wrong with St. Clair?" she asked.

"Nothin' is wrong with him, except that he's different," said Lester. "You know how it is. There ain't nothing wrong with a wolf. But it's different from a dog. It can run farther. It can live on less. It's got three times the strength locked up in its jaws. That's the difference between the rest of men and St. Clair. He's built big and strong, but still he's stronger than he had oughta be. And I know that, too! They call me a gorilla. Maybe I am. But there ain't an electric shock in my fingers the way there is in St. Clair's. You understand?"

"I'm beginning to," said she. "But simply because he's strong, why should that make him wild?"

"He's tasted blood," said the other with conviction. "And he'll sure turn into a man-eater. He can't help it. He's had the taste on the roots of his tongue!"

Then he added: "If you was to marry him, you still wouldn't have him. Because he'd be out wandering again before long. If he run me down, then he might be quiet for a time, but after that he'd have to fill his hands with a fight —maybe a fight with another man, or a gang of men. Maybe a fight with a mountain lion, or a little catch-as-catch-can match with a grizzly. Sooner or later, the lion will scratch his heart right out of his chest, or the bear will smash his head for him. I'd like right well to be on hand when it happens, I can tell you."

She heard his strange, whispering laughter, with just the

suggestion of a snarl buried in it. Then he was silent, and
once again the peace of the night rolled in upon her, and
even the pondering upon the strange ideas of St. Clair could
not disturb her.

CHAPTER 44

She wakened several hours later to find a shaft of moon-
shine striking down upon her face. The old superstition, that
moonlight brings evil dreams, returned to her; certainly her
own dreams had been strange enough, but nothing stranger
than awakening in this place among the mountains and the
dark, straight-standing pines.

She sat up, prepared to move her blankets into the
shadow, and saw that Lester had already moved his own. In
fact, he was not to be seen within the immediate circle of
the trees.

She stood up and walked in the direction in which the
horses had been hobbled out to graze. She wanted some sort
of company, even that of a beast.

But the horses were not there!

They had been placed in a little natural meadow where
the grass grew thick and long, and they were not likely to
wander away from it, hobbled as they were and with
nothing better immediately around them but the needles
thickly packed beneath the trees. Yet, they were not in the
meadow! Neither were they just beyond it.

A sudden, incredible thought came to her.

She turned and, hurrying back into the clearing where
they had made camp, she saw that the entire pack of Spot
Lester was gone. And she uttered a sigh of relief.

Did it not mean in some manner she had been enabled to
touch the heart of Lester? Therefore, he had slipped away
from her and left her alone. He might have made her safe
by a bullet through the head, or a knife stroke in the hollow
of her throat, and perhaps he had leaned over her with the
thought in his mind. Perhaps that was the explanation of
some of the grisly nightmares which had pursued her.

At any rate, she was alone there among the heights, and Lester was gone!

It was not strange that he had taken all the horses. Left on foot, she would have to travel slowly, but she was nevertheless closer to towns than to starvation. He had left her, while he galloped back down the trail to strike a final blow at the three who trailed him, perhaps?

Yes, that must be the explanation. And that would be her own course, also—to get back down the trail as fast as she could. It seemed to her now if she could look a single time on the face of her uncle, with old Bunce and St. Clair at his side, the whole of this dreadful experience would fade suddenly and slip from her mind.

She paid no heed to her pack. She needed to be light for the trail, and she would follow straight back over the country through which she had ridden at the side of Spot Lester. So, at the last, she would either find Durfee and St. Clair, or else she would reach a town and from it raise up a squad of fierce riders to go scouring through the uplands in search of the marauder.

They would not need urging. The blood money on the head of Lester was a fortune large enough to tempt thousands; large enough, also, to split it in twenty parts and still make each part very considerable.

It was a weapon which she could turn against him, the fame of his evil deeds and the desire of the law to catch him, but, as a matter of fact, she did not wish really to strike at him. Not, at least, on her own account. It was only because of the danger which would surely flow out from him toward the three men on her trail that she stepped forward so briskly, eager to do anything which chance might suggest to her mind, in order to succor those who had started out to succor her.

The moon was now past the zenith; the dawn was beginning to dim its light, as the strong summer sunlight dulls a white flower, and she felt that either the dawn alone or the moon alone would be preferable.

As it was, she was always stumbling. Riding boots are not perfect footwear for the pedestrian. And she was walking over broken rocks that turned and twisted beneath her feet. Sometimes she had to wind and twist and break her way through thickets whose thorns ripped her clothes and tore her skin like fishhooks.

At last, she found the sky turning rose, and the day began. After that, the weariness of mind and of body diminished. She felt rested and more assured. When the sun came up a little later, she felt that she had left a world of nightmares and ghosts behind her and had come out into plain reality.

It was hot before the sun was up an hour, and she was then struggling forward up the bottom of a box canyon, when she heard an outburst of rifle fire before her, echoing out of the next ravine.

Her heart failed her with fear and excitement. She knew, somehow, that the noise came from her friends, and that it told how they had struck against Spot Lester.

Perhaps men were already dead or dying on the ground!

She began to run and, still running, reeling, she came to the bottom of the canyon and looked over from its lower lip into the chasm that stepped down beyond it.

It was two hundred yards wide and a mile or two in length. There was not a blade of grass, it seemed, certainly not a scrub, even, in all the length of it. Only, in the center, there was a nest of rocks; and among those rocks her three friends had taken shelter.

There was no firing, now, but she could plainly see what had happened.

Spot Lester, returning down his own outtrail, had waited here on the rim of one side of the box canyon and when the three came on, he opened fire.

He had struck at them, first, farther down the valley. She could see the bodies of three horses near the rocks. And three more lay dead just outside of the ragged circle of the stones.

Were more than horses killed by the bullets of Spot Lester? She could not see a form move, of course. What her eye might see, that of Lester would also strike on.

But it was quite possible that he might have killed the horses only with malice aforethought. Certainly, he did not wish an easy death for his enemies. The torture was going to be long drawn out.

And what more exquisite in the way of a living death than

to coop men up where the sun could be flames to scorch them, where lack of water would soon parch their throats and choke their breathing?

To her left, from the rim of the valley, she heard the double report of a rifle; a single shot answered from the circle of the rocks.

One man at least, therefore was alive among the rocks. And now she had located the position of Lester.

Hatred and fear and admiration rushed up into her mind as she thought of the cunning of the man who had gathered three others into the hollow of his hand. Rancher Bunce might not be formidable, but Durfee was a man in ten thousand, and what could be said of St. Clair? Yet he, with the rest, was harmlessly cooped there, to wait for death.

They were helpless, totally. Such an uncanny expert as Lester might undoubtedly have shot them out of their saddles, one by one. Instead, he preferred to let them taste slow death.

She knew what their death might be. She knew how these canyon walls would gather the sunshine and reflect it with maddening force. The mere glare from the white sand would be almost unendurable. The rocks themselves would become oven-hot. The thermometer could record a hundred and twenty or thirty in the shade, in such an inferno. But there would be no shade! And the gathering strength of the sun's rays, scalding the shoulders, filling the very brain with smoke, would gradually madden them.

Suppose, then, that they managed to live through the day? On the night that followed, the light of the broad moon, nearing the full, would take the place of the sun to guide the rifle of Spot Lester. And if the light were dimmer, still it would be more than sufficient. By this time, he had the range perfectly; he could lie at ease under the shadow of the trees on the rim of the valley and his eyes would never leave his victims.

Sooner or later, tormented past endurance, the three would try to charge from their fortress. They would risk their lives in the conviction that no human being could keep up a constant vigil. But they would be wrong.

More than the patience of a hungry cat beside the rat hole would be the endurance of Spot Lester, now that he had brought his devices to such a happy consummation.

One thing alone could save the hunted three and that would be, during the first night, a thunderstorm to blacken the face of the sky. Under that cover they might dare to venture forth. But would they wait that long, with parched and aching throats?

She doubted it greatly.

What could she do, then, to help them who had tried to help her? Miserably she pondered. She might struggle across the rocky hills with already bruised feet, but she knew of no place nearer than a twenty-hour march where she could confidently expect to find a village. Long before help could come, even at a gallop, the heat of the next day's sun would be scorching the sufferers.

Now it seemed to her that she perfectly understood the scheme of Spot Lester.

He had wished to bring her on slowly to this place, where the sound of rifles would attract her even from a distance. And at this moment he must be confident that she was looking on at his trap and secretly admiring it. In a sense, he was staging an exhibition in the hope that she, of all people in the world, might make up the applauding audience.

As the dizziness and the whirling thought of despair filled her mind, she went back under a broad-limbed pine tree and sat down there, her back against the trunk. She could hear the trickling of water near by, that meant so little to her, but which would be like a direct bit of heaven to the dry throats of the three in the ravine.

Gradually she saw the truth. If she had the will to aid them, it must be by taking some of the water in her canteen, if she could devise no larger carrier, and bringing it to the besieged.

But how bring it when the merciless rifle of Lester commanded the way?

She fell into a torpor; and the sun climbed steadily in the sky, pouring flames down upon the earth.

CHAPTER 45

Time passes swiftly for those who dream or for those who know that they are moving toward destruction. So it was with the girl, postponing from hour to hour the time when she must make her effort and die for it!

But at last she knew that the hour had come, for something burned her hand, and looking down, wincing, she saw that a little spot of sunlight had struck down through the scattering branches of the tree and touched her skin.

Yes, there was fire in the sky, showering down upon the earth. And the three, living or dead in the ravine below her, were tasting the bitter strength of it.

Then she stood up. Her knees buckled under her, and she put out a hand against the rough trunk of the tree to steady herself. She was afraid. Fear made her hollow and empty. Her eyes stared, aching under her brows.

But once more she looked down into the valley.

Up there on the height, even, it was intolerably hot. Yet she had the green heaven of the pine tree above her, and a small breeze cooled her face. But there was no breeze in that house of torment below her!

Once more, with a vague, despairing eye, she scanned the faces of the mountains, one by one. For it might be that she would see the upward mounting puff of thin white which told where moving things were raising the dust, but there was no token of other life in all that landscape! Then she turned back toward the sound of the water. It was a mere trickle, whispering among the rocks and pooling itself in the cool beneath the trees. She lay on her face beside it and drank. She was very thirsty, now that she had a moment to think of herself. It was as though she had eaten much salt meat.

Then she filled the canteen. It held a good quart but what was a quart among three men? Why, it would be no better than a swallow for even one of them! True, it was better than nothing. It would be worth the risk of death to get this supply to them. But what else could she use?

She sat down, took off her broad-brimmed sombrero and fanned her hot face with it, striving to think, until at last it was clear that the water carrier was already in her hand! It was her hat!

The stanch weave of the Stetson would hold water almost as well as metal could. There were the four metal rimmed air holes in the sides of the crown, but they could be plugged. And then, capacious crown having been filled, could she not sew up the whole rim until it was practically water-tight?

She had a small pocket sewing kit in the pocket of her riding skirt, and this she took out at once. Hard twists of the cloth were worked into the four air holes and sewed firmly in place; then, taking the strongest thread and making very small stitches, she sewed up the rim of the hat, leaving only a small aperture. Then, pouring water from the canteen, she filled that hat, literally, to the brim, and sewed up the final aperture.

It made the clumsiest possible sort of a shape to carry, but, after all, it held a surprising weight of water. She was amazed by the solid burden of it!

To be sure, the water sweated through, after a few moments, but she could tell from the way the water oozed that not more than a pint or so would escape during the journey to the rocks. And the moment had now come for the final step!

She took a last deep drink from the spring, refilled the canteen for the last time, picked up the water-filled hat and struck out.

She knew that there was only one possible way of getting to the rocks. The distance from either end of the valley was far, far too long, but near the rocks, on the side of the valley opposite to that where Spot Lester crouched like an eagle on the lookout, the wall of the ravine was broken and an irregular fissure worked downward, broad at the top, and narrowing to nothing at the bottom. In this fissure a few shrubs grew, and many jagged points of rock projected.

These might help to shelter her and give her foot and handholds in the descent. They would screen her somewhat from the keen eye of Lester on the other side of the ravine.

If she could get to the bottom of the cleft unobserved, the distance would be short from that spot to the little group of rocks where the hunted men were sheltered. She would depend on good fortune to get her across the ground rapidly, good fortune and the probability that the great Lester was looking rather to see that the men did not leave the rocks than that others should be prevented from coming toward them.

She was already in movement now.

At last she rounded the side of the valley and came, under the shelter of the rim rocks and the trees, to the crevice which she had examined before from a distance. It was a thousand times better than she had hoped. For the cleft was, in fact, the beginning of a tributary ravine. The throat of it offered a fairly easy descent to the bottom, and a way well shielded from hostile eyes.

So she went down rapidily and stood just inside the shadow at the teeth of the little gorge. There her heart almost failed her. Before her the brilliance of the sunshine was a wall of fire, and the heat of the valley floor beat fiercely up into her face.

If she stepped out into that furnace, how long would it be before the unerring bullets from the rifle of Lester struck her with stunning force and tore at her body like savage teeth.

But if it were impossible to go forward, it was also impossible to turn back. To move away from this danger would be to invite poisonous shame into her life forever.

So she waited, fighting a silent battle for a few seconds. And then she heard the slow splashing of drops as the water oozed through the waterlogged felt of the Stetson. It urged her more than all else, this thought that the supply of water she was carrying was now being exhausted as she stood there, arguing with herself about a thing which in her heart she well knew that she must accomplish.

She measured the distance again. From her lookout on high, it had seemed of little consequence. But now that she was at it, it looked like a vast corridor of flame leading to stones which might shelter against bullets, but never against this terrible sun.

She took a deep breath. Then she stepped out and ran straight ahead with all her might.

The canteen bounced and jangled at her belt. The hat of water was so heavy that she had to carry it in both arms. She sprinted with all her might. Despair nerved her.

And suddenly she was lightened by hope, also, a savage, incredulous hope as the yards of white-flashing sun shot away behind her and the goal drew nearer.

Then a spurt of dust was knocked up before her feet, some of it as high as her hands and stinging with a cutting force.

She knew what had knocked up that dust. She knew it even before the hollow echo of the rifle's report rang at her ears. Her men among the rocks were alive and alert to what was happening, at last.

As she rushed on, wondering how such a marksman as Lester could have missed, the rocks blazed out with a rapid fire of rifle shots. They were combining and searching the valley rim above them from which Lester was shooting, trying to harm him or at least to silence his weapon for an instant.

But again the sand was knocked up at her feet in a high flying jet. She understood now. Even the cruel heart of Lester had relented enough, at the sight of her courage, to give her two warnings. After them, he would strike her down surely.

She wanted to run straight on, but she found herself dodging before the gun of the hunter. Close were those rocks now. Here and there, the sun flared up from them as though reflected from wet surfaces.

And then the blow fell.

It struck her inside the left shoulder with a blow that turned her half around. She would have fallen, except for the impetus of running.

She went on, staggering.

It was as though a red-hot sword had been thrust through her, and the hilt of the sword had struck and shocked her, as the blade passed through her body.

Who had said that a bullet wound was, first, only a numb shock, and afterward a gradually spreading pain?

They were wrong; it was a blinding agony.

She hurried on, gasping. Her left arm could bear no weight now; she had to sustain the heavy bulk of the hat in the crook of her right arm and against her right hip.

And the rifle did not speak against her again! She stumbled and fell forward among the rocks.

CHAPTER 46

She hardly knew what happened in the first few minutes. She only knew that the heat among these rocks was that which rushes out when the oven door is opened. Only, the heat from the oven is a single blast, and this was a steady burning flame. The men were half naked. They had thrown up a quantity of sand behind the largest of the rocks, and above this pit they had stretched their clothes to make an awning.

Now she was lifted in great hands and placed under that awning. St. Clair it was who raised her.

Durfee cut away the bloodstained cloth from her shoulder. His every touch got at the roots of her nerves. She cried out: "I want to be brave, but don't touch me. I'm going to scream. Uncle, don't touch me! You're killing me!"

Her throat ached; darkness swept over her eyes; a needle thrust of sound pierced her ears and she knew that she had screamed long and loud.

Durfee's face, terribly contorted, was close above her, with old Bunce, looking like a frightened boy, his eyes thrusting out of his head. She waved her right hand at them.

"Go away!" she cried. "I don't want to see you. I want Henry. I want to see you, Henry. Where are you? Why don't you come? Why don't you come?"

St. Clair put the other two to one side and kneeled beside her. In his hands strong white cloth was ripping like thin paper.

"I'm here, Mary," he said.

She gripped at him with the one hand she could use.

"I'm going to die, Henry," she said. "I don't want to die! Don't let me die!"

There was that screaming again, so frightful that it almost closed her eyes, and the face of St. Clair was almost lost to her.

When she could see again she was crying: "I don't want to die. I'm too young, Henry. Help me!"

The pain was driving down, down in her lungs. She was burning inside.

When the bullet pricked the lungs, that was the end. The blood reached the breathing, presently, and then there was strangulation.

"Henry, Henry, Henry, why don't you do something? You can save me! You're strong enough to keep me alive!"

He took her jaw between thumb and forefinger of his right hand. He shook her head; the grip of his fingers hurt her badly.

That pain cleared her brain somewhat and enabled her to hear a man gasping and groaning as though in dying pangs.

That was old Bunce, who was slumped down in the sand, with his hands over his face. He was not wounded. What had gone through his heart was the sight of her dying, as she thought.

She could see Durfee, too, close beside her, and his face was not a face at all, but a bit of gray stone, weather carved, the semblance of a human face and no more.

But now, most clearly of all, she could see the handsome face of St. Clair, unperturbed, calm.

"You're letting yourself go," he said. "You're being an hysterical little fool. Stop that idiotic yelling!"

She was stunned.

As she lay still, following him with hurt wonder, shocked, she saw him manipulate the upper arm and the shoulder. His grip was firm, but it gave her no more pain; it even lessened the ache and the thrusting hurt of the wound.

She heard him saying calmly: "You're a lucky girl. No bones broken—"

"The lungs!" she gasped at him. "It's cut through my lungs."

"You'd be frothing at the lips, red froth," he answered her with a stern impatience. "Lie still and don't bother me with your nonsense. I'll tell you what the bullet did and where it went."

She was silent. The cold brutality of his speech seemed

to bludgeon all sensibility out of her. She lay quietly. The breath entered her more deeply.

He took sand, finer than dust, and packed it over both the mouths of the wound, saying: "The bullet clipped straight through you. You'll be using this arm and shoulder as well as ever, in three weeks. You're the luckiest girl in the world. Bunce, stop that blasted whining. Come here and hold the end of this bandage."

She wondered why he did not ask Durfee, of the stone face, to do this. But he paid no attention to Durfee, his old friend. Bunce came, dragging his crippled body. He stole frightened glances at her face, like a guilty child before a parent.

And now St. Clair drew the bandage firmly around the hurt, over the shoulder and under it. The pain settled to a steady ache, subdued, easily endured. At last he finished.

He paid no more heed to her, for the moment, but picked up the canteen she had brought and uncapped it. He said: "Durfee, drink some of this!"

Durfee did not even move his stony eyes from the face of the girl.

"Drink some of this!" repeated St. Clair loudly.

Durfee obeyed. He handed back the canteen, and it was passed to Bunce. Then Durfee said: "How did he treat you, that thing yonder, Lester?" She stared at him, wondering at the husky change in his voice.

"He treated me like a distant relation," she said. "Some one who's a fool and a nuisance, but like a relation."

He lifted the pull of hair at one side of her head. "How did this happen?" he asked.

"He knocked me down when I shouted a warning to you that day."

She heard a deep, humming growl. It came from the throat of St. Clair.

"Don't ask questions," he commanded.

"I've found out what I wanted to know," said Durfee.

"Keep still, then," whispered St. Clair.

He sat down beside her, calm, unperturbed as ever. The sweat ran steadily down his face. Bunce, his back against the big rock, made a slight groan with every breath he drew. The heat was killing him. Even Durfee, iron man that he was, lay back, only half conscious.

She said to St. Clair: "I'm sorry I was such a coward and a fool."

And he answered: "We'd all three be dead, twice over, except for you. I talked like that a while back to buck you up a little. No other woman in the world could have done what you've done. Now lie still."

He gave her water to drink from the canteen, lifting her head with his great hand. It was as though she never before had tasted drink.

She closed her eyes. "I thought you despised me, Henry," said she.

He answered nothing. She did not need any answer, however. For she felt that such praise as he had given to her he would never be able to bestow on another human being. Such words had to be torn from the bottom of his heart and it was hard for them to find a way.

But peace began to descend over her. So frightful was the heat that the skin of her entire body burned, except where St. Clair sprinkled her with water and then fanned her.

It occurred to her that she had not seen him drink a single drop, since her coming with supply.

But she did not speak of this or urge him, for she knew that, of all the days of his life, on this day he was iron and could not be bent or altered.

Then she said: "What time is it?"

"Two o'clock," said St. Clair, "and it's turning cooler already."

But her wide horrified eyes were seeing the truth. At two o'clock the worst of the day's heat was only beginning. She had been hardly a moment in the valley and it seemed already an eternity of torture.

CHAPTER 47

Slow death! No, not for St. Clair. Heat or cold, she felt, would never affect him until his terrible will was broken. But for her it was slow death, and for Bunce and Durfee.

Neither of them complained, but Bunce could not keep the rattle out of his throat. He lay with his mouth twisted open, awry. For hours he made that ghastly sound in the back of his throat, and for hours she expected that each moment would be the last. Her own nerves began to fray out. Her lips began to tremble. She had to close her eyes and hold her breath, and center all her faculties on herself, to keep the tears back. She wanted to whimper like a child.

Then she heard St. Clair saying: "That's all right. You cry, if you want to. You have a right to cry. We're being baked alive. It's frightfully bad. The brain is burning inside my head. No wonder you want to cry!"

She opened her eyes at him in bewilderment. "Do you really feel it so much?" she asked him.

"Aye, it's an inferno. Durfee, do something for Bunce."

The answer of Durfee was a moan, but he moved to obey the order.

St. Clair closed her hand in his. The thin sprinkling of water continued to fall on her. Without ceasing he fanned her.

She saw him turn a brighter and a brighter crimson; then blotches of gray appeared in his face. Yes, St. Clair was dying, too.

She could hear the rattling breath of Bunce drawn more irregularly. Durfee was gasping and cursing in a breathless whisper.

Slow death!

The sun, as it slanted from the west, had not lessened in power; it simply came prying at them from a deadlier angle.

"There's no more water," St. Clair announced finally. "And still an hour to sundown. This will be the hardest part. Keep up your heart. I'd give you my own blood, if that would help you!"

She looked steadily up into his face and knew that he meant what he said. More than water or wine, the words fed and strengthened her. If she had come to love him, almost like a being from another world, he loved her also.

Then the sun went down.

But the moon rose after it.

The coolness began to come out of the air, though the rocks and the sand were still burning. St. Clair propped her up a little. With the upper part of her body away from the ground, she seemed bathed in coolness. Life became a possibility, if only there were not the fatal thought of tomorrow and that burning fire focused upon them again.

The breathing of Bunce grew easier. Durfee seemed quite himself again.

And now the cruel, silver light of the moon was flooding through the valley.

The hours went on. Sleep came over her. A strong, fierce pulse of blood began to hammer at her temples, and she waked to hear a sort of maniacal laughter from Bunce, as he cried: "I tell you, I'm able to read weather. I tell you, it's in the wind—rain! I can smell it. There's rain falling on the mountains right now. It'll be here, before long. Rain, rain, it'll cover the moon."

She looked up and, in fact, there was a moving breeze that touched her body and cooled her face. To the southwest, she saw great cumulus clouds building, swaying toward them across the sky. For an hour they built loftier, blacker, and then with one sudden movement, like water bursting over the lip of a dam, they flowed clear across the sky. The moon went out!

They had prepared the litter before this—a pair of rifles for side pieces and a saddle blanket drawn and knotted across them. On this St. Clair laid her on her right side; he carried her at the head and Durfee at the feet, as they moved across the valley's floor. Not a drop of rain was falling, but the deep river of wind-borne clouds gave them a saving darkness.

They carried her with some little trouble up the floor on the cleft in the canyon wall, and when they came to the upper level St. Clair said: "Here are some trees; they'll keep off the wind, and the rain, too, if it comes. Durfee, you and Bunce stay here, with your rifles ready. You can hear the trickling of water off there, if you want to fill the canteens. I'll be away for a few minutes and come back."

They made a bed of boughs for her; they built up a windbreak and, when the wind and rain came in a torrent together, she was safe and warm.

But all this time she was not thinking of herself or of her own pain; she was thinking of St. Clair.

He had gone to find Lester and something told her that he would meet the criminal. What would happen when they met? She had no doubt. For Lester was a tiger among men, but St. Clair was a lion. No, she had no doubt.

Near by, Bunce lay stretched out, asleep, whimpering sometimes in the depth of his exhaustion. Her uncle sat erect at her feet, a rifle across his knees. He thought that she, like Bunce, was sleeping, for he never spoke to her once. But she preferred to lie like that, silently turning her thoughts over in her brain.

But, in time, as the noise of the rain drew off somewhat, after the first downpour, she heard another trampling sound that drew nearer out of the distance, and at last she whispered: "Do you hear it?"

"Yes," murmured Durfee.

"Horses!" said she.

"Aye," said Durfee. "Henry's comin' back with the horses of Lester."

He spoke in the most matter-of-fact manner, as though the victory of St. Clair were a foregone conclusion. It was more like a sense of accomplished doom when at last her straining eyes made out the dim forms of the horses through the night.

Then she saw a rider with a bulky object before the pommel of his saddle. The rider dismounted, and lifted down the burden from before his saddle.

"Durfee, strike a light," said St. Clair; and Durfee, with a sudden exclamation, leaped up and made a light.

Then she saw that the burden in the hands of St. Clair was a living thing, Spot Lester. He hung slackly, as though vital bones were broken in his body. His head hung down as from a broken neck. She herself rose and stood, forgetful of her wound.

They were both in tatters; and blood from a scalp wound was still running slowly down the face of St. Clair. It had been hand to hand once more. And once more Lester had gone down.

"Look up!" commanded St. Clair.

The limp rag of humanity in his hands lifted its head, groaning. And the wildly wandering eyes found those of the girl. He cast up both his hands before his face and bowed his head again.

Spot Lester? Aye, it was he, and shaking like a frightened girl.

She understood then. It was not his body, but his soul that was broken as on a wheel.

"I wanted to ask you, Mary, and you, Durfee, what to do with him? He was malevolent enough to shoot her; but not enough to send a second bullet into her. I know that he had time for another shot."

"Let him go!" cried Mary. "His heart's broken. He'll never be more than a poor, crawling beggar all the rest of the days of his life."

And Durfee said, in a slow voice of disgust: "Aye, let him be. I never thought a time would come when I'd say that of Lester. But living will be worse than a quick death now for that—thing!"

"Take this horse, then," said St. Clair, and he heaved the bulk up into a saddle, and struck the horse on the flank. Off it moved, but Spot Lester did not straighten in the saddle. He lay slouched forward, with his arms flung out along the mustang's neck.

St. Clair came back and flung himself down on the ground beneath the tree.

"You're hurt, lad," said Durfee.

"Aye—in the brain," said St. Clair. "Because I've seen what can happen to any man that puts too much trust in the strength of his hands and a wild life. I've seen what can happen to a Lester, or to me."

"If you've seen that," said Durfee, "you've seen the way home from all your troubles. It needed a Lester to show you the truth about yourself. Aye, you're on the way home, and I reckon that you'll have company on the way."